DARE TO TAKE

CHURCHILL BRADLEY ACADEMY BOOK TWO

L. ANN
CLAIRE MARTA

DARE TO TAKE

This book is a work of fiction. Names, characters, businesses, organisations, places, events and incidents either are the product of the author's imagination or are used fictitiously. Any resemblance to actual persons, living or dead, events, or locales is entirely coincidental.

Cover design by Honey & Sin

Interior Formatting by Crow Fiction Designs

First Edition: February 2023

ISBN: 9798375410494

This is a dark high school bully romance. The warnings from book one continue for book two.

You've glimpsed the monster of Churchill Bradley Academy behind the school's walls. We warned you this would be no sweet romance. There's darkness, steam, hate, and angst.
Step back into the halls that whisper with secrets. Where bullies rule and the elite students play their games.

Do you dare to continue?

Red or green, dear reader?

Playlist

BAD THINGS - SUMMER KENNEDY
12 ROUNDS - BOHNES
I'M WITH YOU - AVRIL LAVIGNE
REAPER - SILVERBERG
CRAWLING BACK TO YOU - DAUGHTRY
PAPERCUTS - MACHINE GUN KELLY
NUMB LINKIN PARK

Dedication

For the tears of our readers, and the screams of our alpha readers.

This series has become so much more than we could have hoped.

To every crazy idea we had, the obsession with a story that flowed into words. ("*It was only supposed to be a 30k Novella*", and we'll never get tired of laughing over that.)

Ari and Eli's story is a beautiful heartache, and we hope you enjoy it as much as we did writing it.

1

Eli

"The rumors going around school are insane. Why the fuck did you leave that cell phone in your locker?"

I roll onto my back and stare at the ceiling, the phone against my ear as Kellan reports on how the first week back at school went.

"*I* didn't. It wasn't my cell they found. It was *hers.* Someone must have put it in my locker." I can't say her name, can barely even think it without flinching.

"*Hers?*"

"Yeah. Guess she left it in her room. Someone must have found it and looked through everything."

The only positive thing is no one has recognized the guy who is getting his dick sucked on the video. Silver lining? For *me*, maybe. Not for her. She is completely recognizable. On her knees, those plump lips wrapped around my dick, cheeks hollowing out with every long, wet suck.

I groan.

Stop fucking thinking about it.

"Has she come back?" Kellan's question disrupts my thoughts.

I sigh. "No. To her credit, Elena is losing her mind. Dad has hired a PI to try and find her. It's all my fault, of course." My voice is light, but it *is* my fault. I drove her to this.

A few short months ago, I would have celebrated the fact that she's now known as a slut, a whore, and a *cock-sucker*. All my plans to destroy her have come to fruition.

Except, those plans went out of the window the day I tasted her sweetness for the first time.

Then the games I was playing became something else. A desire to fulfill the fantasies she'd written about. To see her smile. To make her come. And *that* turned into an obsession, a desperate need to hear my name on her lips and not the character I was playing.

The sound of her voice moaning my name while she comes haunts my dreams, alongside the guilt of what I've caused. I throw a hand over my face in an attempt to block out the images of her writhing beneath me, clutching at me as she screams how much she hates me while she milks my dick for everything it holds.

"Are you listening to me?" Kellan's voice is sharp.

"No, not really," I admit.

"Do you think they'll let you come back? Everyone is saying you're gone for good."

"I don't know. Dad is on to the principal daily. He's donated a lot of money to Churchill Bradley, so that might sway them in my favor, but he's talking about military school as a secondary option." And even though I'm eighteen and can legally tell him to fuck off, I quite like living at home, so if he does decide to go that route, I'll comply with the decision.

"Eli? Come down here." The man himself calls from outside my bedroom door.

I blow out a breath. "I gotta go. Dad is shouting. He's decided that now is a great time to become a disciplinarian."

Kellan chuckles. "Well, you *did* fuck his stepdaughter."

"He doesn't know that." *Thank fuck.* "Keep me in the loop. I'll text you later." I cut the call and roll off the bed.

My dad is standing in the hallway when I pull the door open. His eyes scan over me, and he shakes his head.

"I blame myself for this. I should have never let you run wild for so long."

I rub the back of my neck.

"Do we have to go through this again?"

We've had the same conversation every day for the past two weeks. Going back and forth, achieving nothing.

"I'm trying to understand, Eli. I am. What possessed you to do it?"

"I told you. I *didn't* do it. Someone planted that phone in my locker."

"I want to believe you, son. I really do."

"Then fucking do it. I'm telling you I *did not* upload that video. I did not have that phone in my possession."

He falls silent, and we walk along the hallway to the staircase. His hand touches my arm just before I put my foot onto the first step.

"Why were you in her bedroom that morning?"

"I was returning something to her." That isn't a lie.

"Her diary. The one you read out in front of the entire class?"

"No. A different one."

He sighs. "Oh, Eli."

I shrug. "I wanted to know if she was aware of Elena's plan to marry you."

"And what did you find?"

A soul desperate to be seen, to be touched, to be desired.

"Nothing about you."

2

Arabella

He kisses me hungrily, his fingers sinking into my hair to anchor my head in place. I pull him closer, grab a fistful of his t-shirt, and kiss him as hard as I can. He tastes of peppermint, and his heady scent is familiar and comforting. His strong arms keep me captive, while his mouth devours mine.

My head spins with need.

His lips roam along my neck as he lifts me by the waist. Hoisting me up against him, his hands cup my backside, forcing my legs to wrap around his waist. I'm burning up with the need for him to touch me in the way I want. Eager to feel his body merging with my own.

A hand slips under my t-shirt to close around my breast. He's breathing hard against my ear. Rocking forward, he rubs the length of his cock against my entrance. Everything within me clenches, and I claw at his shoulders in a silent demand for more.

"Say my name. Let me hear that hate, Princess."

I open my eyes, and meet a smoldering green-eyed gaze ...

I jerk awake with a start, and look around, heart pounding.

Eli isn't here. I'm alone in the bedroom.

How can I hate him so much that it hurts but at the same time want to rip his clothes off and fuck him? I must be out of my mind.

I flop back onto the narrow bed and throw an arm over my eyes to block out the sunlight peeking in through the gap in the curtains. Battling to slow my heart rate, I try to blot out the desperate, needy throb between my legs.

It's been two weeks since I fled the house in the Hamptons—fourteen days since my life became a dumpster fire burning out of control. I haven't been in contact with anyone. I'm too frightened to switch on my phone after the video was released. To make matters worse, my period is late.

My hand slips down to my stomach, and panic consumes me. I took the morning-after pill the second I found a pharmacy but what if it hasn't worked? What if I'm pregnant?

A few months ago, I'd had my life planned out. Then Eli Travers came into it, turning everything upside down. Destroyed my safe, quiet world.

Everything has changed. *I've* changed. I've come to a dead end, and I no longer know how to go forward.

Please, don't let me be pregnant.

I'm the same age as when my mother got pregnant with me. I don't want to be like her. I don't want history to repeat itself.

I have officially hit the rock bottom equivalent of sheer humiliation.

A soft knock sounds on the door. "Arabella, dear, why don't you come down and have some lunch? Do you want to call Amanda and see if she wants to join us?"

My best friend.

I've barely seen her since I arrived. She's too busy with her boyfriend and new friends to spend time with me. I tried to tell her what happened, but it became clear that she is no longer interested in my problems.

So much for best friends forever.

Mrs. Goldmann's voice calling my name again drags me out of my dark and melancholy thoughts.

"I'm coming. I think Amanda was going to the mall with Darren." It's easier than telling her that I don't think Amanda is interested in spending time with me.

I throw the blanket back, crawl out of bed, and tug on my hoodie. I find my sneakers, stuff my feet into them, then head for the door.

She's waiting right outside with a kind smile on her wrinkled face, blue eyes sharp and curious. "It's so nice to have you visiting, but shouldn't you be getting back to that fancy school Elena sent you off to?"

"I explained before. I'm taking a break for a while," I lie.

"Oh, that's right. You did say that."

She leads the way down the stairs, then through the house to the tidy kitchen. A glass of milk and a plate of chocolate chip cookies is waiting for me on the table. I can't help but smile, my mood lightening at the memories of all the times Mrs. Goldmann watched over me when I was little.

I drop down into my seat, and take a sip of the milk, my thoughts heavy with fears and doubts. The envelope of cash I kept hidden for emergencies is running out.

I'm going to have to find a job. Somewhere to live. And if I'm pregnant … what then?

Mrs. Goldmann lowers herself into the chair beside me. "You know you can stay here as long as you like."

I offer her a weak smile, wishing that was possible. "That's kind of you, but I can't stay forever."

"Did you fight with your mom?"

The look of compassion and understanding in her expression wreaks havoc on my fragile control. "I—"

She pats my hand. "It's okay if you have. I practically raised you while Elena was off gallivanting, and I hope you know you can confide in me. I've been waiting for you to say something since you got here."

It's on the tip of my tongue to tell her the truth, but the words die before they can spill out. What would she think of me if she knew what I had done. What I let happen. I bow my head under the weight of shame and guilt.

"Yeah, we argued," I tell her, my eyes stinging with tears.

Mrs. Goldmann sighs. "That woman has always been reckless and selfish. Running off with whatever man flashed her a smile. Thank God you're nothing like her. You have your head screwed on right."

The tears break free to roll down my cheeks, and I scrub at them with my trembling hands. I'm more like my mother than I realized.

I let myself get caught up in excitement. In dark and dangerous pleasure. Now I'm paying for that mistake.

All my dreams and plans for the future are in tatters. All my bright hopes burnt to ash.

Eli Travers and Churchill Bradley Academy have taught me some cruel truths about life.

Fairy tales don't exist.

Prince Charming is dead, and the world is ruled by villains instead.

3

Eli

"How's that?" The tattoo artist hands me a mirror, and I tilt my head to examine the result.

"Perfect." I hand him three folded hundred-dollar bills. More than the tattoo costs, but worth the over-payment for him fitting me in at short notice and not asking questions.

"You know how to look after it?"

I wave a hand at the tattoos covering my arms. "I'm good, thanks."

"Okay. Any problems, you know where to find me."

We shake, bump shoulders, and I walk out. My car is parked a few feet away and someone calls my name just as I reach it.

"Hey, Travers."

I pocket my car key and turn to face Evan Ridley.

Why the fuck is he here and not at school?

"I bet you're wondering what I'm doing here." He echoes my thought and waves a hand behind him. "Had to drive Jace for a check-up and his dad didn't want him stuck with the school medical team. *Someone* attacked him over Thanksgiving. You wouldn't know anything about that, would you?"

I lean against the side of my car. "You know the answer to that." I'm not stupid enough to admit to it out loud.

He chuckles. "True." He turns away, then swings back. "Oh. Say hi to Arabella for me. Everyone misses her at school." He licks his lips. "Especially after that little video. The guys are all lining up for a turn."

I straighten, and he steps back, lifting his hands. "I'm just saying. She might want to watch herself when she comes back. Her friends will look after her, though. We won't let anyone touch her."

"Sure. Like when she trusted you to drive her home and you made her take her top off."

His smile drops away. "You know that wasn't me, Eli. I wouldn't do something like that to her."

"Right." I unlock my car, throw the door open and climb in.

"See you around, Eli. If the school lets you back in."

My car's engine drowns out anything else he has to say, and I slam the door and drive away.

***

I'm barely inside the entrance hall of the house when my dad bellows my name. I swear the fucker has a tracker on my phone. He's breathing down my neck constantly and seems to know the second I return from anywhere.

Instead of heading straight up to my room, I walk down the hallway to his study and knock on the door. I wait for his instruction to go inside before entering.

"Sit down, son."

Great. Another chat.

I pull out the chair opposite his desk and slump onto it. "What am I being blamed for now?"

"No one is blaming you for anything."

"They're not? Because it doesn't fucking look that way from where I'm sitting."

"Language."

"Don't you think it's a bit late to start parenting me now? Why don't you just go back to your fucking trophy wife and leave me to deal with all this bullshit myself?"

"Enough! I am sick and tired of you speaking about Elena that way. She has been nothing but kind to you, especially after what you did to her daughter."

Oh, you have no fucking idea what I did to her.

My jaw clenches. He's not talking about me fucking her, or about her sucking my dick, or me eating her pussy until she begged and screamed and pleaded to come.

"I see we're finally making progress."

"What do you mean?" My fingers are clenched against my thigh. There's a heavy weight in the pit of my stomach.

"You didn't deny releasing the video this time."

And there it is!

"I didn't think I needed to. I've told you a hundred fucking times that I didn't do it."

"And yet the evidence was found in your locker."

"Because someone is fucking setting me up!" I surge to my feet. "Why are you so fucking willing to believe the worst of me?"

"Eli—"

"No! Everything is always my fucking fault. It doesn't matter what it is. You come home with a new wife. A woman half your fucking age and you expect me to smile and make nice. Then you drop another bombshell. She has a fucking daughter, and I'm supposed to just welcome her into our family. And if *that's* not enough, you send her to my fucking school, and I'm supposed to ease her into that. You put so much fucking effort into a girl who's not even related to you, while I'm over here fucking *begging* for attention from you."

I'm panting when I stop shouting. My dad is sitting there, staring at me, one hand pressed to his chest. He doesn't say a word. I shake my head.

"I don't know why I fucking bother." I spin on my heel and stalk to the door.

"Eli … Son." My dad's voice is faint, and I almost miss him whispering my name.

The hairs stand up on the back of my neck and I twist around. He's white, face drained of color, and he's clutching at his chest, mouth wide as he gasps for breath.

"Dad?" All the anger I've been feeling dissipates, replaced by fear as I run across the room. "Dad?" I catch him as he slumps forward, stopping his head from colliding with the desk top.

"Fuck. *Dad*?"

I shake him, but he doesn't respond. My heart is pounding, my eyesight swimming as my throat closes up. I'm with my mom again. Watching the life slip away from her eyes while I drag her away from the car.

I shake my head, the room coming back into focus.

Fuck.

My hand is in my pocket, pulling out my cell on autopilot, and I hit the number for Emergency services.

Curled up on the bed, I stare at my phone where it's on the floor in the corner like it's a viper ready to bite me. I want to reach out to Miles, but I'm terrified of what's waiting for me if I turn it on.

Has Sin released more videos?

His betrayal slices so deeply through me that I feel it right down to my soul. After all the games I played for him. After everything I let him do to me. Everything he made me do to him. I'd loved him through it all.

No tears come. Only memories and regrets.

I need to move. Keeping still only makes me think, and I can't stand being in my head right now. I should go for a run. Focus my mind on that instead of everything else. I put on my sneakers and walk toward the door.

"Arabella, you have a visitor," Mrs. Goldmann calls from the kitchen when I'm halfway down the stairs.

A visitor? Could it be Amanda? Maybe she's decided I'm worth her time now.

I take the last few steps two at a time and follow the hallway to the back of the house. The smile on my face melts away the second I see who it is.

My mother is sitting in the comfortable little kitchen, her face pale, and mouth set in a hard line. Her presence rips the cocoon of safety I've been living in into shreds.

"Elena—"

"How *dare* you scare me like that." She rises from her seat, her voice shrill. "Two weeks. Two *fucking* weeks, and not one word from you."

My chest hurts, and I struggle to speak. "I—"

"Elliot and I have been worried sick about *you*. Thank God the PI he hired found you here."

I swallow, my throat thick with tears. "I'm sorry."

She shakes her head. "Not another word, Arabella. Get your things. You're coming home with me."

My heart slams frantically against my ribs at her demand. "But—"

"I am not in the mood for arguments, young lady."

Mrs. Goldmann gives me an encouraging smile from where she's sitting. "It's okay, dear. Do as your mom says while I talk with her."

I scurry out of the kitchen, and sprint back up the stairs to my room.

My mom is here. She's going to drag me back to the house. Back to Eli.

Do they know what he did? That we had sex?

I crouch down on the floor, and stare blankly at the side of the bed.

He's going to use it against me. Accuse me of being a whore like my mother.

I don't want to go back. I don't want to go back. I don't want to go back. I don't want to go back. The words chant through my head in a sickening rush.

I glance across the room, and my attention fixes on the window.

If I run, she'll find me again. If I did, where would I go? I'm out of options.

Defeat envelops me. I pull myself up off the floor, and numbly pack all my things into my suitcase. I take one long last look around the room, the echoes of my childhood bringing bittersweet memories.

Where's the little girl with a head full of dreams? The one who used to fight dragons and sail on imaginary pirate ships.

She's gone.

That Arabella Gray doesn't exist anymore.

The hollow-eyed girl with the pale face who stares back at me in the mirror each morning is a stranger.

I leave the room and my past behind me. My mother and Mrs. Goldmann are waiting for me in the hallway.

Elena sweeps the older woman with a narrow-eyed glare. "Thank you for looking after my daughter. But in the future, if she ever turns up at your door, you *don't* lie to me about it when I call to ask you if you've seen her. In future, you will call me immediately."

I loop a strand of loose hair behind my ear and shift uneasily at the tension in the air. "Thanks for everything, Mrs. G."

She pulls me into her arms. "You look after yourself, Bella."

Eyes closed, I squeeze her tightly, the small sign of affection meaning so much more to me than she'll ever know. "I'll try."

There's a black SUV waiting for us when we walk outside. My mother walks around to the driver's side, and climbs in. I trail after her, stow my suitcase in the trunk and then take the seat beside her. I keep my head bowed.

"Arabella, look at me."

I pinch my eyes shut.

"Look at me," she demands again, her voice shaky. "What

happened is *not* your fault."

"Yes, it is," I reply.

"No, it's *mine*. Eli hates me for marrying his dad, and he aimed that anger at you. We didn't know he'd been bullying you until we learned about the video. The school found a phone that belonged to you in his locker. He released the video—"

The rest of Elena's words don't register.

Eli released it, *not* Sin. He had my phone.

Tears swim in my eyes, and something tight inside me eases a fraction.

"How could you let someone take photographs of you like that? *Videos*?" she continues. "I thought you were smarter than that."

"I can't go back. Please don't make me go back." A strangled sob breaks free.

Elena sighs. "This place isn't your home anymore, sweetheart. You *have* to come back."

Gulping for air, I shake in my seat, sobbing hysterically. "Mom, please—" The fact I call her *Mom* should tell her how badly I don't want to go back.

"I should have been there for you. I'm sorry—" Her words are cut short as the sound of her ringtone fills the car. She reaches for it, then frowns at the caller ID before answering.

"Hello? Mrs. Travers speaking."

Her face pales as she listens to the voice on the other end of the call.

Dread creeps up my spine, when she drops the phone onto her lap and stares out of the window.

"What's the matter?"

"Elliot's had a heart attack." Elena's eyes are two blue wells of pain when she turns toward me.

I almost don't catch her whispered words. "W-what?"

5

Eli

I summon up a tired smile when the nurse walks past me.

"You should go home and rest." Her voice is pitched low, so my father isn't disturbed. "He's stable now. He's sleeping normally and has done so for the past forty-eight hours. You don't need to be here."

"No. I'll stay. He might need me when he wakes."

The truth is if I go home and find my bed, there's a chance I won't leave it for the next two days. It's my fault he's here. If I hadn't fought with him, if I hadn't fucked up so many times, he wouldn't be lying in a hospital bed.

"You're not going to be any good to him if you make yourself sick with exhaustion and end up in the bed beside him."

"I *said* I'm staying."

I haven't left the hospital for three days, riding here in the ambulance with him and taking up residence in the chair in his private room once they got him stabilized.

"Eli?" His whisper brings me out of my seat, and I cross to his bed. He reaches out a hand to grip mine. "Son."

"I'm sorry." I bow my head to his, and his other hand comes up to palm my cheek.

"Not your fault."

"If I hadn't—"

"The doctors said it could have happened at any time. This wasn't your fault, Eli." His hand slides over my cheek and cups the back of my head to pull me closer. "But you smell, son. You need to go home and shower."

"I don't want to leave."

He smiles, and I've never been so relieved in my life. "I'm not going anywhere. Go home, shower, get some sleep and come back in the morning. I'm in good hands here."

"But—"

"I love you, Eli." He pulls my head down and kisses the top of my head. "Now go home and get some rest. Elena's on her way. She can keep me company and you can take over tomorrow."

Elena. A woman who has been very conspicuous by her absence these past three days.

"It's about time."

"Don't be hard on her. The private investigator I hired found Arabella, and she went to bring her home. They were just getting in the car to drive to the airport when the hospital finally got hold of her."

I still. *Arabella has been found?* The rest of his words sink in. *She's coming back to the Hamptons?*

The surge of relief I feel is followed closely by something else, a darker emotion that swirls through me. She accused me of taking advantage of her, of *forcing* myself on her. Will she also blame me for the video? I'm sure Elena will have told her where her cell phone was found.

I pull out of my father's grip and straighten. "I'll wait until she gets here."

His eyes shift to look beyond me. "That would be now."

"Elliot? Oh my god, *Elliot*." Elena rushes past me in a cloud of expensive perfume. She wraps her arms around my father and presses her forehead to his. "If I'd known something was going to happen, I wouldn't have left." She kisses his cheeks, and his mouth. "Are you okay?"

I turn away, not wanting to see the intimacy between them, and grab my hoodie before slipping out of the door.

I'm outside the hospital before I remember I left my cell at home, and didn't drive here, so I turn and walk back inside to the reception desk.

"Hi. Could you call an Uber for me?"

The woman on the desk gives me a bright, toothy smile. "Of course!"

The Uber driver is understanding about my situation and waits while I go inside the house and find my wallet once we get there. I'm back out a few minutes later, money in hand, to pay him. He takes the folded notes with a smile and backs down the drive. I stand there, watching until it disappears out of sight before turning to trudge back indoors.

I'm fucking exhausted, *drained*, but I detour to the kitchen to let the cook and house staff know how my father is. I spend fifteen minutes fielding their questions before I'm able to extricate myself and climb the stairs to my room. On the periphery of my vision, I see movement, but my gaze is focused on my bed, and I'm honestly too fucking tired to pay attention to anything else around me.

I sit on the edge of the mattress and pull off my sneakers, drag the hoodie over my head and toss it to the floor and then fall back against the sheets. I should take off my clothes and have a shower.

I will do that … I just want to rest my eyes for a few minutes first.

6

Arabella

Standing in the middle of the bedroom, I keep my arms wrapped around my middle. I still can't believe I'm back here. It's creepy the way my room is perfect. The messy bed is remade, and all the clothes I'd left all over the floor have been put away. It's as if the night I fucked Eli didn't happen.

Elena was quiet and subdued the whole journey back to the Hamptons. Her worry for Elliot had been tangible.

Maybe she does actually care about him? Or maybe she's worried about Eli getting control of everything if he dies.

The cynical little voice in my head twists my lips. My mother has always cared more about herself than anything else. Why would that change now? She won't let herself lose all this without a fight.

It would be just another reason for my stepbrother to hate me.

Please let Elliot be okay.

I send up the silent prayer with a guilt-ridden heart. I'm the cause of his heart attack. If I hadn't run away, he'd be here right now.

With a ragged breath, I sink to the floor. I want to go to the hospital to see him, but my mother has forbidden me from leaving the house unless I'm accompanied. She made sure the staff was under strict instructions not to let me leave before she'd gone to see Elliot.

Where am I going to go? I have nowhere left.

A helpless laugh escapes me. This might be a castle of luxury, but it's still a cage.

I find my phone and sit with it clenched between my hands. I can't hide from what's out there anymore. No matter what I do, it will still be waiting for me. I take a deep breath, switch it on, and watch the screen spring to life. It only takes a moment for the texts and notifications to start to flood in.

Miles: What the hell, Bella? What did you do?

Miles: Who are the men in the video?

Miles: I thought we were friends. Why didn't you tell me? I can't believe you'd do something like this.

Miles: I tried to call you, but it's going to voicemail. Call me back.

Miles: Bella, where are you?

Miles: Everyone is asking me where you are. They think I'm one of the guys in the video. I'm fucking denying it. All the cheerleaders and jocks are giving me hell.

Miles: Everyone is saying Eli leaked the video. Did he make you do those things? Did he hurt you?

Miles: Where are you? Eli's dad had the school contact me to see if I knew. No one knows where you are.

Miles: Just let me know you're ok.

My heart feels like it's squeezing out of my chest, and my lips tremble. He won't want to be friends with me now. Not after what's happened.

I click on the notifications for the school's social media app, and stare down at the comments and posts.

Arabella Gray—cock-sucking whore.

This girl is going to be popular down on her knees.

Look at the tits on her.

I can't wait to have those lips wrapped around my dick.

I see a gangbang in her future.

The cruel and lurid commentary goes on and on. The video of me naked, on my knees giving Sin a blowjob, is everywhere.

Disgust and shame build within me. I wipe a tear off my cheek, but more fall.

What happens if I *am* pregnant?

From the way she acted, my mom doesn't know Eli and I had sex. He could easily deny it now with the video exposed. Say one of the men in it fucked me and got me pregnant.

Will Elena and Elliot arrange to have it terminated? Just like my dad wanted to get rid of me when she got knocked up.

Another round of texts pops up.

`Lacy: You are no longer a member of the cheer squad. It was a unanimous vote.`

`Lacy: The school has agreed to give me another room. Nothing personal, but I have a reputation to keep.`

Even though it's not a surprise, it still hurts. I scrub my eyes with the back of my hand and force myself to stop crying. If I'm going to survive this, something has to change. I sniff and sit up straighter. I need to protect myself.

An idea forms, and ignoring the rest of the hurtful messages, I click away from the app and open an internet browser.

An hour later, I have everything I need ordered and delivery scheduled for the next few days. The Arabella who first set foot in this house was naive and trusting. I'm not going to be that girl anymore.

There's movement on the landing outside my door. I drop my phone and get to my feet. It's too early for Elena to be back, but when I peer out of the door, it's to see Eli on his way into his room. His clothes are crumpled, and he looks exhausted.

Guilt eats at me again. He must have been at the hospital with his dad. I move along the hallway until I'm standing on the threshold of his door. He's sprawled out on his bed with his eyes closed.

"How's your dad?" I keep my voice low, empty of emotion.

Eli doesn't move. "Alive."

"That's good."

His eyes open to slits, the green a thin gleam between thick black eyelashes. "You don't need to pretend you're relieved. I'm sure you and your mother are disappointed that you're not getting your hands on his money."

I grit my teeth, and don't bother to deny it. Elliot is in the hospital because of me. Nothing I do will change his mind. Eli's hate is too deep to believe anything I say.

"You got what you wanted. The whole school knows what I am now because of the video you posted. I can't believe you took the phone from my room. Have you been watching me? Is that how you knew about it?" My voice is calm—the complete opposite of what I feel inside.

"For fuck's sake." Eli sits up and pins me with a glare. "I did *not* post that fucking video. I'm sick and tired of being blamed for things I didn't do."

Sparks flicker between us. There's no way to deny the pull I feel between us, and I hate him even more for the attraction I feel. My anger scalds me with tiny embers. It's all his fault.

Tears burn the back of my eyes, but I resist shedding them. "Why are you such an asshole?"

"Why did you accuse me of taking advantage of you when you're the one that begged me to fuck you?"

"I was drunk."

His gaze doesn't leave mine, and his hands move to palm himself in the front of his jeans. "You weren't that drunk. You knew exactly what you were doing. You had your hand on my dick. You said you wanted me—"

I can't stop my eyes from following the movement as he squeezes himself through the denim. "Shut up. I don't want you."

He bares his teeth. "Liar."

My attention snaps up. I glare at him with all the hate burning inside me. "Bite me."

"Already have, Princess. More than once."

7

Eli

She turns to leave, and I'm off the bed and blocking her escape in a heartbeat.

"Why did you come back?"

"You think I *wanted* to come back here?"

"You're eighteen. You could have refused."

The surprise on her face is enough to tell me that she didn't even think of that. I laugh, the sound hard and lacking humor.

"Too focused on the money to even think about that, I guess."

Her hand swings out, but she's too slow. I catch her wrist and pull it down to her side. "You know, you hit me a lot. You should see someone about that temper of yours." I step forward, driving her back a step. "Or did I hit a nerve, Princess? Was I too close to the truth?"

"I don't care about your fucking money!"

I know she doesn't, but I'm too tired, too stressed, and too fucking angry to care about anything but making her bleed alongside me.

"If that's the case, how did you pay for your flight to Nowhere, Hicksville?" I hike an eyebrow. "Or did you suck the pilot's dick in exchange for a seat on the plane?"

She twists out of my grip. "You're such a fucking asshole. It's no wonder everyone hates you."

"And yet you want to fuck me anyway."

"It'll be a cold day in hell before I let you near me again."

I smirk, my eyes dropping to her breasts. "You're practically begging for it right now." It's a throwaway line. I can't see a thing through the thick hoodie she's wearing.

She folds her arms, covering her chest. "Stop looking at me."

I take another step toward her. "Stop imagining my dick in your pussy."

Her cheeks turn pink. "Don't be disgusting." She starts to walk past me. My hand flashes out to grab her arm, and I haul her around.

"What's disgusting is that I could bend you over right now, pull down your panties and slide my dick right in. You'd be wet and ready for it."

This time she *does* slap me. Pain radiates across my cheek, and something snaps inside me.

My fingers curl around her throat, my thumb pushing her chin up. There's a flash of something—fear?—in her eyes and then I'm kissing her, my tongue forcing its way past her lips. There's a risk of her biting it off, but I don't fucking care. I need to feel something, *anything*. Something other than the guilt that's been eating me alive for the past two days.

She doesn't move. Doesn't push me away. Doesn't kiss me back. At least, not until I raise my head. The second my lips leave hers, her arms lift, hook around my neck and pulls me back down.

And then the battle is on.

This isn't a kiss. It's a fucking war for dominance. I suck her lip into my mouth, she *bites* mine. Our tongues duel. Our teeth bite, clash, *draw blood* … and then she's dragging my hoodie up. Our mouths part long enough for her to pull it over my head and then I go back for more, wrapping my arms around her waist and dragging her closer against me.

My fingers find the hem of her top and slide beneath it, up her spine to the hook on her bra. Her hands are *everywhere*. Roaming over my chest, down my arms, my hips and then she touches my spine.

I freeze for a second, and that moment is long enough for her palm to run over one of the scars littering my back. I'm too late when I reach back and pull her hand away so I can shove her away from me.

She blinks at me, eyes hazy with lust and confusion. "Eli?" My name on her lips is like a knife to the gut.

I reach deep inside and pull out a smile. My tone is rich with derision when I speak. "What was that about not wanting me, Princess?" I make a show of wiping the back of my hand across my mouth. "Seems like you're just as hot for me sober as you were drunk." I crouch for my hoodie and pull it on. "Get the fuck out of my room."

Her bottom lip drops, her face turns red, and the desire in her eyes turns back to hate.

How pathetic is it that I'd rather she hate me than ask me about the scars?

"You make me sick, Eli Travers," she spits at me, and runs from the room.

There's a pain behind my eyes, a throbbing that pulses in time with the beat of my heart, and nausea threatens. With tired steps, I walk to the door and close it, then turn toward the bathroom.

A shower, sleep, then food, and maybe … *maybe* … I'll feel human enough to deal with the rest of the fucking day.

8

Arabella

I rush into my bedroom and slam the door shut behind me. Wiping my mouth with the back of my hand, I try to get rid of the taste of Eli. A familiar throb pulses between my legs.

How can I still want him? After everything he's done. All the hate between us.

My body doesn't seem to understand. All it wants is to feel him up against me. To take the pleasure it can get from his touch. If he hadn't stopped, I'd still be in there now, naked, and writhing beneath him.

What had been on his back?

My fingers twitch, as I recall the rough edges of his skin. Scars? Is that why he's always covered up in a hoodie with no inch of him on show?

A hazy memory surfaces. Eli naked on top of me, his arms covered in tattoos. Expression twisted in pleasure as he pounded in and out of me with relentless thrusts.

The image makes my panties wet, and the pulsing between my legs turns into sweet torture. A feeling cut short by a flash of rage.

How dare he make me want him. Who the fuck does he think he is? I blink back tears of fury, of exhaustion and fear. I need to start thinking with my head, instead of acting impulsively and letting my emotions rule my actions.

Do I tell him about my late period?

Don't be ridiculous, Bella.

It would just be more fuel to the fire of his hatred. I know for certain, I need to keep it a secret from everyone.

The kiss we've just shared forces its way to the forefront of my mind. I remember the way I'd moaned into his mouth. The feel of something smooth, round, and hard on his tongue. *A new piercing?*

Humiliation kicks in. I should have slapped him harder.

You're not a blameless little victim in this war. Elliot is in the hospital because of you. You deserve Eli's torment.

Hugging myself, I cross the room to the bathroom to run a bath. I add a dollop of bubble bath and strip out of my clothes before descending into the water while it's still running. Some of my stress ebbs in the heat, and I wait until the tub is full before turning off the water. Laying back, I close my eyes, sinking until the only thing above the surface is my face. It feels as though I'm in a watery embrace. I can feel it warming every inch of my skin. Sounds are dulled. It's peaceful and calm. My attraction for Eli is still there, making my pussy clench needily and my nipples hard, but I don't want to touch myself.

Because you want Eli to do it. You want his mouth on your breasts, between your legs. You want him to block out the world. The same way your secret lover used to pleasure you when you were together, but your stepbrother isn't Sin. A tiny voice reminds me.

I shouldn't be physically attracted to Eli.

Not when Sin has my heart, even if his rejection has left it battered and bruised.

I'm so mixed up.

Holding my breath, I pull my head right under. Strands of hair float around my face caressing my cheeks. Everything is muted, the world above distorted.

Eli Travers is the enemy.

Kissing him is a bad idea.

Fantasizing about having sex with him again is even worse.

My chest tightens, and my lungs burn with the need for air. I lurch upward, break the surface and suck in a mouthful of oxygen. Wiping the water out of my eyes, I slick back my wet hair. And then sink back down so I can stare up at the light above me.

Has Sin seen the video?

Now I know he didn't post it, I'm desperate to see him.

I wish I could contact him. He must have heard about what happened.

Has he been back to the tomb? Has he thought about me at all?

Without the phone he gave me, I have no way of contacting him.

Will I ever get to talk to him again?

9

Eli

I wake up disoriented. The headache that had been threatening has arrived with a vengeance. My head is pounding, and it feels like a dead weight when I lift it from the pillow. The room is in darkness, and I grope around for my cell.

"Time?" My voice is a rough croak, but thankfully my phone app recognizes it.

"One am," the robotic voice tells me.

There are three missed calls and numerous text notifications, so I drop back against the mattress and tap through to see what's going on. My heart is hammering when I see two of the calls are from the hospital, and relief sweeps through me when the voicemail tells me they're just calling to give me a positive update on my dad's health. The third call is from Kellan, as are the messages.

`Kellan: Call me.`

`Kellan: Is everything okay? Is your dad okay? Call me when you get this.`

`Kellan: Fine, I'll tell you this way. Miles hasn't fucked Arabella.`

I snort quietly. *No shit, Sherlock.*

`Kellan: Okay, you're scaring me now. You're never silent for this long. Fucking call me.`

The rest of the texts are pretty much the same thing, with more swearing. I hit dial on his number. Unsurprisingly, he answers on the second ring.

"What the fuck? Where have you been?"

"Sorry, I crashed. Just woke up." I rub my temple, trying to ease the ache. "Dad's okay. The hospital called to say he can come home in a couple of days."

"That's good news."

"Yeah." I close my eyes.

"Has the school made a decision on whether you can come back?"

"Not that I've heard." I yawn, scratching my jaw. "Elena brought Arabella back earlier today … *yesterday*, I mean." I haven't told him what happened between us, only that she ran away after the video was leaked.

"So, you get to play happy families for Christmas."

After what happened earlier, somehow, I doubt that.

"I'm going to do my best. My dad will be home. The last thing I want is to put him back in the hospital. Next time he might not survive." And I don't think I'd survive the guilt of that.

There's a noise outside my door, footsteps followed by a low voice that I can't quite hear clearly. I frown. It's late. None of the house staff live here and will have left hours ago. That leaves two people.

"I'm gonna go. I'll call you later if there's any news." I end the call and drop my cell onto the bed, then roll to my feet.

Grabbing a t-shirt off the back of a chair, I pull it over my head as I cross the carpet and open the door. Elena is standing in the doorway to Arabella's room, and they're talking quietly. Elena's head turns toward me when I step into the hallway.

"Eli! Did I wake you? I'm sorry. I've just got back from the hospital."

I drag a hand through my hair, shoving it off my face. "How's Dad?"

She smiles, and it actually looks like genuine relief in her eyes. "Much better. I had the hospital leave you a message. Did you get it? It was only after you left that I realized I didn't have your number, so I couldn't call you myself."

"I did. Thank you."

Movement beside her draws my eye and I find Arabella leaning against the doorframe, her gaze trained on me. She looks away when she sees me looking.

"I'm going back to bed," she tells her mother. "I'll see you in the morning, Elena." She closes the door on the pair of us.

Silence thickens the air between us, awkward and heavy. "I was just going to sneak downstairs for a hot chocolate. It's far too late for coffee, although I could definitely kill for one. Do you want to join me?" The olive branch is offered in a hesitant voice, but I recognize it for what it is. And, for my father's health, I accept it.

"Sure. I was thinking about making a sandwich anyway."

We walk through the hallway and down the stairs to the kitchen. I'm sure the cook will have words to say when she arrives in the morning to find we've raided her supplies, but I'll deal with that later. The woman practically raised me. As I pull open the refrigerator to see what I can eat, my gaze lands on a plate of sandwiches covered in Saran wrap and a little label. The message makes me smile.

Eli, you're going to be hungry when you wake up. I did pop my head around your door earlier but didn't want to disturb you. I expect this plate to be empty and in the dishwasher when I come in. Make sure you drink something non-alcoholic! Poppy x

I take it out, unwrap it, and place it on the table. Elena moves around the other end of the kitchen, quietly preparing two mugs. It feels weird. Like I'm betraying my mom by allowing this woman to do something she'd always done for me. I push down the instinct to lash out and thank her quietly when she places the mug in front of me. She perches on a chair on the opposite side of the table.

"We didn't get off to the greatest start," she says.

I nod.

"I'm sure Arabella has been vocal about what a terrible mother I am."

I wait for her to defend herself. She surprises me when she doesn't.

"She isn't wrong. I was little more than a child when I had her, and I wasn't prepared to have a baby. I spent a lot of time running from the fact I'm a mom." She pauses to sip her drink and sighs. "Lucky for her, she never needed me. Sometimes I wonder whether she would have been better off if I never came home."

I take a bite out of my sandwich, chew, swallow and then look at her. "Why are you telling me this?"

"Because I think you and Arabella are more alike than you realize. I know you don't like me but give her a chance."

I laugh. "You think she wants anything to do with me? That video—"

"I don't think you did it."

That silences me.

"I *thought* you did at first. You're angry at me for marrying your dad. Maybe you think I'm trying to take your mom's place. Taking your anger out on Arabella makes sense." She shakes her head. "But the more I thought about it, the more I realized that it's not what you would do. I don't think you'd hide, and I think you'd admit to it if you were the one to blame. Especially now, after Elliot's heart attack."

She sets her mug down and props her chin on one hand. "I spoke to your dad earlier tonight. We're going to do everything we can to get you back into Churchill Bradley. Arabella will be going back after Christmas. Hopefully, you'll be able to return as well."

10

Arabella

Applying the last coat of nail polish to my nails, I sit back to let them dry. 'Bad Things' by Summer Kennedy is playing on my phone next to me on the desk.

It's been a week since Eli and I had our run-in, and I've hidden in my room since then. Elliot has been home on bedrest for the last few days, and Elena told me he wants us all to have a family dinner tonight. I've been permitted to see him once under my mother's supervision. She still insists I've done nothing wrong, but she makes me feel like I'm a criminal. My anger and guilt have hardened into a shell around my heart. A shield I'm grateful for to hide my pain.

I make sure my nails are dry before I leave the seat and move to my bed. A few unopened parcels and packages are on the floor in the corner of the room—clothes I'd ordered online to go with my mood.

My attention darts to the clock. I'm expected to be downstairs in the next ten minutes. I have no doubt that Elena will come to get me if I don't turn up. The only reason I'm going to this family dinner is because I don't want to cause Elliot any more stress.

My phone is on the desk, I press stop on the music and put it in my pocket and pull open my door. I don't see anyone when I leave my room and walk along the hallway. Elena and Eli are in the dining room when I enter.

My mother glances my way, then does a double take when she sees what I'm wearing.

"*Black* lipstick?"

"It goes with my nails." I wiggle my fingers, showing them off.

"And what are you wearing? Is that a spiked *dog* collar around your neck?"

I look down at the tight black jeans hugging my legs and the long-sleeved t-shirt with rips along the arms. "Clothes."

Eli snickers.

I shoot a quick look in his direction, but that's all the acknowledgement I give him.

Elena sighs. "Go and change. This isn't Halloween."

"If Eli can wear whatever he wants." I point out without any hint of the irritation I'm feeling inside. "I can too."

Before she can answer, Elliot enters the room. He looks pale and a little older since he got out of the hospital. His gaze meets mine, and for one brief second, I swear I see a flicker of pity in them. The pain inside me writhes, trying to escape its cage, but I bury it back down among the ice.

Feel nothing, then nothing can hurt you.

"Is this something new, Arabella?" He smiles. "What do they call it? A goth phase?"

I return his smile, but it feels stiff on my face. "Something like that."

"I like it. It suits you."

Elena steps toward him to fuss with the collar of his shirt. "Are you sure you're up to this? You should rest."

"I am resting." He raises his hand and curls his fingers around hers. "And I want to have dinner with my family tonight."

We all move to take our seats, and I'm acutely aware that Eli is sitting directly across from me. All I need to do is stretch out my leg and I could touch him. I do everything in my power not to look his way.

"You're very pale, Bella," my mother comments. "Or is that makeup too?"

I tilt my head and meet her stare. "Oh, no. *That's* all natural."

"It's been a rough few weeks for all of us." Elliot points out from the other end of the table. "I'm sure once Arabella gets back to school—"

"Wait, what?" My head snaps around to him.

"Your mother didn't tell you that you're going back after Christmas?"

I open my mouth to argue, then close it again. Instead, I turn to Elena. "But I don't want to go back."

The maids sweep into the room carrying trays of food. I don't even bother to see what's placed in front of me. My whole focus is on my mother's tight expression.

"We've spoken to the school, and they are dealing with what happened. You just need to get to graduation." Her voice is low and calm, as if I'm a difficult child. "It's not long. A few months."

A fucking lifetime for me. She really doesn't give a fuck about me.

She doesn't flinch under my glare. "It will be fine, Bella. You'll have a counselor you can talk to at any time. If the other students pick on you, you'll have someone to tell immediately. It's going to be okay."

"And how do you know that? Are you a fucking mind reader now?"

Her lips flatten into a thin white line. "Arabella, please don't spoil tonight with a tantrum."

Don't ruin this for Elliot.

I pick up my fork and prod at the pasta in front of me. My stomach is tight, and I'm not sure I will be able to keep food down.

Eli is watching me from across the table.

He must be enjoying himself immensely.

Has he seen the comments on the video? Does he know what's waiting for me back at Churchill Bradley Academy?

What all the boys have said?

At least he won't be there to see it.

11

Eli

I'm thankful as fuck that Elena didn't replace the old dining table with a glass-topped one because my dick is standing at attention, and my jeans are doing nothing to hide it. Arabella is sitting across from me and every time her black-coated lips part to take another mouthful of whatever we're eating, showing her little pink tongue, I have to bite back a groan. She walked into the room looking like she took a stroll through my fucking dreams and picked out clothes I wanted to see her in.

Tight jeans that hug her ass. A top that, with every turn or twist of her body flashes creamy skin. The collar around her throat draws my gaze more than once. I want to hook my fingers in it, pull her to me and hold her in place while she sucks my dick.

My fork clatters to the table, silencing the conversation around me, and I surge to my feet.

"Eli?" My dad frowns at me.

"Sorry. Just hot. Need to take my hoodie off."

I turn so that the back of the chair hides my dick and pull the hoodie over my head. Retaking my seat, I drape it across my legs. A smile flickers across Arabella's lips, and I wonder if she knows what she's doing to me.

"Elena and I have been talking. Christmas is almost here. I know we usually have dinner at home." My dad glances over at me. "But with everything that's happened, we thought it'd be nice to show that we are a family and go to the club."

I groan. The Country Club is one of the places I hate the most. Full of rich idiots who think their bank balance makes them important.

"Do we have to?"

"It's Christmas, Eli. We can't expect Poppy and her staff to spend the entire holiday here working."

"Surely it's not outside of Elena's skillset to cook Christmas dinner for four of us." My gaze flicks to Arabella. "Or maybe *she* can do it. If I recall, she was cooking up a storm when we were introduced."

"I was baking." Her voice is crisp and cool.

"Baking, cooking …" I shrug. "Same thing."

"Actually, it isn't. But since you've probably never set foot near a stove or tried to make a meal for yourself, I'm not surprised you have no idea."

Silence falls. I refuse to rise to the bait she's laying out. She wants me to cause a scene. I can see it in the set of her features, the way her chin is tipped, the provocative curl to her lip.

"I like this new you." I point my knife at her, and smile. "It's a better reflection of your inner darkness. It's good that you're not hiding behind the pink and pretty princess exterior anymore. You'll need a new nickname, of course. *Princess* just isn't … appropriate for this." I wave my knife in a circle in front of her.

Her eyes narrow, something sparking deep in their depths. I hold her gaze. The silence lengthens, thickens, as we stare at each other, and then Elena clears her throat and Arabella looks away.

"The plan is to go to the Club for Christmas dinner, then we'll come home and open gifts," Elena says.

I frown. Gifts? We haven't done the gift thing in years. Dad usually just lets me buy what I want. I can't remember the last time I actually opened a wrapped present.

"You mean like *actual* physical gifts?" I can't stop the question from breaking free.

Elena's brows pull together. "Of course, actual gifts. You kids should start thinking about what you'd like."

"You know I'm eighteen, right, and have access to millions of dollars on a daily basis? I *have* everything I could ever want." My voice is dry, and she has the good grace to blush.

"And that's why we're setting a budget. I want you to write a list of twenty things you'd like, the total cannot come to more than one thousand dollars, and me and your father will choose the ones we want to get for you."

The idea of budgeting money brings me out in a cold sweat.

She turns to Arabella. "The same goes for you." Her eyes drift over her daughter's clothes. "Maybe a new wardrobe?" She doesn't wait for a reply, turning back to me. "And I want you to buy each other a gift. Your budget for that is a hundred dollars each."

"No way." Arabella snaps.

"What the fuck?" I say at the same time. "We don't even know each other."

Everything I know about Arabella Gray are not things I can share with her mother. How she likes to be touched, how she tastes, the sounds she makes, how her entire body flushes when she comes.

Fuck. My erection, which had died down, wakes up again.

Elena casts a stern look at each of us. "Then I suggest you get to know each other."

12

Arabella

I scroll through the items on the website I have open on my phone. A hundred bucks. Whatever I get, Eli is going to hate it, so what's the point of putting some actual thought into it? He's been spoiled his whole life. He'll just see my gift as tacky and cheap.

I shudder at the thought of what he'll get for me.

Something embarrassing.

I hadn't missed his reaction to me at dinner last night.

I like this new you. It's a better reflection of your inner darkness. It's good that you're not hiding behind the pink and pretty princess exterior anymore.

The new me. He forged this new version out of his hate and taunting. This Arabella is done with taking shit from him or anyone else.

A tap at my door ends my search, and a second later, Elena enters my room. Her gaze runs over me, taking in the figure-hugging long-sleeved black top, down to the short black leather skirt adorned with a silver chain. Beneath that, thigh-high black socks are matched with a pair of flat black ballet shoes.

"If this is about me not coming down to breakfast, I wasn't hungry." Leaving the side of the bed, I move to the makeup bag on my desk.

She steps further into my room and closes the door. "You and Eli are spending the day together."

I drop into my seat, and find my lipstick. "I don't want anything to do with him."

My mother sighs. "He's your brother."

"Stepbrother." I correct her automatically, applying a coat of black to my lips. "You know what he did. Why is he even under the same roof as me?"

"Eli didn't share the video."

I don't look up from sorting through my new makeup. "Bullshit."

"I believe him."

Elena's soft, confident words are enough to make me spin in my seat and face her. "I'm your *daughter*. You should be on my side."

An emotion I can't define flickers in her eyes. "I am but don't you want those responsible to be punished? I know Eli has bullied you and treated you badly, but he wouldn't go this far."

"So, you know him well now, do you?"

"I've been making an effort to get to know him. Something you need to do too."

My anger boils over, and I don't even try to leash it. "This is unbelievable."

"Arabella, you need to be an adult. This—" She gestures up and down at me. "Sulking doesn't help anyone."

I grit my teeth. "I am *not* sulking."

"Good, then prove it. Spend the day with Eli."

"Why don't you just gouge my eyes out with a pen? That will be less painful."

Elena rolls her eyes. "Stop being so dramatic."

"If you like him so much, why don't you spend some more time with him?" I pick out eyeshadow and mascara, rise from my chair and walk into the bathroom.

"This act of rebellion isn't going to get you anywhere, sweetheart. If not for me, then for Elliot's sake, make an effort with his son."

My eyes move to hers through the mirror. She's standing in the doorway, watching me. I put on my eyeshadow and then a sweep of mascara on my eyelashes, admiring the way the makeup gives my eyes a dramatic smokey effect, and take a step back. "Fine. I'll spend the day with him."

I'm going to regret this.

Elena smiles. "Good, I'll have him downstairs in ten minutes."

I turn to face her. "Can we leave the grounds?"

She thinks about it for a moment before she nods. "I'll allow it."

"Be ready with bail money for when one of us murders the other."

Her response is a laugh and nothing more.

When she leaves, I finish getting ready. I fasten the dog collar around my neck, straighten my shoulders, raise my chin, and pull my mental armor in place.

Eli is waiting for me in the main hall when I descend the stairs. Dressed all in black, just as I am. He's in a hoodie, the padlock he always wears visible on its chain around his neck. He smiles when he sees me, those green eyes lingering on what I'm wearing, and his tongue touching the ring piercing his lip.

"I'm told we're supposed to spend time together." There's nothing in his voice to tell me how he feels about it.

"Do you have your car keys?" I step off the last stair.

Reaching into his pocket, he shows them to me. "You want to go for a drive?"

"I want to get out of this fucking cage for a couple of hours." I walk past him and open the front door.

Eli comes up behind me and leans in before I can move, brushing his lips over the side of my neck. My body comes to life in response, and my pulse trips over itself. He steps around me before I can react.

I send him a glare. "Fuck you."

That only makes him smirk. "Maybe later, if you ask me nicely. Now, where do you want to go?"

I gape for a second, and then snap my teeth closed. I flip my hair over my shoulder. "Do you know any good tattoo artists?"

"You want to get a tattoo?"

I shrug. "Why the fuck not?"

13

Eli

It's a good thing I know the way to my favorite tattoo parlor because my gaze keeps leaving the road to track up Arabella's legs. She pays no attention to me, fiddling with her cell for the entire drive and only looks up when I cut off the engine.

"We're here."

"Here being …?" One blonde eyebrow lifts.

"You requested a tattoo parlor. This is the best place around. Do you know what you want?"

"No."

"Okay, well …" I unclip my seatbelt and open the door. "They have albums of artwork that you can flick through. If you don't want something custom, then you can get a flash piece."

"Flash?"

"Designs they've already made and are available either to get as they are or to help inspire what you want. Come on. We'll need to see if they have any walk-in appointments. You might need to come back for an appointment."

She follows me out of the car and keeps pace beside me as I head down the sidewalk.

"Are they expensive?"

"Depends on the piece."

"What if I just get something small. How much will it cost?"

I glance over at her. "I have no idea."

"But you *have* tattoos!"

One side of my mouth tips up into a smile. "Remember those, do you?" My voice is soft and her cheeks turn pink. I guess the old Arabella is still in there somewhere. "I just hand over my credit card. I don't ask what the cost is."

Her laugh is brittle. "Of course. The pretty little rich boy doesn't need to check if he has the right amount of cash."

I hike an eyebrow. "You think I'm pretty?"

"It wasn't a compliment," she mutters.

"In here." I stop by a blacked-out door, and push the handle, then sweep one hand out. "After you."

She throws me a look from beneath her eyelashes and walks past me. The scent of her perfume hits my nose. It's different from the floral one I'm used to. This one is richer, heavier, and suits her far more.

Once she's inside, I let the door swing closed and follow her.

"Eli!" The man behind the counter jumps up and strides around. "Didn't expect to see you again so soon. And who's this pretty little lady?"

"So soon? When were you here?" Arabella turns to look at me, eyes sweeping over me curiously.

"Up here." I tap the side of my throat and her eyes zero in on the marks there.

"I thought they were scratches." Her brow pleats.

"They were. *You* gave them to me. I had them immortalized."

Her jaw drops. "Are you *insane?* Why would you do that?"

I shrug. *Because I wanted something to remember her by.*

"It seemed like a good idea at the time. Terry." I turn to the man waiting patiently. "This is Arabella. She wants a tattoo but isn't sure what to get."

"Then let's get the albums out." He drapes an arm over Arabella's shoulders and leads her through the archway into the back room.

I flop down onto one of the overstuffed chairs and prop my feet up on the table. Maybe I should get some more work while I'm here. "Hey, Terry?" I call out.

He appears through the archway.

"Do you have time to add some script to my side?"

"Sure. Let me get your girlfriend settled with the books, so she can have a look, and then I'll do it for you. How many words is it?"

"Just three. I have the design I want on my cell." I tap through and turn it around to show him.

He nods. "That's simple enough. Won't take long. Come through and get set up."

I follow him into the back room. Arabella is tucked into a chair in one corner, head bowed over an album of artwork. She doesn't look up when I walk past her and sit on one of the tattoo couches and strip out of my hoodie. I don't remove the t-shirt I'm wearing, but I lay on my side facing Arabella and drag it up, so the right side of my ribs are on show.

"Send me the image."

I email the design to him, and he prints it off and sets up a template. Setting it to one side, he preps my side, then puts the template on my skin. "There?" He shows me in the mirror, and I nod.

"Perfect."

"Let's do this then."

"Can you put these three letters in red?" I point at the ones I mean.

"Sure thing."

A minute later, the buzz of the tattoo pen fills the air, and that familiar sensation hits my skin. I let my eyes drift closed, the repetitive swipe of the pen lulling me into an almost meditative state.

It feels like I've just closed my eyes when he announces it's done. He wipes it clean and grabs the mirror.

"What do you think?"

I read the words and smile, nodding. "That's exactly what I wanted."

19

Arabella

Eli has the scratches I'd left tattooed on his neck? Wounds I'd made when we had sex.

I stare blindly down at the book in front of me, not really seeing the images, my mind puzzling over the mystery of his actions.

Why? As a trophy? Something to immortalize taking my virginity?

I should be angry, but instead, I find a strange, perverse pleasure that they are now permanently marked on his body for all to see.

A buzzing sound penetrates my thoughts, and I glance up to see Eli stretched on the tattoo couch. His black t-shirt has been tugged up, and the tattooist is busy inking something into his skin. I lick my lips at the tanned and toned skin on display, then catch myself, and redirect my attention to the tattoo pen moving over him.

A thread of nervousness winds around me.

Does it hurt?

I take in the expression on Eli's face. His eyes are closed, and there's a look of almost- pleasure on his face.

Of course, he likes the pain. That's probably why he has so many tattoos. He's addicted to it.

Tearing my attention away from him, I return it to the book in front of me. I flip through the pages, seeing design after design, but nothing catches my eye. I'm halfway through when I finally find what I want.

"What do you think?"

Terry's question draws my gaze back toward them. The tattooist is holding up a mirror, but the angle they're standing at means I can't see what Eli's tattoo is.

Eli smiles. "Perfect."

And then he turns … and my mind blanks when I see what has been tattooed over his ribs.

Nasty Little Monster in black and red is stark against his tanned skin in flowing letters.

I'm pretty certain my confusion is unguarded on my face. My mouth dries up, and I force myself to look back at the pictures in the book on the table.

That's what I called him the morning I ran away. I want to ask him why he has it, but I'm wary of the tattooist listening.

Why should I even care why he's done it? Another taunt at me for what happened. Another reminder of the hate between us.

"Have you picked a design, honey?"

Raising my head, I find Terry beside me.

"I want this." I tap my finger over the image of a butterfly that looks so real it almost flutters off the page. "Just a small one. And could it be blue?"

His attention roams up my arm as I pull up the sleeve of my top. "Over the cigarette burns?"

I nod.

He rubs his chin. "How's your pain tolerance? It'll hurt more because the skin has been damaged and will be more susceptible to pain. Maybe you'd prefer it somewhere else?"

The second he mentions pain, I change my mind. I flip my arm over and pat my forearm. "Here, then."

The guy smiles. "That I can do. Blue, you say? Let me get the template prepared, and we'll get started."

My gaze moves nervously to the tattoo couch.

How much is this going to hurt?

Eli pulls down his top and turns.

"Ready?"

I stand, slip off my chair and walk toward him. "More than ready."

The tattooist jerks his chin at the couch. "On you get."

One hand on my skirt to keep it in place, I somehow manage to get up onto it. Not without flashing the skin between my thigh-high socks and the hem of my skirt, though. When I'm finally settled, I turn to see Eli and the guy both watching me.

I give them both a flirty smile. "Let's get this over with."

Sitting down on his stool, the tattooists position the design on my forearm. "Here, okay?"

"Yes." My voice is small, and I hate the nervousness I can hear in it.

I avoid Eli's gaze and look up at the ceiling. My heart pounds as I fight to hold onto the courage that had brought me here.

Terry wipes my arm with something wet. "Here we go."

Eyes closed, I bite down hard on my lower lip, as the buzzing fills my ears. The first touch of the needle makes me yelp, but I force myself to lie still. It feels like a bunch of bees are stinging their way over my skin.

Fingers entwine with mine. "Do you think it hurts?"

"Not as much as I thought it would." I keep my eyes shut,

squeeze Eli's fingers and dig my nails into his skin as hard as I can. I'm grateful for the grounding contact, but at the same time, I hate that he's the one here giving it to me.

He likes to see you hurting. I remind myself.

"Let me guess. You chose it because it's pretty?"

I can almost hear his eyes roll.

"It is pretty." I agree. "But butterflies also feed on the dead."

"They're attracted to the sodium," Terry says.

I smile and nod. "Which makes them macabre as well as beautiful."

Just like the new me.

The heat and sting become more noticeable over time, but I hold still.

"All done," Terry announces after what feels like forever.

Eli immediately lets go of my hand.

I open my eyes while Terry wipes down my arm and inspect the image on my skin. The thin lines, color, and shading bring it to life. The delicate blue butterfly looks ready to flutter right off my forearm. It's angled in such a way that it adds realism to the tattoo.

"Wash it in non-perfumed warm soapy water a couple of times a day, and don't scratch it when it itches," the tattooist tells me.

He smooths cocoa butter over the butterfly before he covers it in Saran wrap. Carefully tugging the sleeve of my top down, I hop off the couch.

I can only imagine what my mother will say when she sees the tattoo. A smirk tugs my lips up at the thought.

"What else can you do around here for some fun?"

15

Eli

"Define fun." I drop my credit card onto the counter. "Take the payment for both tattoos and your usual tip."

"I can pay for my tattoo." The defensiveness in her tone is clear.

"I know that." I keep my voice mild.

I don't want to fight with her in front of Terry, and I'm trying *very hard* not to let her bait me. The last thing I need is her to go back home and report how awful I was. Maybe she knows the threat I'm under and that's why she's being so antagonistic.

When Elena told me she wanted me to spend the day with Arabella so we could get to know each other better, I said no. My mere presence brings out the devil in her, which, if I'm honest with myself, I like *a lot,* but I don't think spending the day with my dick buried inside her daughter is what Elena had in mind.

But then she told me that my father is looking at brochures for military school to ensure I don't *return to my bullying ways* when she goes back to Churchill Bradley, and her hope is that by proving we can spend time together without fighting, he will change his mind.

She repeated that she believed me when I said I didn't leak the videos, but that I need to prove to my dad I can be trusted.

So here I am … trying to tame the kitten from hell.

"Always a pleasure, Eli." Terry hands back my card and tips a wink at Arabella. "If you want to pay him back, you could always pay for whatever you do next today."

I roll my eyes. "Don't give her ideas." I pocket my card and walk to the door. "Come on, then. What does my little Hellcat want to do now?"

She doesn't comment on the nickname. "You live here. What is there to do?"

We walk back to my car, and I lean against the side. "Well, there's the beach, if you want to relax. Shopping, if retail therapy is your thing. Or are you looking for something tourists would do?"

"How do *you* spend your time here?"

"Painting, sketching, hiding out in my bedroom."

"Don't you ever leave the house?"

I shrug. "Only if I have to."

I could tell her that before my mom died, I rode horses, swam in the pool, and spent almost every waking moment out in the sun, but very rarely left the grounds of our house. I could tell her how I avoided all the other kids because they were likely to beat the shit out of me because I was small, quiet, and weird. But she wouldn't believe a word of it. And why would she? The kid I was is not who I am now. That quiet, shy boy who was scared of the world died alongside his mother.

"There must be *something* to do."

"We could drive up to the Montauk Point Lighthouse and smoke a joint on the rocks." I throw out the flippant suggestion, not really expecting her to say yes.

"You have …" her voice drops, "marijuana?"

"Weed."

"I want to do that."

My gaze cuts to her, eyes narrowing. "You want to get stoned?"

She nods.

"Have you ever smoked it before?"

"Not really."

"Have you ever smoked *anything* before?"

She shakes her head. I purse my lips, tongue flicking at my lip piercing.

"Okay," I say eventually. "If that's what you want to do. Get in the car."

***

It takes around forty minutes to reach Montauk Point. I park the car, open the glovebox, and take out a small tin. Reaching into the back seat, I grab a spare hoodie and toss it at her.

"It's fucking freezing. I'd rather not be accused of bringing you here to catch pneumonia, so put this on."

Instead of leading her up to the lighthouse, I take her down toward the beach. There are fewer people there. The breeze from the sea is icy and Arabella is shivering by the time we find a place to sit. My hoodie swamps her, making it easy for her to draw her legs up and pull it over the top of them so only the tips of her feet are on show.

I flip open the case and take out a joint. "Are you sure about this?"

She nods from the depths of her hood. Shielding the flame of the lighter from the wind, I light the joint and take in a lungful of the smoke, then pass it to her. Her first drag on it has her coughing and spluttering. I laugh.

"Try again." I settle back against the rocks, stretching out with one hand tucked beneath my head and look up at the sky.

When she hands the joint back to me, I take a long slow pull on it and let my eyes close, letting the drug do its work. We pass it back and forth in silence, apart from the occasional cough from her, and after a short while she lays down beside me.

"I don't feel so cold now."

I chuckle. "Do you feel anything?"

"Relaxed." She rolls onto her side to face me. "Did you get a tongue piercing?"

I push my tongue out and wiggle the piercing against my bottom lip. "Day after you ran."

I take another pull on the joint and blow out smoke rings. She giggles.

"Teach me how to do that!"

16

Arabella

Eli watches me through half-closed eyes. "Draw in a mouthful of smoke. Then press your tongue to the bottom of your mouth. Hollow your cheeks out like you're sucking on a lollipop and open your mouth to form an O." He follows his own instructions, and a smoke ring pops from his mouth and hangs between us.

I take the joint from him, follow his instructions, giggling when I blow out, but the smoke is just a cloud. "It's hard."

He takes the joint back from me. "Not bad for your first time."

My head feels odd, *buzzy*, and I'm happy. All my worries are so far away. This doesn't seem real. Maybe I've stepped into an alternate universe where my stepbrother isn't an asshole. *Maybe it's a dream?*

I rest my chin on my palm and stare at the boy beside me on the rocks, studying his features. Boy doesn't really fit. Not with those sharp cheekbones, shadowed jawline, and firm lips. "You're much prettier than the other boys at school."

I'm either losing my mind, or Eli just blushed.

"I thought you had a thing for swimmers and jocks?" He takes another drag from the joint.

"They have a thing for me." I sit up and climb, a little clumsily, over his legs to straddle his hips.

Eli's free hand snakes up to cup my backside. "What are you up to, Hellcat?"

I smile at the nickname, liking it more than Princess. It makes me sound like something sinful and naughty.

"Getting more comfortable." I rock myself experimentally against him, and moan at the friction of his jeans against the scrap of lace I'm wearing. "I want to feel good."

And do bad things to you.

He swears under his breath and pushes up against me. "And only my dick will do, huh?"

I try to keep a straight face, but a giggle escapes me. "Your dick is the only one around."

"I think you like being on top of me."

"Maybe I like having you beneath me."

"Do you?"

"Yes, I do."

I grind against him, rolling my hips back and forth in a steady rhythm. The hard ridge of Eli's cock swells beneath his zipper, and my whole focus centers on rubbing myself against it.

The hand on my ass dips beneath the skirt, and he groans. "A thong?"

I grin at the tortured sound of his voice. "I bought a ton of them. All different colors."

He props the joint between his lips, lifts his other hand and slides it under my top. His fingers hook over the cup of my bra and tug it down. He pinches my nipple.

My pussy clenches in response, and I suck in an unsteady breath. I rock against him harder, to chase the building pleasure.

I'm so wet, but I don't care. The joint we've shared has taken away any embarrassment about the way I'm soaking the front of his jeans. My pace and pressure increases as I push harder and harder into him.

Eli grunts with my movements. He toys with my nipple, and his hand on my ass encourages my movements. Back and forth, I go over his cock beneath the denim.

My climax hits, and I stiffen. Eyes closed, I cry out while my orgasm courses through me.

Eli sits up, his lips finding mine, the joint gone. I sigh into his mouth, as heat washes through me. He devours me with his mouth, swallowing my moans.

He's still moving beneath me, and when he reaches for the button of his jeans, I grab his wrists.

I pull my lips from his and pout. "I'm hungry."

He blinks. "Hungry?"

I bend my head to his throat, and push the soft cotton of his hoodie away, so I can latch onto his neck and suck at him. "Uh-huh."

His hands find my hips. "Let's finish what you started, then I'll feed you."

I flick his earlobe with my tongue. "I'm not in the mood anymore."

"Not in the mood?" he repeats.

"Nope, and if you don't have a condom, it's never going to happen. Not after last time."

Eli stills at my words.

I sit back on his lap, and gently drag my nails over his cheek. "No protection. No pussy."

Rolling off him, I land on the rocks beside him and stare up at the sky, giggling. The sound of my laughter is slightly hysterical.

17

I look at the girl giggling like a crazy person beside me. She's fucking high as a kite, and she's only had a few pulls on the joint we shared. Her body is shaking with laughter, and I have to fight not to smile. Her giggling is infectious, light-hearted, and warm.

Schooling my expression, I shift until our positions are reversed. Now *I'm* straddling *her* hips with my palms either side of her head. Her giggles hiccup to a stop and she stares up at me out of huge blue eyes, still glazed from the weed and her orgasm.

"No protection. No pussy. That's the rule you're setting?" I lean down to stroke my nose along hers while I reach into the back pocket of my jeans and pull out a foil wrapper. I wave it in front of her face. "Good thing I came prepared."

Her eyes follow the packet as it moves in front of her eyes and her lips part. "Oh."

"Mmhmm." I stroke my fingers over her lips, tracing the cupid's bow.

"Do you want to fuck me in public, Eli?" The smile on her lips suggests that she doesn't think I would do it.

"Oh, I want to do a lot of things to you, *Arabella*." I whisper the words against her lips. "Feeling you come all over my dick again is *definitely* on the list."

I slip my hand beneath her top and cup her breast. Her breath hitches. "Have you ever been eaten out by someone with a tongue piercing, Hellcat?" I nip her bottom lip. "Oh, no. That's right. You were a virgin. Makes me wonder what else you haven't done. I know you've opened your mouth for someone's dick, but have you spread your legs for someone else's tongue?"

I wonder if she'll admit to sneaking out at night to let a stranger make her come, but she stays silent. My thumb swipes over her nipple and her entire body shudders beneath me.

Lifting my head, I take a quick look around. No one is nearby. The cold weather is probably keeping most people away. I withdraw my hand and take hold of the hem of her top and pull it up, revealing her stomach. Sliding down her body, I lower my head and kiss just above the waistband of her skirt. My tongue licks around her navel, dips into the hollowed indent, then up. I draw the material higher until my lips touch the soft underside of her breast. She hisses when I nudge the material of her bra away with my nose and suck her nipple into my mouth.

My other hand smooths down her leg, over her thigh and then reverses direction beneath the short skirt. The crotch of her panties is soaked, and her hips jerk when I stroke over them.

"Dirty little Hellcat." My lips brush against her breast as I speak, and her fingers curl into my hair to drag my mouth back to her nipple. I laugh and catch it between my teeth, tugging at it until her back arches.

I hook a finger into her panties and pull them to one side.

"You're so wet. I bet my dick could slide right in without any foreplay at all. Is your clit aching? Does it need to be touched?" My thumb dips into her wetness, but I don't touch her clit. Instead, I stroke a circle around it. "Do you want to come again, Hellcat?"

"Eli!" Her nails dig into my scalp.

Lust burns like lava through my veins, but I shove it down ruthlessly. Sealing my lips to her breast, I suck and bite until I leave a hickey. She moans, hips jerking as she tries to get my thumb to where she needs it most.

I pull my hand free from her panties and lick my thumb. "You taste delicious." My voice is a low growl. Her lips curve up, and her eyes are sultry with desire as she looks at me.

I smile and roll to my feet. "But I'm fucking starving," I say in a more regular tone. I hold out a hand. "Let's go find something to eat."

It takes a second for my words to sink into her weed-impaired lust-soaked mind, but when they do her jaw drops.

"What the fuck, Eli?"

I shrug, pushing my hands into my pockets and stare down at her. "Fair's fair. If I don't get to come, nor do you." I reach down and pull her to her feet, adjust her top so she's covered, and tug her skirt down to a more reasonable level. "I know a great place just up the coast from here." I link my fingers with hers and set off, tugging her along with me.

She's glaring at me every time I glance at her. Guess my Hellcat doesn't like payback.

When we reach the car, I unlock it and open the door for her to climb in, then crouch down. She ignores me, clicking the seatbelt into place. I run my fingers up her leg.

"How close to the edge are you right now? If you can hold out until we reach where I want to go, I can always book a room …" I don't wait for her to answer, springing to my feet and striding around to the driver's side. When I'm behind the wheel, I glance over at her. "Or you could just pull your skirt up and finish the job while I drive. That would be a shame though. Your pretty little pussy deserves more than your own fingers getting you off."

I start the car and reverse out of the parking lot.

18

Arabella

My fingers twitch with the need to touch myself, but I keep them in my lap. I'm so horny I can't keep still in my seat. All I can think about is having Eli's tongue piercing on my clit.

Is this the effect of the joint we smoked?

Nothing seems real.

What would it feel like? Would it feel as good as Sin's mouth?

A messy tangle of emotion blocks in my throat. Sin isn't here, and I'm aching so much. I don't even know if he'll see me again when I go back to school.

My body is attracted to Eli, but it doesn't mean anything. I'm just scratching an itch. I'm hungry for another orgasm, and I know he can give it to me. I might lust after him, but that doesn't mean I like him.

I say quiet as he drives, aware of him sending me glances from time to time. By the time we reach the place he's talking about, I'm ready to explode.

He switches off the engine. "What's it going to be, Hellcat?"

"The room." The words come out in a breathless rush.

A smirk curves his lips, and he tugs a lock of my blonde hair. "And the food?"

I inhale a ragged breath. "If you don't fuck me right now, I'm going to kick you where it hurts. Food after."

He laughs. The need to punch him fills me, and I half-raise my hand to slap him.

Eli grabs my wrist. "Save your anger for the bedroom."

He exits out of the driver's side, and I climb shakily out of my own. I eye the expensive-looking hotel. "This is where you want to eat?"

He moves past me toward the main door. "They serve good food in the restaurant, which is also available with room service."

Where no one can see us.

I giggle at the thought. "I'm not sure this is what Elena had meant by us getting to know each other."

Not that I give a fuck what she thinks anymore.

Eli's fingers curl around my elbow, to steer me in the right direction. "She doesn't have to know."

"I like being stoned," I say as we pass an elderly couple.

The man with silver hair gives me a stern look, so I blow him a kiss. The woman, probably his wife, grabs him by the arm and hauls him away.

We cross the parking lot. Our appearance draws glances from a few of the other guests milling around the reception area. Eli ignores them, striding over to the desk. I wrap my arms around myself and hang back while he books a room. The relaxed mood the joint has left me in continues to buzz through me. I'm so aroused I don't feel comfortable in my skin, and I can barely think past my lust.

I lick my lips and ignore the look the woman behind the desk gives me. A moment later, Eli walks toward me with a keycard clutched between his fingers. Catching my hand, he leads me toward a bank of elevators.

I jab the button, and we wait for a beat before a set of doors whooshes open.

Eli presses the button for the top floor. "You look hungry, Hellcat."

He's staring at my lips, and I'm aching everywhere. I want him to kiss me so badly. A tingle begins in the space between my thighs.

I inch closer, eating up the space between us until it disappears. "I don't remember the first time we had sex, which makes me think you have a small dick."

His eyebrow raises. "Did it feel small to you out there on the beach?"

I shrug. "I wasn't that impressed."

"Ohhh, the things I'm going to do to that mouth of yours." Eli closes in on me, to trap me against the wall of the elevator. His mouth meets mine, and I open to him, feeling the press of his tongue against mine. A delicious liquid heat spreads through my belly the longer we battle with the kiss.

Eli strokes the edge of my jaw and over my lips.

I nip at the end of it with my teeth. "Kiss me until I'm sick of it. Fuck me until I can't stand it anymore."

Eli

"But what if you don't get sick of it? What if you become addicted?" I kiss along her cheek to her ear. "What if you can't get enough?"

Her hands dip beneath my shirt, and I grab her wrist to stop her from touching the fresh tattoo on my ribs.

"Won't happen." Her teeth sink into my bottom lip, and she sucks it into her mouth, while her hand burrows beneath the waistband of my jeans.

"You think so?" I pull my mouth free and check the floor number. Two more until we reach the penthouse.

"You're not as addictive as you think you are."

The doors swish open, and I catch her hand to draw her out. "You keep coming back for more. You're more addicted to me than you think."

She laughs. "The weed has made me horny, and you're the only one here."

"Ahh." I tap the keycard against the lock and push the door open. "So, if someone else came along, you'd dump me for them?"

"I don't know. Do they have a tongue piercing?" She sashays past me, hips swaying and a smile on her lips.

I close the door and lean against it, watching as she wanders around the room. Her fingers trail across the back of the couch on her path to the floor-to-ceiling windows set in one wall. She slides one door open and steps out onto the balcony beyond and leans over the railing to look out at the view. I cross the room and move up behind her, resting one hand either side of her body.

"It's beautiful."

I brush the hair away from her neck and press my lips against it. "Yes." I'm not talking about the view.

Dropping one hand, I run my palm up her thigh, push her skirt up over her ass and then hook my fingers into the thong nestled against her skin and drag it down. I crouch behind her, holding first one ankle, then the other and lift her leg to remove the lacy scrap of material.

"Someone might see."

I kiss one ass cheek, straighten, and nudge her legs apart with one knee. "We're too high up. Take the hoodie off."

She pulls it over her head.

"Now, your shirt."

"It's too cold to be naked out here."

I drag it up, baring her breasts. "I'll keep you warm." She doesn't stop me from stripping her out of her shirt and bra, and I wrap one arm around her waist and pull her back into my body.

"You're still dressed. That's not fair."

"All you want is my tongue and my dick. I don't need to take my clothes off to give you those."

My palm slides over her stomach and down between her legs. She's already wet. Her stance widens, giving me easier access and I push a finger inside her. Her head drops back against my shoulder and her eyes close.

"Tell me how you feel."

"Cold."

I pinch a nipple. “So, these tight little nipples are hard because you’re cold and not because you’re turned on?”

“That’s right.”

I chuckle against her throat. “You’re such a fucking liar. Your greedy little pussy is begging for more.” I push a second finger into her willing body, and she moans. “Do you think you can take another?”

“I can take anything you want to give.”

I kiss along her shoulder. “That sounds like a challenge, Hellcat.” A third finger joins the two already pumping in and out of her.

Her gasp sparks my nerve-endings to life.

“I lied about being too far up to be seen. If anyone looks up from the parking lot, they’re going to see my fingers buried in your pretty little pussy, and my hand groping your tits. Do you think it’ll turn them on?”

“Eli!”

“Do you like the thought of being seen?” I’ve read her diary; I *know* she’s fantasized about it. “Spread open, your clit on display for all to see while you fuck my fingers.”

“Fuck me.” The demand is delivered with a groan.

“Do you want my dick inside you?”

“Yes!”

“Right here? On the balcony. Do you want me to bend you over the railing and fuck you until your screams echo around the parking lot?”

“Stop talking and *fuck me*.”

“Say please. Please, Eli, feed me your dick and make me come.”

“Fuck you!” But she’s grinding her ass against my dick.

"No, the idea is for *me* to fuck *you*. But not until you ask, Hellcat." My thumb flicks over her clit and her breath hitches. "Do you like that?"

"Do it again."

I repeat the action and pinch her nipple with my other hand. "Reach back and take my dick out."

Her hand finds the button on my jeans and pops it open, then shoves inside to curl around my dick.

"Good girl."

"Condom," she gasps. "Eli, please. Fuck me now."

I pull my fingers free and pluck the condom from my pocket "You got it, Hellcat. Hold on to the railing and bend over."

I rip open the packet, roll the condom on and place the head of my dick against her opening and push forward. We groan in tandem as I thrust inside.

20

Arabella

I clutch the railing, my eyes fixed on the sea, the expanse of blue expanding out to the horizon. I can feel every thick inch of him stretching me, and my body adjusts to his cock. I'm cold, but the heat that burns off Eli melts it away.

"You feel so fucking good, Hellcat." He thrusts all the way in.

The movement steals my breath away. The fingers holding my hips dig roughly into my skin. His cock moves in and out of me in slow, deep thrusts. It's leisurely and torturous and not what I want.

Why is he going so slow?

I press back against him. "Faster."

He chuckles but continues his languid pace. "You wanted me to fuck you, and I am."

I grind into him, and yelp when his hand comes down hard on my ass.

"Fuck me properly."

"Tell me what you want."

"Fuck me with your hate." His speed doesn't change, and I whine. "Give it to me, Eli."

He pulls back, and for a second, I think he's going to stop, but a beat later, he slams back into me. I cry out, and claw at the metal of the railing wishing it was his flesh. In this position, I can't touch him. I'm desperate to scratch him and bite him and hurt him until it feels good.

Eli drives into me over and over. My pussy clenches with each thrust, and I revel in the primitive rawness. Eyes closed, I absorb the sensation of him moving inside me, only vaguely aware of the mewls and moans that leave my lips.

Anyone can hear us, and I just don't care. If anything, it arouses me more knowing anyone who looks up can see what we're doing.

His hand snakes down between my legs. "Tell me how badly you want to come."

"So bad," I wail.

His thumb circles my clit. "Beg for it. Say, Eli, let me come."

I shake my head. "No."

His pace slows and his fingers move from my clit. "Then no orgasm for my dirty little Hellcat."

Panic snaps my eyes open, and my attention drops to the view below. We're so far up. If I fall, I'll end up as a red splatter on the ground below.

"Please, Eli." The words leave me on a whimper. "Let me come on your cock. I need it so badly. Don't stop. Please don't stop."

"Good girl." He picks up a steady rhythm.

My eyes threaten to roll up into the back of my head as the need to come grows. It builds and builds with each of his thrusts. I'm right there, standing on a dangerous precipice which isn't just the drop over the rail if I should fall. I'm on the verge of tumbling into an orgasm which I shouldn't be allowing to happen. My release hits, and I plummet through a kaleidoscope of color.

He groans behind me, and a second later, he shudders. I feel his cock pulsing, sending aftershocks through me. I pant, clutch the railing, and savor every second of it.

He pulls out of me and steps back. "It's cold. We should get back inside. I don't think Elena will be happy if you get hypothermia."

Heart still hammering against my ribs, I step away from the railing. My knees go weak, and he catches me before I hit the floor.

"Oops." I giggle, drunk and intoxicated on my orgasm.

He sweeps me up in his arms and carries me back into the penthouse and through to the bedroom.

"I want to do it again," I tell him as I'm deposited on the huge bed. I roll onto my back, naked in nothing but black knee-high socks and my ballet shoes.

"I think I've created a monster."

His words tug my eyes up to the smirk on his face. "Do you like fucking me? Did watching the video you leaked get you hard? Did you watch the other ones?"

Something dark shifts over his expression. "For the last time. I did not release that fucking video."

I stretch out on the mattress, to watch him through half-closed eyes. "Maybe you did. Maybe you didn't. But you didn't answer my other questions."

He turns on his heels, to stalk out of the room without reply. The glass door in the other room bangs closed. He doesn't return straight away, and I lay listening to him moving around outside the room.

"Yes, the video of you sucking someone's dick made me hard," he tells me from the doorway when he finally reappears. "I bet all the guys at school who saw it jerked off and pretended their hands were your mouth." His words are crude. "Who is he?"

He's still denying it? Why isn't he rubbing it in my face and calling me a whore. That's what he thinks I am. A whore like Elena.

I shrug, trying to act casual and not show my true emotions. "I don't know. A stranger in the dark."

Why deny it now when everyone has seen the video? I can't pretend it wasn't me. There's no going back in time to change what happened, no matter how much I wish I could.

Shame and arousal mix with the memories of everything Sin had made me do. I'd done them willingly. First out of a forbidden thrill, and then out of an irresistible urge to please him.

Eli stares at me, eyes intense. "You opened that pretty mouth to take some guy's dick, and you don't know who it is?"

"You saw the blindfold, right?" A wave of shame makes me glance away from him.

"Did it turn you on?"

"You said you watched the video. You know the answer to that."

"Was it the first time you'd met him? You just stripped and got on your knees for him?"

"It wasn't like that." Warmth heats my cheeks. "I guess everyone knows Arabella Gray isn't so sweet and innocent anymore."

The mattress moves as Eli drops down beside me. "Sweet and innocent are overrated, Hellcat."

"How many condoms do you have?" I roll over onto my side and reach for the button of his jeans. I want to purge the thought of all the boys at school watching the intimate moment I shared with Sin. "I think the weed has turned me into a nymphomaniac."

Eli grabs my wrist, the fingers of his free hand trace over the cigarette burns on my skin. "Where did you get these?"

I glance at them. "One of Elena's boyfriends when I was six. He was drunk and used me as an ashtray. He broke my arm when I cried out."

I force away the painful recollection of Elena driving me to the hospital, and I go back to unbuttoning his jeans. My hand slips beneath his boxer briefs, and I curl my fingers around the hard, hot girth of his cock.

"Put your dirty hands and mouth all over me again."

21

Eli

"You've already had my dirty hands all over you. I think it's time you returned the favor, don't you?" I settle onto my back and tuck my hands behind my head. "You're already an orgasm ahead of me."

"You're keeping count?" Her fingers are warm around my dick, but her grip is gentle.

"Someone has to." I smirk at her scowl. "What are you doing down there?" I direct my gaze to where her hand is in my jeans. "Touch me like you mean it, Hellcat."

"I don't want to hurt you."

That makes me laugh. "Yes, you do. You want to see me bleed." I push my hand beneath the denim and curl my fingers around hers. "Grip harder." I adjust her hold on my dick and show her how to pump up and down.

My head drops back against the pillow, eyes closing, as we both stroke my erection.

"That's it. Take it out and wrap your lips around it."

"You want me to suck your dick, Eli?"

"Pretty sure that's what I just said." I grunt when she pulls my dick free of my jeans, her fingers squeezing around my length. "Mouth, Hellcat."

"I like that better than Princess."

My lip curls. "It fits you better than Princess. But I always knew there was a hellcat lurking beneath the pretty pink shell." I open my eyes to find her staring at me. "What?"

She shakes her head. "Nothing. You just reminded me of someone for a second."

"Oh? Who?" I need to be more careful. We seem to be on the precarious edge of… *something* right now. But if she links me to Sin, she'll hate me more than she already does.

"Doesn't matter." Her head turns away, and her tongue sweeps across her lips. "I've only done this once." She kneels beside my hip and slowly lowers her head. "What should I do?"

Fuck.

The whispered question sends all the blood in my body straight down to my dick.

"Lick the head."

My gaze is riveted to her as her tongue comes out and touches the tip of my dick. The sensation is like a bolt of lightning, burning its way through my veins. "Use your tongue to make me wet." My voice comes out as a rough growl. "Then wrap your lips around me and suck me into your mouth."

She follows my instruction, licking her way up one side and down the other before parting her lips and engulfing my dick into the hot, wet depths of her mouth.

"Fuck." The curse is ripped from me.

Watching my dick disappear into her mouth almost makes me lose control, and I close my eyes against the incredible visual. "Bring your ass up here."

She releases my dick with a wet pop. "How?"

"I want you to sit on my face. Legs either side of my head. Bring your pussy to me, Hellcat. Then get my dick back in your mouth."

The mattress bounces as she moves, and I open my eyes just as she takes the position I demanded.

"Perfect." The word is a guttural groan as my hands curve over her ass, and I pull her down onto my face, tongue searching out her clit.

The only sounds in the room are her muffled whimpers as I feast on her while she sucks my dick. She tries to escape twice, her body twitching and shaking with the force of her orgasm, and I hold her in place, thrusting my tongue in and out of her pussy in time with her mouth sliding up and down my dick.

When my nerves start to tighten, I reach down and pull her head off me. I don't want to come in her mouth … not this time. "Turn around. There are two more condoms in my pocket. Get one out and roll it on."

She climbs off me, finds the packet and tears it open, but doesn't do anything with it.

"Huh, I forgot. You've never done that." I hold out my hand. "I'll show you." I take the condom out of the packet and roll it over my dick, then toss her a smile. "Climb on board, Hellcat."

"You're still dressed."

"I told you, you don't need me to take my clothes off. All you want is my dick." I wave a hand toward where it's jutting out of my jeans, condom-wrapped and ready to go. "And that's readily available."

"Take your jeans off."

"*You* take my jeans off."

She hooks her fingers into the belt loops and drags the denim down my legs. Her scowl when she discovers I'm still wearing sneakers is hilarious, but I manage not to laugh out loud. She pulls them off, yanks my jeans the rest of the way down and then straddles my hips.

I reach down and wrap a hand around my erection. "Lower yourself onto my dick. Keep your eyes on me." I want to see the expression on her face when I fill her up.

Her blue eyes darken as my dick stretches her open. Her teeth sink into her bottom lip and, once I'm fully seated inside her, she throws her head back.

"Ride me. The way you did back at the lighthouse." I run a finger around a nipple, feeling it harden beneath my touch. "You should get these pierced." I pinch it. "Little hoops so I can tug them. Or maybe you should get this pierced." I tap her clit with my other hand, and she twitches. "But that means I wouldn't be able to eat you out for at least six weeks." I rub in a small circle. "You're not moving, Hellcat. I'm not doing all the work for you. If you want to come, you need to fuck me."

Her hips rock forward, and my hands drop to her hips. I push down, driving my dick deeper inside her.

"Fuck me like you hate me." I toss her own words back at her.

22

Arabella

"I *do* hate you." Undulating my hips, I thrust up and down on his length. "Do you want me pierced, Eli?"

"You've already got a tattoo." He glances at the Saran wrap still on my arm.

My butterfly.

I grind down hard on top of him, moaning at the way he fills me. "Are you trying to turn me into your toy?"

"I think you enjoy being my toy to play with." He cups my breasts, and fondles my nipples, twisting them between his fingers.

Anger stirs beneath the pleasure that washes through my body. "Do you enjoy turning me into a whore?"

It's so fucked up that we're making each other feel good. He's been a bastard to me from day one. I can't forget that through the blissful haze of having his cock buried inside me.

"Enjoying sex doesn't make you a whore." Eli stares up at me and tugs on my nipples, sending a sharp dart of pain straight down to my core.

That's not what everyone else thinks.

"How to please a rich man so I can get a ring on my finger, just like Elena." The words flow without thought out of my mouth. "That's what you think I want, right?"

I throw the taunts back in his face with a smile.

In one swift movement, he knocks me sideways and off him. I

land on my side on the mattress, only to be flipped onto my front. Hands drag my ass up into the air, and Eli slams back into me hard. My cry of pleasure is half-muffled when my face is pushed down into the pillow. He fucks me roughly with long steady strokes. Eyes screwed shut, I savor the sensation, anticipating the building tension.

"You want me to fuck you like you're a whore, *Arabella?"* There's a bite to his voice. "Then take my fucking dick like the paid-for fucktoy you are."

He's using me just like I'm using him. He hates me, but I make him hard. My orgasm rolls through me. A few thrusts later, he follows me over, finding his release.

"Fuck," he groans, and pulls out of me.

I roll onto my back, my entire body pulsing in euphoric mush.

Eli climbs off the bed, taking the spent condom off his cock. He's naked from the waist down and I greedily take my fill of staring at him. Just as he returns from the bathroom, his phone rings.

He finds his jeans on the floor and pulls his cell out of his pocket. A smile curves his lips when he sees who's calling and answers.

"Hello, Elena."

My eyes widen at my mother's name, and I press a hand over my mouth to muffle my giggle.

"She's not answering her phone?" Eli strolls toward the bed, gaze locked with mine. "She says she has it on silent. That's why she didn't hear you calling."

He reaches out and trails his fingers up my thigh. "We are working out our differences. Yeah, we're talking things through."

His fingers push into me, and I have to bite my lip to stop myself from moaning.

"We won't be back for dinner," he continues. "In fact, we won't be back tonight at all. I've promised to take her to the Americana Mall in Manhasset and do some Christmas shopping tomorrow, and it's easier if we stay in a hotel."

Americana Mall? I give him a questioning look.

He's silent for a beat and then holds the phone out to me. "She wants to talk to you."

I try to hold in my giggle. If she realizes I'm naked in a hotel with Eli there will be hell to pay.

I press the phone to my ear. "Hello?"

"I'm so happy you and Eli are getting along," Elena gushes on the other end of the line.

Eli pulls my legs apart. His gaze burns into mine up the length of my body.

"We're talking a lot," I tell her, as he lowers his head. My mouth drops open in a silent moan at the first lick of his tongue over my clit.

"So, you're no longer fighting?" my mother asks.

He licks me again.

"N-no. Not fighting."

Eli raises his head and grins, mouthing the words *'hate fucking.'*

"I must admit I was a little worried about sending you off together." She laughs. "Even Elliot had his doubts about the two of you getting along."

"Hmmm." My free hand reaches down to tangle in his hair as he presses kisses along my thigh. "I think we're finding s-some common g-ground."

His hungry mouth returns to torment me, and I grind my pussy against his face.

"I'll leave you to your bonding time. See you tomorrow."

"Okay. Bye." The line goes dead.

His hands wrap around my thighs, and he pulls my legs over his shoulders. I cry out in pleasure, his tongue lapping and licking over my clit, as an orgasm crashes through me.

"Your pussy is still so fucking hungry, even after I've just fed her my dick."

"Are we really staying here tonight?"

He nips at my other thigh with his teeth. "Do you have a problem with that?"

"No. But you might run out of condoms."

"I'll go out and buy more. First, we should order some food. You need to keep your strength up if you want to ride my dick all night."

23

Eli

"It might fall off." She giggles.

"I'm more likely to destroy your pussy before my dick falls off, Hellcat." I roll off the bed and grab my jeans.

Her eyes are on me as I bend to drag them up my legs. "If you keep looking at me like that, the only thing you'll be eating for dinner is me."

Her laugh is low and warm. "Feed me. Fuck me. Fight me."

"That should be your next tattoo."

Her eyes drop to where she knows *Nasty Little Monster* is tattooed across my ribs beneath my t-shirt. "You're the one who keeps marking his body with reminders of me. *You* get it tattooed on yourself."

My smile is lazy. "Maybe I will. It seems like a good motto to live by."

I leave her sprawled on the bed and go into the main room of the suite. There should be a room-service menu somewhere. I turn in a circle, until I spot it beside the house phone. Crossing the carpet, I pick it up and flick through it as I walk back to the bedroom.

"Do you want to order room service or go down to—" I stop in the doorway.

Arabella is curled onto her side, eyes closed, and one hand tucked beneath her cheek. I move closer.

"Arabella?" She doesn't stir. "Ari?" My voice is softer this time.

Nothing. No acknowledgment at all. I am sure she wouldn't be able to resist responding to me shortening her name if she's faking being asleep, but she remains still.

With careful movements, I drag the sheet, which has been pushed to the bottom of the bed by our fucking, up and over her, then brush the hair off her cheek and press a kiss there.

"Pleasant dreams, Kitten."

I retrace my steps out into the other room, pulling the door closed behind me and drop down onto the couch. I'm hungry, but I can wait until she wakes up before ordering food, unless she decides to sleep the entire day away. I pick up the television remote control off the coffee table, turn on the TV, and flick through the stations until I find an old black-and-white horror movie playing.

Leaving that to play in the background, I take my cell out of my pocket and call Kellan. He picks up on the second ring.

"I need you to do something for me."

***

I'm in the middle of a Christopher Lee movie marathon when a shadow falls over me. I turn my head to find Arabella standing at the end of the couch, wrapped in a sheet. Her hair is a tumbled mess around her face.

"I fell asleep."

"I know. You were snoring like a wild boar. I'm surprised we haven't had noise complaints."

She comes toward me, smiling, lets the sheet drop and straddles my lap.

"I was going to ask if you're hungry, but I see what the answer is." I tip my head back against the couch's headrest and look at her.

"I *am* hungry."

"I meant for food."

Her lips nibble a path down my throat, and I angle my head to give her more access. "I could eat."

"The menu is on the coffee table. Do you want to order room service or go down to the restaurant?"

"Room service." She parts her mouth from my neck long enough to answer me.

"What's happening here, Hellcat?" I tangle a hand into her hair and tug her head up.

"Elena wanted us to get to know each other better."

"Pretty sure she didn't mean biblically."

"Then she should have been more specific."

I laugh at that, wrap a lock of her hair around one finger, and use it to draw her closer to me. Just as our lips meet, my cell bursts into life with Kellan's ringtone.

"Ignore it." Arabella winds her arms around my neck, and I'm tempted … so fucking tempted … but this is important.

Dropping my hands to her waist, I lift her off me. "I need to take this. Pick what you want to eat, and I'll order it once I'm done." I stand up, connect the call, and walk into the bedroom.

"Well?"

"The cloud is empty."

"Good."

"No, you don't understand. *I* didn't do it. It had already been wiped. It took me a while to get into the folder. Someone changed the password."

"Fuck. Do you think the school deleted everything?"

"There's no easy way to tell. Given some time, I can probably find out who logged in, the IP address, and whether copies were taken before it was all deleted."

"How *much* time?"

"Not sure. It depends on how well whoever did it covered their tracks."

"Then why the fuck are you wasting time telling me about it? I want to know what happened to those files."

"You got it." He paused. "There's talk that Arabella is coming back to school after Christmas. Is that true?"

"Yeah."

"What about you?"

"Don't know yet. They're still discussing it. When I find out, I'll let you know."

"Okay."

"Kellan?"

"Yeah?"

"I need you to watch over her when she comes back to school. You've seen the social media. They're not done with her yet."

"You got it."

Dare To Take

29

Arabella

Eli is quiet when he comes back from the bedroom, and it makes me wonder who he talked to. I push the thought aside, and stare down at the menu from my place on the sofa.

Huddled back under the bed sheet, I eye the selection in front of me. "Grilled salmon. Chicken souvlaki, lobster risotto. Don't they do any normal food?"

Eli laughs. "Define normal."

"Pizza, burgers, steak?"

He takes a seat beside me and taps the menu in my hands. "Turn it over."

I flip it over, to run my gaze over what's on offer. "Cheddar stuffed burger in a brioche bun?"

He lays his arm along the back of the couch and plays with my hair. "Keep going to the bottom, and you'll find the … less fancy stuff."

I do as instructed and find what I'm looking for. "I'll have a cheeseburger and fries, please."

"Burgers and fries for both of us." He takes the menu from me and rises smoothly from the couch. I watch him pick up the phone and order our food, with an easy confidence. Something that comes with power and money. I bet he's never had to struggle to find his next meal and hope his parent left food in the fridge so he could eat.

My attention moves to the TV, and my eyes widen when I see what's playing across the screen. "Christopher Lee! I love these movies."

Eli retakes his seat beside me. "You do?"

"Uh-huh."

"You like horror movies?"

I scrunch up my nose at the disbelieving tone in his voice. "Not modern ones, but these are classics. He's one of the best Dracula's ever, in my opinion, followed by Bella Lugosi and, of course, Gary Oldman."

"You like Bella Lugosi?" The surprise in his voice is clear.

"With that slow, thick accent, his penetrating eyes, and the way he moved. It's mesmerizing." I keep my eyes on the TV. "His Dracula is a little more sophisticated than Christopher Lee's sexy Dracula."

"So, you're into vampires?"

I turn my head and find him studying me. "Vampires. Old black-and-white movies. *The Maltese Falcon, Singing in the Rain, Some like it Hot*. Mrs. Goldmann adored watching them."

Amusement dances in his eyes. "Who?"

"Our neighbor who lived next door to us back in Michigan. She looked after me when Elena wasn't there." I draw my knees up under the sheet and I hug them to my chest.

Eli falls silent beside me, and we both watch the movie. It's easy to pretend that we don't hate each other. The lines between us are blurring. Everything has shifted and right now, we're just two people hanging out, watching a bunch of people get chased by a vampire. I snicker when one of the women gets covered in blood.

"That looks so fake."

"They used to blend water, food dye, and corn syrup to make it," he says. "Not quite in today's league with the special effects, but I think that's what makes them so much fun to watch."

He jumps up when there's a knock at the door. Instead of letting the waiter in, he accepts the trolley and brings it in himself. "Want to eat at the table?"

I shake my head. "We won't be able to see the TV from over there."

"You want to watch the rest of the movie marathon?" He uncovers the plates that hold our food. "It's not all his vampire stuff."

"I don't mind."

"I thought you wanted my dick."

"I do, but I also want to watch TV while I eat."

He shakes his head and chuckles. "Fine."

He brings the plates over to the couch and places them on the low glass coffee table, before joining me on the cushions. I secure the sheet around my body and perch on the edge. The movie slides into another classic horror movie as we eat.

Taking a sip of my drink, I sense eyes on me. I glance in Eli's direction. My pulse picks up and butterflies take off in my stomach at the look in his eyes. The sexual awareness between us is palpable. This attraction I feel for him is messing with my head. We've already fucked twice; I shouldn't want him again.

His smile is knowing. I catch my lower lip between my teeth and wonder if he can somehow read my mind.

In an effort to shake it off, I pluck a fry from my plate and toss it at him. I laugh when it bounces off his chest.

25

Eli

After she throws a fry at me, I retaliate. The gloves come off and we end up tussling on the floor. Tussling turns into touching, and the movie is soon forgotten in favor of fucking. When we finally separate, panting and sweaty, the movie is over, the food is cold, and the sun has set. I stand and reach down to pull her to her feet.

"You have ketchup in your hair." I brush a finger over the tangled curls. "Why don't you go and take a shower? I'll clean up in here."

"I haven't got anything to wear, other than the clothes I came in."

My lips quirk at her wording, but I refrain from making a joke. "It's the penthouse, Hellcat. There'll be complimentary robes in the bathroom."

"Oh! I didn't think of that."

"I guessed that from your make-shift toga." I wave toward the sheet, now discarded on the floor. "Rules of the world. The richer you are, the more they give you for free. The robes come with the suite booking. We can take them with us when we leave. There will also be toiletries in there. Take whatever you want."

"What about you?"

"What about me?"

Her fingers run up my arm and tug at my t-shirt. "Don't you need to shower, too?"

"I will. Once I'm done in here."

"You could shower with me?"

I press a finger to her chin and tilt her head up. "You're fucking insatiable. Aren't you sore?" I hike an eyebrow. "Or did you fuck half of Michigan when you ran away?"

Hurt flashes across her face and she pulls away.

I catch her hand and tug her back to me. "I'm joking. I don't think you fucked half of Michigan."

"It wasn't funny."

I dip my head to kiss her, but she turns her face away. "Come on, it was just a joke."

"A bad one."

My lips find her ear and I nip it gently. "I'm sorry."

"I'm not a whore, Eli."

"I never said you are. Those were your words, not mine."

"You're the only guy I've fucked."

"But not the only one whose dick you've sucked." But I know that's a lie. Because I know whose dick she was sucking on the video that was shared.

"You're such a fucking asshole." She shoves me away and storms off to the bathroom.

I consider going after her and telling her that it's me in the video but decide against it. Trying to explain why I did it—how to begin with, it was to punish her and that my original intention *was* to share the footage with the school—will just make her more convinced that I am guilty of releasing it.

How could I explain that our meetings stopped being about getting ammunition to prove she was a money-hungry gold-digger and turned into a need to fulfill the fantasies she talked about in her diary? The more I read, the more time I spent with her as Sin, the more I realized she hadn't *lived,* and I wanted to give her all those experiences she was missing out on and dreamed about.

Telling her that the second I touched her, *tasted* her, all my plans shifted and became something else will sound like a lie and the fragile friendship we seem to be building will crash and burn before it even takes root.

I clear up the food, dump it all in the trash and walk through to the bedroom. The shower is running, and I'm so fucking tempted to strip off and join her. But that will open the door to a whole new set of problems, so I distract myself by tidying up the bed.

When she finally comes out of the bathroom, wrapped in a fluffy white robe, her cheeks pink from the heat of the water, I'm lying on the bed messing with my cell.

"Bathroom's free." Her words are stilted.

Still angry with me, then.

"I should hope so. The room costs enough. I'd hate to have to pay extra for bathroom perks." My voice is dry as I swing my legs off the bed.

She rolls her eyes, but I see her lips twitch as she fights to stop a smile. I tweak a lock of damp hair on my way past her to the door, and head into the bathroom to take a shower.

***

I wake up to the strangest sensation, and it takes a little while for my brain to decipher what is happening. First thing I register is that I'm lying face down, my face buried into the pillow. Second thing that comes to mind is that I'm naked. But it's the third thing that has me snapping my eyes open and shoving upright.

Someone is touching me. More specifically, my back.

There's a soft exhalation of air as I knock whoever is there away from me, and that's when sleep finally releases its grip and my mind catches up to where I am.

"Fuck." I twist on the mattress to see Arabella on her back, staring up at me, eyes startled. "Sorry. Did I hurt you?"

She shakes her head.

"What time is it?" I search around for my cell, spot it on the floor and reach down to grab it, but I don't ask it to tell me the time. "Get dressed. We'll go down to the restaurant for breakfast." I stand and snatch my clothes up, dragging the t-shirt over my head.

"Eli." Her voice is soft.

Tension zips through me. I pull on my underwear and jeans.

"Eli—" she tries again, and I *know* what she's going to say so I speak over her.

"Fuck it. Manhasset is around a ninety-minute drive from here. We'll skip breakfast and go straight there. We can find somewhere to eat once we arrive." I drag a hand through my hair and go into the bathroom to brush my teeth.

Movement in the mirror brings my head up as I spit out the water. Arabella. Staring at me out of big blue eyes, bottom lip caught between her teeth. Our eyes meet in the reflection, and her lips part.

"No." I swing around, catch her by her shoulders, and propel her backward out of the room.

"What happened?" Her eyes track across my face. Her voice is still soft, so fucking gentle it twists my insides.

"I *said* no. We're not having that conversation. Get dressed. I'm leaving in ten minutes. With or without you."

"Is that why you never take off your shirt?"

I ignore her, striding out into the main room and searching for my sneakers and hoodie.

"Eli, stop. Talk to me."

Shoving my feet into my shoes, I throw on my hoodie. "No. It's not open for discussion. I'll be in the car." Without waiting for another reply, I walk out, letting the door slam behind me.

Am I being unreasonable? Maybe. But the scars on my back are not something I want to talk about, least of all with a girl who wants nothing from me except the pleasure I can give her.

26

Arabella

I sit in the car beside Eli, the silence strained between us. My body is aching, and between my legs is sore, from all the sex we've had. I should be relaxed, but I can't stop thinking about the scars on his back. The skin had been messy and uneven, a darker shade of pink than the rest of his body. Whatever happened to him must have been agony.

I take a sneaky look at him from the corner of my eye. His lips pressed together, and his gaze is glued to the road ahead, yet he still notices my glance.

"Don't," he growls.

I drag my gaze away and look down at my hands. "I was just going to ask how much longer we have until we get to Manhasset."

"Not sure."

"Okay." I turn toward the window and watch the passing scenery. I want to ask questions, but it will only piss him off more. This truce between us is fragile, and I'm not sure I want to destroy it. Not yet.

By the time we reach the city, excitement has overtaken my concern. I've never been to the Americana Mall. Eli finds a private parking lot and leaves the keys with one of the valets. I shiver with the cold when I step out of the car. I should have worn something warmer than my leather skirt.

"Buy some jeans and a coat, then change into them."

"I should have thought about comfort instead of wanting to show off my new outfit."

"It wouldn't have been as much fun having you get yourself off on my dick if you hadn't worn that skirt."

His rough words make me smile, and a blush warms my cheeks.

We walk along the street together, my attention roving over the brightly decorated Christmas storefronts. "What are you going to get your dad for Christmas?"

Eli shrugs. "No idea."

"You don't do gifts?"

"We used to when my mom was alive."

His words make me realize I don't even know anything about his mother. I don't even know how she died. It's on the tip of my tongue to ask, but from his closed-off expression, it's easy to tell that it's another conversation he doesn't want to have.

Seeing him like this makes him more normal, just like any other regular boy. We both have trauma. Different baggage we're carrying around weighing us both down. Things that have shaped who we are.

My heart gives an odd little jolt in my chest. I feel compassion for the Monster of Churchill Bradley Academy. My tormentor. My enemy. The stepbrother from Hell I never wanted.

Remember what he did to you, how he hurt you. Remember how that felt.

The voice is a weak warning in the back of my head, but I ignore it. It's almost Christmas, and as much as I dislike him, I don't want to have a war between us over the holidays. His dad is still recovering from his heart attack and needs a calm environment.

How tranquil will that be if he finds out I'm fucking his son?

The thought dulls my mellow mood. What happened yesterday

can't happen again. A hotel is one thing, but if Elena or Elliot caught us messing around at the house, it would be disastrous. Once we get home, things will return to reality. Eli hasn't touched me since he woke up. He's already losing interest.

I ignore the slither of disappointment that creeps through me.

"Elena and I did gifts when she was home. Sometimes she just left them with Mrs. Goldmann if she wasn't going to be with me over the holidays."

So many moments she wasn't there. The few memories I have are scattered among her absences. A sad smile pulls my lips up.

"I want to buy a Christmas decoration," I tell him. "To hang on the tree when we put it up."

Eli gives me a sideways glance. "The staff usually put the tree up, but between you vanishing and my dad's heart attack, I doubt anyone has thought about it."

Guilt flares up inside me. "What? No! We have to do it. That's part of the fun. I have a bunch of decorations in a box I've collected. I add to it once a year. It's a tradition. As soon as we get back, I'll start decorating."

It feels natural to grab his hand and drag him into the first big department store we see. We head to the women's department, and I find a pair of black jeans in my size.

A long black flowing coat with faux fur lapels catches my eye, and I check the price tag. "Two hundred dollars. Ouch."

Eli brushes his fingers along the fur. "It would suit you."

"It's too much."

"Two hundred dollars is pocket change."

I sigh. "Maybe to you. I'm used to second-hand clothes and

thrift stores."

He catches my wrist, to stop me from putting it back on the rail. "Try it on."

I search his gaze, losing myself a little in those intoxicating green eyes. "Okay."

I slip my arms into the coat, the warmth of the material enveloping me. My thumbs caress the softness of the lapels, and I push them up until they brush my cheeks.

"It's perfect." I twirl around and around in front of a nearby mirror, watching the way the bottom of the coat swirls around my ankles.

The second I take it off to put it back on its hanger, Eli takes it from me, along with the jeans. He strolls past me through the store. I rush after him only to find him paying for everything with his card by the time I get there.

I accept the bag he hands me. "You didn't need to do that."

He shrugs. "If I didn't, you wouldn't have bought them. Let's call it a gift."

My stomach lurches, and suspicion creeps in. "Payment for the sex?"

Something dark flickers in Eli's eyes. "You're the one who wanted to have sex, and I'm pretty sure you'd never make me pay for it." His lip curls. "Not with money, anyway. Blood, maybe. Stop reading too much into it. It's just clothes, Hellcat. Now go put them on so you don't get cold."

"Thank you for the gift." Awkwardness has me turning toward the changing rooms without another word. I change into the jeans and pull the coat on. Stuffing my skirt in the bag, I emerge onto the store floor to find Eli leaning against a pillar playing with his phone.

"Mistletoe!" I point out lightly as I join him. "You know what that means."

Eli tilts his head up to look at the decoration hanging right above his head and down to meet my gaze, with a frown. "No?"

"If someone stands under the mistletoe, you have to kiss them." When he doesn't make a move, I pout. "Fine, I'll kiss you then."

I curl my fingers in the front of his hoodie and drag him down so I can press my lips to his. I push my tongue into his mouth, flicking it against the ring in his. Eli mutters something against my mouth. His arms come around my waist, and the kiss deepens into something hungrier and urgent.

27

Eli

When someone jostles me from behind, I lift my head. Arabella's arms are looped around my neck, her eyes half-closed. My gaze tracks over her face, following the path of her tongue as it licks over her lips. Reaching back, I unhook her hands and take a step away.

"You're dangerous, Hellcat." I turn away, and a second later her arm creeps around my waist and she leans into my side. My immediate impulse is to push her away, but I fight against it, and drape my arm across her shoulders instead. "Let's get out of here. Christmas decorations you said, right? I know a place you might like."

We weave through the other shoppers and back out into the cold. There's a store off the beaten track, away from the tourists that Poppy brought me to when I was a kid. I'm not sure if it's still there, but if I remember it right, Arabella will love the things it sells.

It takes me a few wrong turns, but eventually, I find the right street and guide her through the door. The interior looks like someone raided Santa's grotto. Everything is Christmas-related. Toys, decorations, train sets, trees. Anything you can imagine.

Arabella gasps, eyes wide as she stares around. I let my arm drop from her shoulders and wave a hand.

"Go nuts." I find a relatively clear space by a wall and lean against it, while she darts around the store, looking at everything.

I push my earbuds in while she's browsing, tap play on my music, and close my eyes. '12 Rounds' by Bohnes fills my ears.

I lose track of time as one song flows into another and it's only when there's a tap on my arm that I open my eyes. Arabella is standing in front of me, holding a small bag.

"Is that all you bought?"

"I told you. I buy one new decoration a year."

"Seems like a long-winded way to decorate a tree."

She rolls her eyes and punches my arm. "Are you being purposely dense? I *have* other decorations. I just buy a special one every year."

"What makes it special?" I follow her out of the store.

She doesn't answer until we're back on the sidewalk. "I like to pick something that represents the year I've had."

I flick a finger toward the bag. "So that's a torture device, then? Should I worry?"

She stops and turns to me. "Did you just make a joke? Does Eli Travers have a sense of humor? Oh my god, is the world about to end?" She slaps a palm to her chest and smirks at me.

"Now, who's the asshole?"

She pats my cheek. "The answer to that question will always be you."

I can't stop the laugh that breaks free. "You're so fucking weird."

***

We stop for lunch in a small cafe, at Arabella's insistence, where she takes forever to decide what to eat. When she finally settles on grilled cheese and a hot chocolate, I double the order.

I have a moment of panic when I realize the cafe doesn't take cards and wants cash. Logically, I *know* what each bill means, but putting it into practice without time and warning sends me into a spin.

I stare down at the folded bills in my hand, then up at the cash register for what feels like an hour before two fingers pluck a couple of them out of my grip and hand them to the server.

"Do you use money so little that you forgot what it means?"

I know she's teasing, I can hear it in her voice, so I force a laugh and nod. "You caught me. I rarely use anything other than a card." I turn and guide her over to a table. "What do you want to do next?" I stretch out my legs beneath the table and hook my ankles around hers.

She frowns at me but doesn't pull away. "We should get gifts for your dad and Elena."

"We don't really—"

"You are *not* about to tell me you don't buy your dad something for Christmas!"

I shrug. "Would you prefer I lie?"

"What about when your mom was alive?"

My mind blanks, immediately closing down any thoughts of my mom, and something must have shown on my face because she covers her mouth with one hand. "I'm sorry."

I force myself to shake my head. "It's fine." My voice is clipped. "Let's just eat, grab whatever you want to get and get out of here. I'm surprised your mom isn't blowing up my phone wanting to know where you are."

She laughs. "It'll take a couple of days for Elena to notice I haven't come home. We're not that close."

"She seemed interested in what you were doing yesterday."

"No, she's interested in what *you're* doing. She's desperate for us to play happy families."

"Why do you think that is?" I lean back when the server arrives with our food and drinks. "Thank you." I give her a smile when she sets it down in front of us.

"I know why *you* think it is." She lifts the mug of hot chocolate to her lips and takes a sip. The throaty moan that erupts from her throat makes my dick hard.

"And why is that?" I keep my voice light.

"I think gold-digger was one of the terms you threw at me."

"You don't think she married my dad to make life easier for herself?"

"Oh, I definitely think she did that."

I'm surprised by her ready agreement.

"But seeing her reaction when the hospital called to tell her about Elliot's heart attack, I think maybe she might like him more than I thought."

"Even money-hungry bitches can fall in love, right?" I pick up my own drink. "For what it's worth, I think my dad could have picked someone worse."

"Wow, is that an admission that you were wrong to be such a bastard to me?"

"I thought we were talking about your mom." I smirk at her over the rim of the mug.

She shakes her head. "You're such an asshole." But there's a smile on her lips and warmth in her voice.

We fall into a companionable silence while we eat and once our plates are clear, gather up her bags and walk back to the car to deposit them.

"I guess you're going to insist on searching for gifts for Dad and Elena?" I lean against the side of the car and look at her.

"It's not Christmas without presents to open, Eli."

28

Arabella

We're almost back at the house when I remember I haven't bothered to turn my phone on today. I hadn't given it a moment's thought while we've been shopping for gifts. Now we're back, my mind is already thinking about what might be waiting for me. After all the hateful and cruel comments over the last week, it's made me wary of checking it.

Rummaging through my bags, I fish it out and turn it on. The screen lights up, and a moment later, it buzzes with incoming notifications.

Unknown number: It's open season on you, Arabella. When you get back to school, we all want a taste of what those lips can do.

Unknown number: Is that little cunt of yours hungry for cock?

Unknown number: Tick tock. See you soon.

My heart pounds in my chest. Unease crawls across my skin. It's a sharp reminder of what awaits me when I get back to Churchill Bradley Academy. Eli has helped me forget, but I've been kidding myself if I thought it was all going to go away. Every second that passes brings me one step closer to going back.

I need to focus on Christmas. One day at a time.

"Everything okay?" Eli's voice is quiet.

I force a smile onto my face when he glances my way.

"Just Miles checking up on me." I'm not sure why I lie.

"I wonder what everyone would think if they knew your boyfriend was gay."

"He's not gay." Panic at what might happen if his secret got out forces me to lie again.

He glances at me quickly, before returning his gaze to the road. "Then why didn't he fuck you?"

His question is enough to hike up my heart rate. "I was the one who didn't want to have sex."

"But you were ready to suck someone else's dick."

"Jealous I didn't suck yours first?"

Eli laughs, his attention on the turn as we swing around into the circular drive of the house. "I got plenty of your other firsts, Hellcat."

Ones I gave him freely and eagerly.

Cheeks hot, I wait until he's cut the engine, then scramble out of the door. Elena appears in the doorway while I'm pulling bags out of the back, and Eli is rounding the car.

"Did you have a nice time?" she asks.

I step back, and pass Eli. "It was fun." Not a lie.

Hanging out with him has been two of the best days I've ever had. Not that I'm about to admit that out loud. How long can I hold onto the illusion that things aren't going to revert to how they were?

"I bought a decoration to mark the year." I walk towards her and into the house. "I thought we could put the tree up."

Elena laughs. "*Up*? Bella, we don't have one of those cheap plastic things you used to buy each year with the lopsided branches. I thought you'd thrown that box of old baubles out when we moved."

Eli joins us, kicking the front door closed with his foot.

"But we need a tree." The thought of not doing something safe and normal spirals me into alarm. "It's not Christmas without one. I always decorate it. It's tradition."

My mother sighs. "I will see if the staff can sort something out, but it's a bit last minute."

"No! We need to do it and decorate it."

"Arabella, you aren't a child anymore."

Every muscle in my body tenses. "It's the one thing we always used to do when you were home, or if I was with Mrs. Goldmann." My protest comes out as a whisper.

"Stop panicking. I ordered one when you were up to your neck in Christmas baubles." Eli's voice is smooth behind me. "It should be here within the hour. That gives you enough time to unpack and figure out where you want it to go."

My smile is so wide my cheeks hurt. I have to stop myself from throwing my arms around his neck and covering his face in grateful kisses. "Thank you."

"No problem." He heads up the stairs.

Elena arches an eyebrow, watching him go. "There's a lot less tension between the two of you. You look a lot more relaxed than when you left yesterday."

"Shopping therapy works wonders." I hurry past her.

The last forty-eight hours don't seem real.

Did I really have a tattoo done, smoke a joint and have unforgettable sex with my stepbrother?

I go up to my room and close the door. Placing the bags on the floor, I open the door to my walk-in closet, find the battered shoe box I hid at the back, and carry it over to the bed. I sit down and flip off the lid. There are thirteen ornaments inside. A wooden reindeer I found in a dollar store. Dried round pieces of pasta stuck together and painted green and red, which I'd made when I was six. The resin gingerbread man is a little worn, hanging on his red string. A selection of colorful baubles crowds the bottom of the box, all different sizes, patterns, and designs. I take the knitted Santa and squeeze his tummy between my fingers.

The ringtone on my phone shatters the silence. Still holding the decoration, I grope for the cell with my free hand and answer.

"Oh, so *now* you answer." Miles' voice booms down the line. "You haven't called. You haven't texted."

I wince. "I'm sorry."

"Are you okay?"

"As fine as can be expected."

"Who was the guy in the video?"

"I don't know." *At least not his real name.*

"How could you—"

"I've already had enough lectures about how stupid I was. I don't need another one."

"Are you coming back after Christmas? Is that true?"

I huff out a breath, roll onto my back, and close my eyes. "Yes. My mom and Eli's dad have arranged for me to come back, even though I don't want to."

"Rumors are flying all over the place. The school has tripled security. Some of the students think it's a teacher's dick you're sucking. Mr. Drake has been questioned over it—"

My lips curl in disgust at the image. "That's just gross."

"I've heard some of the boys talking about you. Not nice stuff. You need to watch yourself when you come back." His voice drops, becoming lower and thicker with some undefined emotion. "And we can't date anymore. I love you, Bella, but I need to stay off people's radar."

I'm silent for a moment absorbing his words, not as shocked as I should be. "I thought we were friends?"

"We are. Just not in public. You'll still be my best friend."

In secret, where no one knows. How many of those do I have now? So much of my life is hidden beneath lies and deception.

"Sure." My voice is light, concealing the pain washing through me. "Whatever."

"Bella—"

"I have to go. See you at school." I end the call.

My happy mood is tainted by the texts and the conversation with Miles. I roll onto my side, stare at the wall, and hug the knitted Santa to my chest.

Don't think about it. Don't think about it. Don't think about it. Don't think about it. I chant over and over in my head.

How bad is it going to be when I go back? Will anyone talk to me at all?

I'm scared.

29

Eli

I walk down the stairs to find the entrance hall in chaos. The Christmas tree I ordered takes up the entire arched alcove beside the staircase and Arabella is standing in front of it. Elena is near the front door, thanking the delivery guys, and there's a trail of spruce needles leading from the door to the tree.

I move up behind Arabella and cast a critical look over the tree. I may have gone overboard picking one.

"You're going to need a ladder to put an angel or star or whatever at the top."

She jumps and spins to face me, clutching a ratty old Santa in her fingers. "It's *real*!"

"Hate to break it to you, Hellcat, but Santa isn't real. It's just a lie told by parents, so they don't have to try too hard. They can blame the guy in red when their kids don't get the gifts they want."

She blinks. "That's a really cynical view, Eli. But I mean the tree."

I frown. "You know trees aren't mythical things, right? They're not unicorns. Of course, it's real."

She gives an exasperated huff, and I school my expression, so she doesn't see me laughing at her.

"I meant it's not a fake tree."

"I don't even know why you want one," Elena says from behind us. "It's not like you have enough of those silly decorations to cover it anyway. It's going to look ridiculous."

Hurt flashes across Arabella's face, followed by disappointment. I'm talking before I even think about it.

"We have a huge box of tree decorations. I'll ask Poppy to get them out for you. Come on." I sling an arm over her shoulders and guide her past Elena. "I suppose you're going to want to play Christmas carols and drink eggnog while you do your decorating?"

Her smile is like the sun rising. "Can we?"

I laugh. Her smile fades.

"Oh … you didn't mean it."

"If that's how you want to spend the afternoon, then who am I to stop you?"

The kitchen is a hive of activity when we enter, but Poppy spots us and stops what she's doing.

"What are you doing in here, Eli? I'm not baking cookies today."

"I thought we agreed part of your contract was cookies on tap?" I toss the older woman a grin.

"Too many cookies, and all those girls will stop sending you dreamy-eyed looks."

"I'm not seeing the downside." I tug Arabella forward. "Ari here wants to decorate the tree. It's out in the hall, but she only has a couple of things. Do you know where the box is?"

"I do. Let me call Matthew to get it for you." She walks to the opposite end of the kitchen and throws open a door.

"Matthew is the gardener," I explain to Arabella, who's staring at me with a weird expression. "What?"

"Nothing."

***

As predicted, she needs a ladder to reach the top of the tree. I hold it steady while she climbs up and places the angel at the top. As she climbs back down, I check to see if anyone is around, and let my hand slide up over her stomach, under her t-shirt and palm her breast.

"You should turn around. You're at the perfect height for me to eat your pussy."

"In the hallway? Where *anyone*, including your dad and Elena, could walk past and see?"

"They might learn some new tricks."

Her laugh is shocked. My fingers slip beneath the lace of her bra and stroke over her nipple. It beads under my touch.

"Tell me you're not wet at the thought of it." I push up her t-shirt with my nose and kiss along her spine. "Maybe we should sneak back down here later tonight, and I could fuck you under the tree. Now that's a Christmas gift I'd be happy to give you."

"Shhh! Someone might hear you."

I laugh against her skin. "Let me see your tits, at least. Turn around and show me. It's been hours, and I'm hungry for a taste."

"Eli!" But she turns on the steps, casting wild glances around as I lift her top up to bare her breasts.

"Merry Christmas to me." My lips close over a nipple, and I suck it into my mouth, flicking my tongue over the tip.

Her hands land in my hair, curling against my scalp and she lets out a soft whine when I bite down, just hard enough to sting. With my other hand, I reach back to unhook her bra and drag it down until both her breasts are free. "That's better." I lean back to look at her.

Her eyelashes shield her eyes. Her lips are slightly parted. Her nipples are hard, pointed, and wet from my tongue.

"I dare you to go upstairs just like that."

Her eyes lift, a slight frown pulling her brows together. I don't react, realizing my choice of words too late to take them back.

"Why would I do that?"

"Because seeing your tits bounce under your shirt as you walk makes my dick hard. Without the shirt, I might just come in my jeans." I smirk at her. "And then you'd have to lick me clean."

30

Arabella

All my problems have been playing on a constant loop in the back of my mind, while I was decorating the tree. The text messages, the fact my period *still* hasn't started, and the loss of Miles as an ally. And yet, they go quiet the second Eli puts his mouth on me.

Does he know how wet I already am from having him suck my nipples? Does he still want to do this, even with the threat of getting caught?

I bite my lip, the danger of someone walking past only making my arousal stronger.

I glance from him to the stairs.

A dare.

I haven't done one of those since ...

I push the memory of Sin aside.

It's crazy that this is exactly what I need, and it's Eli who's giving it to me. A little thrill curls low through my belly. No one is around, but I'm not sure how long that will last.

He called me Ari. No one has ever shortened my name like that before, and I can't help but like it.

"What do I get if I do it?" I ask.

Eli smiles slyly. "What do you want?"

"*You* eating me out upstairs where no one can see us."

He flicks my nipple, making me moan. "Deal."

He takes a step back, and I quickly pull my shirt up over my

Grasping the material in one hand, I tug my bra off all the way. The cool air of the hallway skates over my skin, and I shiver.

Eli cups my breasts, holding my eyes as he squeezes and plumps them in his palms. "A perfect handful." His thumbs sweep over my nipples, and then he lets me go and steps back.

"Don't rush," His voice is a deep murmur as I walk past him. "I want to see those tits bouncing for me."

My heart is hammering, and my butterflies perform somersaults in my stomach. His eyes are hot, glued to my breasts as I sashay past him and take the first two steps.

The thought of Elena, Elliot, or a member of staff discovering me half-naked is both terrifying and exhilarating. Eli makes a strangled groan, and I turn my head, to see him still standing in front of the ladder, one hand inside his jeans.

"Keep going, Hellcat." His attention is riveted to my chest. "All the way up the stairs ... *slowly*."

I'm shaking with adrenaline, one hand gliding up the banister, as I ascend a few more steps.

"Impressive tree. You've both done an amazing job. Where's Arabella?"

My skin goes cold at the sound of Elliot's voice somewhere below.

Eli's quick to move his hand, his focus settling on something down the hallway. "She went to put her phone on charge in her bedroom."

Footsteps move closer. "We should get you both to decorate the tree every year."

I tiptoe faster up the staircase, heart beating a loud rhythm in my ears.

Oh my god. What if he looks this way?

Eli's lips are curved in a smile, and I'm pretty sure he's trying not to laugh. My breath hitches when I see the top of his dad's head appear below me.

He's going to see me.

I hurry the rest of the way up the stairs, unable to look away from Eli's face as I do. His gaze locks on mine, and the second it does, his dad starts to turn. I put on a burst of speed, and, *somehow*, make it to the top of the landing before he spots me.

I go from cold to hot to cold again, as I sprint down the hallway and into my room. I slam the door and throw myself down onto my bed.

"Oh my god. Oh my god." I cover my burning cheeks with my hands. My heart is racing. My skin is flushed … My nipples are so hard, they ache, and my panties are soaking wet.

He'd almost seen me. What would he have thought?

He's already seen the video of me naked, down on my knees, touching myself while I'd suck a guy's cock.

Dizzy with adrenaline, I try to catch my racing thoughts. As my heartbeat slows, the rush is slowly polluted with shame. My head spins out of control. I jump when a hand touches my foot. I roll over, to find Eli watching me from the end of the bed.

He grins, grabs my ankles, and pulls me toward him to the edge of the mattress. "Do you know how fucking hot you looked walking up those stairs like that?"

My legs go around his waist, the feel of his strong body between my thighs overwhelming and intoxicating.

"Eli, he saw me!"

His knees come down on the bed, and he looms over me. "He didn't see you."

"He was going to see me." I wind my arms around his neck and tangle my fingers in his hair.

Eli bends his head to lick one nipple. "Ari, he didn't see you."

"I don't want to give him another heart attack."

He crawls up my body, until we're face to face, and then his mouth covers mine, silencing my words. There's nothing soft about the branding contact. He parts my lips with his tongue, plunges inside, and his hand moves to encircle my throat.

31

Eli

"Ari, look at me." I tilt her head up with my thumb and wait for her gaze to meet mine. "Dad's heart attack wasn't your fault. That's all on me." I capture her lips again, and this time she kisses me back, her legs tightening around my waist.

I press against her, letting her feel how hard my dick is and then pull my mouth from hers. "We've been summoned down to dinner, so as much as I'd love to feast on you right now, you're going to have to be dessert later instead." I roll off her, and hand her the t-shirt she must have tossed to the floor. "Get dressed, Hellcat."

She sits up and my eyes dip to look at her breasts. "Wait."

Her head comes up. "What?"

"Stand up." I look around the room, then smile when I see the pen on the nightstand. "Come here." I take the pen and hook my hand into the front of her jeans so I can pull her closer.

In black pen, I write 'suck' over each breast, then pop the button on her jeans and pull them down her thighs. Holding her gaze with mine, I smile and drag her panties down. Pressing the pen against the skin just above her pussy, I write 'fuck', then bend my head to give one long lick between her legs.

"*Eli!*" She gasps, clutching at my shoulder.

I press one final kiss to her pussy and straighten. "Let's go."

"Clothes first."

My gaze tracks over her. "But you look so good like that."

"Don't think Elena or your dad will agree."

I huff a laugh. "Probably not."

"Eli? Arabella? Hurry up, Cook wants to serve dinner," Elena's voice calls up the stairs.

I smile at Arabella. "You heard her."

She pulls up her jeans, finds her bra and puts it on while I watch, then pulls her t-shirt over her head.

"Lift your arms."

She frowns but does as I ask. I laugh and flick a finger against her stomach. "You'll need to be careful. Whenever you lift your arm, they'll see the writing. Not what it says, but enough to be curious."

She turns toward the bathroom. "I'll wash it off."

I catch her arm. "No, you won't. I want to look at you across the table and know you're thinking about me sucking your nipples and eating your pussy every time you move." I lead her to the door. She resists, her face still turned toward the bathroom. "Come on, Ari. It'll be fun."

Her features soften into a smile. "Fine. Okay. But I want at least two orgasms."

"You got it."

For the first time in longer than I can remember dinner doesn't end in an argument between me and my dad. I spend most of it trading smiles with Arabella across the table, while my dad and Elena talk about … whatever it is they talk about. I don't pay them any attention. My focus is purely on Arabella and how quickly I can excuse myself.

"I don't want dessert, thank you," I tell the maid when she takes my plate away and see Arabella's cheeks turn pink. "It's been a busy couple of days. I'm going to have an early night."

"It's Christmas Eve tomorrow. I thought we could play some board games as a family," Elena says.

"Board games?" Arabella repeats.

"Scrabble, Monopoly …"

"I *know* what board games are. You've just never shown any interest in playing them before."

"I like Scrabble," I say before they can get into an argument. "Not so good at Monopoly. Dad cheats."

"I do not." My dad laughs. "It's not my fault I've been in banking all my life and know how to play the game."

"Arabella, would you do some baking? The cook and staff have tomorrow and Christmas Day off. I'm sure Elliot and Eli would appreciate some of your baked treats."

"I'd love to sample your cookies." I deliver the words with absolutely no inflection, timed to coincide with Arabella lifting a glass of water to her lips.

She chokes. Both our parents turn their attention to her, and I slip out of the dining room and head upstairs to take a shower.

When I walk back into my bedroom, Arabella is sitting cross-legged on my bed. I hike an eyebrow.

"You made me a promise, Eli Travers."

"Did I?" I cross the room and kick my door shut. When I turn back to my bed, she's topless.

"You said if I walked upstairs with no top on, you'd eat me out."

"Hmm. Did I? I don't remember that conversation." I tap a finger against my lips. "When did I say that?"

"Just before your dad nearly saw me naked."

I move closer to the bed. "Sounds vaguely familiar." I wave a hand toward her jeans. "Maybe you should let me see what I promised to eat. It might jog my memory."

She wriggles out of her jeans. I lick my lips.

"Nope. Sorry. Still don't recall. Take off your panties."

My mouth waters as she drags the scrap of lace down her legs.

"Things are starting to look familiar." I kneel on the end of the bed and curl my fingers around her ankles. "Open your legs, Ari. I think it's time for dessert."

32

Arabella

Eli winks at me as he walks around the car to my side. Elena and Elliot are holding hands, moving toward the entrance of the Country Club ahead of us in the dark. From the sound of the music, the Christmas Eve party is in full swing.

Everything feels surreal. The day had passed, playing board games and me baking up a storm. My mother even helped me in the kitchen, which has never happened, *ever*. We all tucked the gifts under the Christmas tree, ready to be opened tomorrow. We actually felt like a proper family, which made me realize how broken we'd been before.

Fingers brush the back of my hand as I walk. Giving Eli a sideways glance, I smile. His face is cast in shadows from the lights of the building, and I catch the smirk on his lips. I woke up this morning, with his hungry mouth between my legs and on the brink of an orgasm. The second my body tipped over the edge, he'd rose and settled between my thighs. The image of his green eyes boring into mine as he held my hips and sank deep inside of me is seared into my brain.

He leans close to whisper in my ear. "I'll find somewhere later to bend you over, shove my dick inside you and fuck your brains out."

"Eli!" I nudge his shoulder with mine.

"Are you going to tell me that the idea of sneaking out in the dark and coming on my dick doesn't make you wet?"

My attention darts to our parents, but they're far enough away not to hear us. "You know it does."

His hand caresses my ass, then drops away. "Maybe I'll just put you on your knees and you can suck my dick. There are plenty of places around here we could go."

"You've done it before?" I'm not sure why the thought leaves me unsettled.

This is just fun. Nothing more. I don't even know why we're still having sex.

Because I like it. I like Eli's cock buried so deep inside me that I forget everything else.

Eli's gaze flicks over my face, and he frowns. "I wasn't born knowing how to get you off. I'm not innocent, Hellcat. You must have worked out by now that there have been plenty of girls who've had a taste of me."

How many girls? I want to ask, but I keep my mouth shut.

We've almost reached the entrance to the club, the strings of colored lights making the cheerful Christmas decorations gleam. The place is busy. People are gathered in groups sipping drinks and around tables filled with food, or dancing, the excited hum of voices filling the air with the music.

The woman behind the coat-checking desk greets Elliot warmly, asking about his health. After a brief conversation, he hands his long woolen coat to her.

"I wish you'd wear a happy color, Bella." Elena sighs, giving her jacket over to the woman. "It's Christmas Eve after all, and black is so depressing."

She eyed the long black dress when I descended the stairs back at the house, ready to go out. The fact she's waited this long to say something is amusing.

I slip out of my coat and place it on the desk. "I like black. It goes with everything."

The hairs on the back of my neck rise. I sense eyes on me and scan the faces of the other partygoers until several familiar ones come into view. Tina, Evan, Bret, and his roommate, Garrett, are watching me from across the room.

The shock of seeing them freezes the smile on my lips.

Disjointed memories fill my head. The texts, the messages, and the video. Nausea rolls in my stomach, and I struggle to breathe.

I tear my attention away from them. "I'm going to use the restroom."

As I step away from Elena, I catch Eli's frown. Weaving my way quickly through the crowd of people toward the back of the building, I don't stop until I'm in the restroom, shut behind the door of one of the stalls. I lean back, eyes closed, and rest my head against the smooth wood.

I'm shaking.

Reality snaps back, ugly and stark, with everything that lies ahead. An overwhelming sense of dread clutches me, my head a mess of anxiety and fear that I'm struggling to subdue.

This is what they want. I have to be strong. No emotions. Don't feel, and they can't hurt me.

I focus on the words.

To survive, I need to bury everything deep, just like I've done in the past. Show no weakness and live behind a hardened shell. Shut my emotions down.

Being with Eli has made me forget that. When we go back to school, will he fall back into his role as the Monster of Churchill Bradley Academy? Will I be cut loose, a passing distraction while we're at home?

Will I become an outcast?

A door bangs beyond my stall.

"Did you see her? What was she wearing?"

I open my eyes at the sound of Tina's voice and clench my hands.

"I still can't believe she's coming back," another female voice replies. "I thought she would have slithered back to wherever she came from."

"I bet her mom and Eli's dad just want to get rid of her. That video is everywhere. I knew she was a slut from the beginning. There was no way she was as innocent as she pretended. Thank god, Lacy had the sense to remove her from the cheerleading squad."

"I want to know if Eli is coming back to school." Tina's friend sighs. "I miss that thing he can do with his tongue."

Tina giggles. "Maybe we could talk him into a threesome. He won't say no to having two girls at the same time. At least that's what I've heard."

Something hard and cold solidifies inside me, crushing every other emotion. I straighten, turn, unlock the door, and saunter out. The second they see me, they stop talking.

"Hey, Arabella." Tina flicks her hair over her shoulder. "I heard Miles dumped you over the phone."

I move past them, wash my hands in the sink and dry them. "And?"

She blinks at my response. "You must be broken up about it."

I shrug. "Plenty more fish in the sea."

"Like anyone will want you now." Her friend snickers. "At least not as a girlfriend."

I walk toward the door, and I don't let any of the hurt or pain show on my face.

I hate them. But this is just a taste of what I'm going back to. I have no doubts in my head that Tina and her friends are going to make my life a living hell.

When I step out of the restroom, I turn in the direction of my mother, only for someone to grab my wrist. I expect it to be Eli, but wariness hits me when I find it's Bret instead. His friend, Garrett, is just behind him, watching me intently.

"Want to come and suck our cocks?" Bret tugs me toward him, the pressure he's exerting on my wrist giving me no choice.

I try not to panic and pin a smile on my face. "I don't think there would be much to suck."

His other hand moves to grip my waist. "We've seen what a horny little slut you can be. Two guys at once. Maybe you can take three. One for each hole."

The sour smell of beer is on his breath. My skin crawls at the way his hand squeezes my hip. Garrett moves to circle behind me. He's so close I can feel the heat from his front warming my back. I'm wedged between them with nowhere to go.

Everyone around us is absorbed in drinking and chatting, not paying us any attention.

Bret tugs at my hand. "Come on, let's go outside."

"If you don't let me go, I'm going to scream."

"No, you won't." The confidence in his tone sets my anger alight. Does he really think I'm going to go with them?

"One." The word comes out steadily.

Bret grins and pulls at my arm again.

"Two."

"Three." I open my mouth, and Bret releases his hold on me. The second I'm free, I hurry away from them, my heart thudding wildly in my chest.

33

Eli

I'm leaning against a wall, near the doors which lead out into the private garden area at the back of the club, when Arabella weaves her way back through the crowds to join us. My dad and Elena are sitting at a table nearby, their heads close together as they talk.

"Hey, Eli." My gaze moves from Arabella to the brunette standing in front of me. When I don't speak, she twirls a lock of hair around her finger. "You look as bored as me. Want to go into the maze and …" Her tongue sweeps over her bottom lip.

"And what?"

"Make me see stars?" Her giggle sets my teeth on edge.

"I'd rather grind down my teeth with a dull file."

Her lips part and she frowns at me. "I don't know what that means."

I sigh. "It *means* fuck off."

I push away from the wall and stride past her, looking left and right for Arabella. She hasn't returned to the table, and I can't see any sign of her inside the ballroom, so I step through the open doors which lead outside. A flash of blonde hair to my right turns me sideways, and I stride along the patio to the end of the building and around the corner and almost crash into her.

"What are you doing out here?"

She spins to face me. "What happens when we go back to school?"

"What do you mean?"

"Everyone thinks I'm a slut."

I snort. "Everyone is jealous. Fuck what they think."

"*Jealous*?" Her voice is shrill.

"You really think any of the guys who watched that video didn't want to be m—the guy whose dick you were sucking? All the girls wanted what you were getting."

She laughs, the sound high-pitched. "Sure. *That's* what they're all thinking."

"Have you any idea how many women fantasize about two men giving them all their attention?"

"I don't!"

I throw my head back, laughing. "Did you forget that I read your diary, Hellcat? You wrote all about that night and how it made you feel."

"Oh my god, you knew all about it before the video was leaked. You read about everything I did with him."

"Sin, you mean? That's what you call him, right?" I need to stop talking, but I can't stop the words from leaving my lips. "The guy who made you realize making yourself come was nothing compared to someone else's mouth on your pussy."

"And you wonder why I don't believe you about the video!" Her hand lifts and I catch her wrist before her palm connects with my cheek.

"Didn't I warn you before about slapping me?" I drag her toward me. "I don't know what the fucking problem is. I didn't release the video, and you already know I read your diary."

"But you went into my room and *stole* my diary! You could have taken the cell phone, too."

"I didn't need to go into your room. Lacy gave me your diary." My words surprise her.

Her jaw drops, and a flash of hurt crosses her face. "Lacy?"

I shrug. "She wanted me to paint a mural for her ridiculous Halloween party. In return, I told her I wanted your diary."

She twists out of my grip and walks away. I set off after her.

"Where are you going?"

"Leave me alone."

"You're seriously throwing a tantrum over something that happened months ago?"

She skirts around the fountain and walks into the garden maze beyond it. I stride along beside her.

"I'm not throwing a tantrum."

"Then what do you call this? You're storming off like a woman scorned."

Her laugh is brittle. "You read my diary, picked out a paragraph and shared it with the entire class. You traded a painting for my private thoughts."

"That painting took me an entire fucking week."

"Oh, boo hoo!"

"I could have accepted her offer to suck my dick instead."

She flinches, stops, and turns to face me. Her blue eyes are burning with fury. "Thank you for reminding me why they call you the Monster of Churchill Bradley."

My jaw clenches. "You need a reminder of that, Arabella?" I wrap my hands around the tops of her arms and back her deeper into the maze.

"How many times has Lacy sucked your cock?"

"More than you have."

She shoves at my chest. “I fucking hate you.”

39

Arabella

All the hate that's been bubbling up through the cracks since my clash with Bret and Garrett turns to molten fury in my veins. Eli drags me deeper into the shadowy maze, the illuminations from the fairy lights strung through it guiding his way.

"Get off me." The words leave me in a high-pitched shriek.

He thinks a fucking painting is more important than my inner thoughts. There's no remorse on his face for everything he's done to me. I've been blind even to consider he'd be sorry.

His grip tightens on the top of my arms. "If you don't stop talking, I'll stuff your mouth with your panties."

Lunging at him, I claw at his shoulders channeling all the emotions threatening to shatter me. "I should scratch out your eyes for everything you've done. I can't believe you've tricked me into thinking you were different."

Eli's laugh is hollow. "You can try, Hellcat."

"There's not a remorseful bone in your body, is there?"

"I'm a monster, remember? Why would I feel remorse?"

His angry eyes meet mine and his gaze flicks to my mouth. I know what's going to happen a split second before he kisses me. The hands around the tops of my arms grip harder, as his lips find mine. I kiss him back; I can't help myself.

He releases my arms and grabs a fistful of my dress to drag it up over my hips.

I dig my nails into his neck. He shudders and bites down on my lip, then slams me back against something cold and hard. My legs wrap around his hips, my fingers tangling in his hair. One hand spreads out across my ass while he makes fast movements with the other beneath me.

I'm so lost in the frenzied kiss that I don't fully register him shoving the scrap of lace between my legs aside. I rip my mouth from his, with a gasp at the feel of his cock at my entrance.

"You're so fucking wet." Eli snarls, and shoves deep inside me.

I cling to him as he pumps into me in harsh, short thrusts, the stone at my back keeping me in place.

His lips are against my ear. "You might hate me, but your body still craves what I give it. There's no denying that."

My lips part to cry out.

His hand flies up to cover my mouth, to smother my words as he rolls his hips forward, driving his cock deeper into me. My moan of pleasure is muffled by his palm.

"Just look at how much you love my dick. You're fucking insatiable," he whispers against my neck, picking up the pace and biting down hard on my flesh. "All it takes is one touch and you go up in flames. What the fuck does it matter what's happened before when *this* is the result?" His teeth sink into the base of my throat.

I soak it all in.

It hurts.

It overwhelms me.

The pleasure and pain destroy me as my world comes undone.

An orgasm erupts through me, leaving my body shaking and

bathed in pleasure.

Eli continues to fuck me, his movements becoming more frantic and uncoordinated. A beat later, he growls, bites the lobe of my ear, and a shudder wracks his body.

He drops his forehead to my shoulder, one arm wrapped around my waist. The only sound is that of our heavy breathing. His semi-hard cock still buried inside me. I throw my head back and stare up at the starry sky.

I *hate* him for making me want this. I've never felt so out of control. Lost in the heat of the moment.

He's my nemesis.

My bully.

My lover.

My stepbrother.

He's everything I shouldn't want. Dangerous, violent, aggressive. And whatever this craziness is between us, he's going to twist it up and use it against me as a weapon, eventually.

He releases me gently, lowering my legs to the ground and lets me go. I sway on my feet, and step away from him. Only then do I see what he just fucked me against. An angel. A beacon of purity … and we've just tainted it.

Eli's cock juts up from the open jeans hanging low on his lean hips. His eyes are dark and stormy in the soft glow of the fairy lights, and a lock of hair has tumbled onto his forehead.

And that's when it hits me. The warm wetness dripping down my thigh. The laugh which bubbles up holds a hint of hysteria. He didn't use a condom.

"Ari—" He reaches for me.

I slap him before he can stop me, the sting in my palm nothing compared to the pain in my chest. I glare at him, as my eyes drown in tears. My laughter cuts off.

"I'm *never* going to forgive you for what you've done. Thank you for the reminder of who you really are."

I turn on my heels, and don't wait for him to retaliate.

35

Eli

I let her go without a fight, and turn in the opposite direction, tucking my dick back into my pants.

What the fuck just happened? How did we end up arguing?

I scrub a hand down my face, replaying the fight in my head.

Oh yeah. She called me a monster.

I thought we were beyond that, but once again, she threw it into my face and, fucking idiot that I am, I reacted.

I sink down onto the stone wall circling the center of the maze and drop my head into my hands. Music and laughter from the party inside the Country Club reach me as people celebrate the last few hours of Christmas Eve.

My mind goes back to Arabella's face. The horror and hurt when she realized I hadn't used a condom, and my stomach twists. I hadn't even thought about it, hadn't really considered much of anything beyond the need to be close to her, to show her that we had something beyond the hate she feels.

Exhaustion weighs me down. No matter what I fucking do, I can't shed the monster title I've been given. Everything untoward that happens at school or at home, and fingers are pointed at me. Most of the time, I'm not to blame. But once you start being accused of things, it's hard not to behave badly just so that there's a fucking reason for the accusation.

I want to go home. I want to get away from everyone. But I'm stuck here because I stupidly agreed to travel as a family.

"Eli?"

My head snaps up at the sound of my name, and my eyes zero in on the girl coming toward me. Tina Rafferty, head cheerleader, full-time bitch. She's dressed in a festively red dress that leaves very little to the imagination, cut low on the breasts and high on the thighs.

I let her come close to me before I stand. Her fingers reach out and trail down the front of my shirt.

"I haven't seen you around for a while." She looks up at me through her lashes.

"Getting thrown out of school will do that."

"You did a public service. That slut was trying to fool everyone with her sweet and innocent act."

Her words rouse my temper. "How many videos of you sucking dick are out there, Tina?"

"At least I'm only sucking the dick of one person. There are two guys in that video with their hands all over her."

I cant my head, and let a smirk pull my lips up. "Jealous?"

"No!"

"Did your pussy get wet watching her?"

Her cheeks flush.

"Are you secretly wishing it was you in that video?"

"I'm not a slut."

"Arabella isn't a slut. She just knows what she likes."

"And she likes getting off with two men."

I snort. "Like you have never been spit-roasted. I remember a party last year …" I tap a finger against my lips. "You were wearing a dress a lot like the one you have on now. What happened? Let me think. Kellan was here."

"Shut up."

"Oh, that's right. You were on your hands and knees, with Kellan's dick in your pussy and mine in your mouth."

"I said shut up."

"Why? Don't like the reminder that it could have been you in that video? I'm pretty sure we recorded it, didn't we? Let me text Kellan. I'm sure he'll still have a copy." I reach for my cell.

Tina grabs my wrist. "There's no need for that!"

My laugh is hard and brittle. "Oh yeah, I forgot. Can't let your precious cheer squad or the guys you hang with know that you let the monster and his friend fuck you." I pat her cheek. "Don't worry. You're not the only girl on the squad that's sampled my dick."

I turn toward the exit.

"What about Arabella?"

Her question has me looking back. "What about her?"

"Has *she* sampled your dick?"

"What if she has?" I walk away.

***

Arabella avoids talking to me for the rest of the evening, and it's clear Elena and my dad have noticed because they both keep casting questioning looks at me. I ignore them, and the rest of the world, by pushing my earbuds in and listening to music, but I'm conscious of Arabella sitting opposite me. Every time she reaches for a drink, shifts on her seat, and glances at me. My body is attuned to her every move, and my nerves are frayed by the time we leave. Not because

I think she's about to tell everyone I fucked her in the maze, but because I don't think the clash we had is over yet. There's more coming. There's a promise, a *threat*, in her eyes warning me that she's not done chewing me out.

We sit at opposite ends of the back seat in the car, and I stare out of the window. My dad and Elena talk quietly in the front. Elena is driving. She hasn't touched a drop of alcohol tonight. I frown. In fact, I don't think I've seen her drink at all since Dad's heart attack.

"Are you two okay?" she asks, raising her voice to be heard above the roar of the car's engine.

"Fine," I snap.

"Tired." Arabella's voice is just as clipped as mine.

"Well, you both should go straight to bed then. I'd like you to be happy tomorrow. It's Christmas."

"When did you start caring about that?" Arabella mutters.

I don't think Elena hears her, the words were too low, but I do. I glance over at her. She's stiff on the seat, shoulders back, head turned toward the window, hands tucked between her thighs. All she needs is a blindfold, and her position would match how she waited for me … for *Sin* … on the bench.

I rest my head against the back of the seat, the words she tossed at me earlier echoing around my head.

"I'm never going to forgive you for what you've done. Thank you for the reminder of who you really are."

Who I really am. What a fucking joke. She has no idea who I really am. All she sees is what everyone else sees. For a time, I thought that maybe she saw beneath that. Saw *me*.

I don't realize I laugh aloud until her head turns toward me. The look she rakes over me is like fire against my skin, burning me. When our eyes meet, her lips move into a tight sneer, and then she looks away, dismissing me from her attention.

I pull out my cell.

Me: You can't ignore me forever. You're going to come looking for my dick before the week is over. Your pussy knows what it wants.

She wants the monster? Fine. That's what she can have.

36

Arabella

"Arabella, it's time to get up," Elena taps on my bedroom door. "I'm surprised you aren't already downstairs poking around the presents."

I wipe the tears from my cheeks and uncover my head from under the warmth of my blanket. "I'm coming."

I keep a hand pressed to the dull, cramping pain low in my abdomen. My period finally started this morning, which is a blessing. The discovery brought a torrent of tears with it. And I don't know whether I'm crying with relief or anger.

I'm still furious over what Eli did yesterday, and the text he sent me in the car only stoked the flames further. I'm sure my mother must have given him my number. I've saved him in my contacts as *Nasty Little Monster.*

I am not addicted to his dick. Hell will freeze over first before I let him fuck me again.

I grope for my phone on the bedside table, and finally send him a response to his message.

`Me: Just because you get me wet doesn't mean your dick is the only one in the world.`

A second later, it pings.

`NLM: But they won't fuck you the way I do.`

I grit my teeth, my fingers flying over the keys.

`Me: Guess I won't know until I try.`

NLM: Sin and his friend? Are you going to ask them to spit roast you? A dick in your mouth and pussy? Maybe that little virgin ass.

Me: A first you're never going to get, asshole.

I discard my phone on my pillow, shove the blanket aside and crawl out of bed. The sharp, stabbing pain my movements cause makes me grimace. It's Christmas Day, and I should be excited, but I'm not. I'm miserable and grumpy, and all I want to do is remain under the blankets.

I find a pair of comfortable black sweats, a t-shirt, and a baggy hoodie. I add fresh underwear to my pile but don't bother with a bra. I leave everything on my bed and go to take a shower.

The hot water cascading over me brings some relief, and I take my time washing my hair, lingering as long as I can before stepping out and drying off. Wrapped in a towel, I return to my room and get dressed. A chunky pair of fluffy socks with sparkly unicorns are enough to keep my feet warm, so I don't bother with my sneakers.

I leave my room to go and join the others, flipping my hood up over my head as I descend the stairs.

Eli is already in the kitchen when I enter, sipping coffee at the table. Elliot is at the stove, cooking, while my mother is busy setting out plates.

I flip Eli a middle finger when our parents aren't looking. His eyes gleam, but he gives me no response at all.

Elena turns and catches me standing in the doorway. "There you are, Bella."

"This looks very domestic." I shuffle into the room, take a seat at the table, and help myself to coffee and a piece of toast from the rack.

"With the staff away, we need to fend for ourselves." Elliot smiles at me over his shoulder. "And believe it or not. I *do* know how to cook more than a boiled egg."

"We thought we could open the presents this morning." My mother carries two plates over to where Eli and I are sat and places them in front of us. "Instead of after dinner."

I take a slice of the crispy bacon, bite, chew, and swallow it before I answer. "If that's what you want to do."

Her smile dims. "I thought you two would be a little more enthusiastic. Especially *you*, sweetheart, after the song and dance about having a tree. You always loved Christmas."

A snide remark burns on my tongue, but I keep silent. For all the Christmases she was actually home, I'm surprised she remembers anything about how I feel about it.

Elliot joins us, bringing the last two plates over for himself and my mother. I eat in silence, but I can sense Eli boring a hole into the side of my head. I'm more than happy to ignore him.

When we're finished eating, I help my stepdad load up the dishwasher and wipe down the kitchen counters, to leave them ready for lunchtime. Eli remains at the table, fiddling with his phone. I'm half tempted to see if he's sent me another message, but my cell is in my room.

Elliot and my mother make a big fuss about herding us into the hallway, where all the presents are tucked beneath the tree. We fill our arms with the brightly wrapped packages and carry them into the living room.

Elliot acts as gift-giver, reading out the names on the tags while Christmas music plays quietly in the background. His happy smile brightens my mood even though I'm still in pain. Wrapping paper gets strewn in a mess across the floor as we all rip open present after present. For once, my mother actually seems happy with what I bought her, stroking the colorful, expensive oriental scarf with her fingers.

"Arabella, you're very quiet," she says from her place on the couch to my right. "Didn't you like your presents?"

I glance at all the open boxes around me. Clothes, jewelry, perfume, and boots to match my new style. A shoulder bag in the shape of a coffin with a black cat purse and a mix of different chokers.

"I love them." I manage a weak smile. "I'm not feeling very well."

She sits forward, to press a hand to my forehead. "You're not hot."

"Cramps."

Understanding softens her expression. "Why didn't you say anything earlier? Are they bad?"

I nod. "I didn't want to spoil the day. I think I'm going to go back to bed for a while."

"You and Eli still need to swap gifts," Elliot points out when I move to rise.

My heart sinks at his words. I've been trying to avoid it. I collect the two parcels wrapped in silvery paper and give them to Eli. "Merry Christmas."

He arches an eyebrow but doesn't reply.

I retake my seat on the couch beside my mother and watch him rip open the paper. The personalized leather roll-out case to carry his pencils is handmade and adorned with the initials E.T. embossed on the front in a fancy cursive script. Eli caresses it, his fingertips lingering over the E.

The surprise on his face is clear, but he doesn't say a word.

Without looking up at me, he opens the second bulkier gift.

A box set of Christopher Lee movies, including the ones we'd watched together when we'd stayed at the hotel.

Hunching my shoulders at the memory of everything we'd done together there, I drop my attention to the floor. I don't care if he thinks my gifts are lame. It doesn't matter if he hates them.

Who are you trying to convince?

Because it mattered when you bought them. A voice whispers in the back of my head.

And, as much as I despise him right now, I liked the secret side of himself he'd shared with me. And it hurts my heart to admit that I *do* care what he thinks.

37

Eli

I can feel her staring at me as I sit with the box set and leather case on my lap. My fingers stroke over the details embossed into the material. I'm pretty sure she's spent over the one-hundred-dollar limit Elena set us, which suits me because I ignored it as well.

It's only when my dad says my name that I realize I've been lost in my own thoughts, and I blink, refocusing on the room.

"Thank you." My voice is rougher than I want, so I clear my throat, stand, and walk out to where the tree stands in the entrance hall. The gifts I wrapped for her are at the back, tucked out of sight, and it takes me a minute or two to get them. Returning to the living room, I stop in front of her and place the biggest one at my feet.

I rub my jaw and look at her. "I need a promise from you before you open these."

Her eyes narrow. "What kind of promise?"

I slap one of her gifts against my palm. "No screaming and no hitting."

"I don't think you need to worry about that. Arabella doesn't have a violent bone in her body," Elena speaks up from behind me.

I laugh at that and touch the tattoo on my throat. Neither of the adults can see what I'm doing, but Arabella's eyes follow the movement. "I'm sure even Arabella has her triggers." I hold out one of the gifts, just out of her reach. "Well?"

"I won't scream at you or hit you *today*."

I give a faint smile at the qualifier. "Good enough." I hand her the first gift.

She opens it slowly, picking at the tape, suspicion written all over her face when she unwraps a dark wooden box, padlocked closed with a small silver key. "What is it?"

"Open it and find out."

She turns the lock and lifts the lid. A leather diary is nestled inside. Her eyes fly up to meet mine.

"I've always thought the way they put little locks on paper covers is pointless." I wave a hand toward the box. "At least that's harder to break into." I hand her the second gift.

This one cost me nothing but time, and as her gaze tracks over it, I wonder if she'll throw it back at me.

It's a sketch of her standing in front of a mirror. She's wearing a pink t-shirt and black yoga pants. Her hair is in a ponytail, and her face is bare of any makeup. There's a frown on her face as she stares at her reflection.

The Arabella in the mirror has her hair in pigtails, there's a choker around her throat, and her makeup is dark and heavy. She's wearing the short skirt she had on when we went out for the day, as well as the long stockings and a cropped top that shows the barest hint of her breasts. A knowing smile tips her lips up.

She doesn't say anything, tucking the sketch beneath the diary.

I nudge the third gift toward her with my foot, then move back to take my seat. She stares down in confusion at the black and silver brocade that spills out of the paper when she tears it open.

"You're designing a dress for your art project," I say into the silence. "I caught a look at it during a class. There's enough material there for you to make it with."

"Oh my gosh!" Elena claps her hands, saving both of us from speaking further. "I'm so proud of you both. Look at how much thought you put into those gifts."

I shift uncomfortably on my chair. "Yeah, well …" I glance at the clock mounted on the wall. A pointless action, since I have no fucking idea what it says. "I promised Kellan I'd call him. If you don't mind …"

"Be back down at three," my dad says.

I'm off my seat and out of the room before he can change his mind.

Yes, I'm running. I don't want to stick around for Arabella to throw everything back at me. I take the stairs two at a time and lock my bedroom door behind me once I'm inside. I hit Kellan's number on my cell and lift it to my ear.

"Merry Christmas, asshole," he greets me.

"How's it going?" I sprawl onto my bed and stare up at the ceiling.

"Oh, you know. Everyone loves me as long as I'm paying for everything. I'm thinking about buying a house somewhere … maybe a deserted island."

"You should have come here."

He sighs down the line. "And then I'd have had to listen to the wails of despair. God forbid, they think I'm upset with them. I might cut them off."

I chuckle. "Are they really that bad?"

Kellan is silent for half a second. "No, not really. It's just a little claustrophobic having such ridiculous amounts of attention paid to me. Usually being the recipient of this much affection means I'm going to at least get my dick sucked."

"I'm sure there's someone willing to get on their knees for you."

"How scandalous, Eli. This is my family you're talking about." His mock outrage makes me laugh. "Paragons of the back of beyond town they live in. They would never dare do something so … *taboo*. Anyway, it would break Miles' heart if I cheated on him."

I laugh harder. "Sure, it would."

"You doubt me, my friend? That boy is crazy for me."

"Crazy for your dick or just crazy. Have you spoken to him at all?"

"Yeah." His voice turns serious. "He mentioned breaking up with Arabella. Can't be seen with the school whore, you know? It'll damage his reputation."

I squash down my anger at his words. I know it's not what Kellan thinks. "More than coming out as gay will?"

"He's *still* in denial. Gay for me, he says, but usually likes girls. Yet, other than Arabella, he can't name a single girlfriend he's had. Funny that." He doesn't laugh.

There's something in his tone that bothers me. "Have you caught feelings, Kell?"

"Don't be ridiculous." But his denial comes too quickly.

"If you have, you need to be fucking careful. If he's not willing to admit he's gay because of his friends, you know it's for a reason. I'm not going to be there to watch your back."

"Don't worry about me. I have it under control. Anyway, you'll be back soon enough. There's no way they're going to keep you out of the school. Doesn't your father own at least half of it?"

"He's donated enough money for that to be true."

"Well, there you go then." A voice, soft and feminine, calls his name. "And that's my cue to leave. I'm being summoned to play lord of the manor and oversee the gift-giving. I'll call you later."

I toss my cell down beside me. I'm not as confident as Kellan. Everyone believes I leaked that video. I can't see any way that my dad will be able to convince them to allow me back unless I admit to it and accept a punishment.

Would it be worth doing that? Do I want to go back to Churchill Bradley?

38

Arabella

My phone pinging distracts me from the Christmas movie I have playing on the TV. I brush my finger over the screen and open my messages.

`Miles: Merry Christmas. I hope Eli isn't giving you hell.`

I'm tempted not to respond, but after a few minutes, I give in to the urge to reply to him.

`Me: Merry Christmas.`

I go back to the movie, but my cell vibrates a minute later.

`Miles: Please don't be angry with me.`

Anger rolls through me. Why shouldn't I be angry? He said he'd always have my back, but I'm not even at school yet, and he's officially dumped and unfriended me.

`Miles: I got you a present.`

Because he feels guilty? I'm not going to make him feel good about sneaking around to stay friends.

`Me: You didn't have to do that.`

`Miles: Yes, I did. I'm a shitty friend.`

`Me: Yes, you are.`

`Miles: We're still Ant-man and The Wasp. Daredevil and Elektra, just not in public.`

`Me: I'd rather be the Invisible Woman.`

I toss the phone onto the blanket, drag the pillow down and hug it to my chest. My attention darts to my table, where I left the dark wooden box with the diary Eli had given me. The black and silver brocade is on the seat beneath it. Both are beautiful, but it's the drawing he's done of me that holds all my attention. I've seen a few of his sketches before, but it hits me now just how talented he is. I hadn't expected him to put so much thought into my gifts. The fact he has makes me frown.

Had he done it just to appease his dad and Elena?

I stare at the sketch, which is propped up against the wall.

When did he draw it? After our trip to the hotel?

I roll onto my back, stare up at the ceiling and then reach for my phone again. Finding Eli's messages, I type out a text.

`Me: Thank you for the presents. I loved them.`

I've literally just pressed send when a notification pops up. A second later, three more appear. More start to blow up my phone.

Dread washes over me.

I click on the first one. A photo fills my screen. A *familiar* photo. One I took in the shower in my room at school and sent to Sin.

I'm naked under the cascading water, one hand cups my left breast and a teasing pout is on my lips.

The caption attached to it drives a cold wedge through my ribs.

Merry fucking Christmas. Do you like my stepsister's tits?

39

Eli

"Eli!" My door bangs off the wall as my dad strides in. "What is *wrong* with you?"

"I don't think the list has changed since the last time you asked." I swing my legs off the bed and stand. "Why?"

"Why? *Why?* How can you stand there and behave like Elena's daughter is not distraught in the other room."

"Arabella?" I start past my father, only for him to grab my arm and haul me back.

"Stop pretending. Just *stop it*. I get it. You're not happy I married Elena. And you're taking it out on Arabella. I honestly thought after the past week that you'd come to terms with it, but I see now you were just setting her up."

"I have no fucking idea what you're talking about."

He folds his arms and glares at me. "Okay, Eli. We'll do this your way."

"Do *what* my way?"

"I want your cell phone and your laptop. Unlock them both. Then pack enough clothes for the next month. I'm sending you to stay with your uncle in Rhode Island until—"

"What the fuck?"

"I thought I'd raised you better than this, but I can see those few years after your mom died—"

"Don't you fucking dare," I snarl.

He has the decency to not finish his sentence. "You're going to stay with Edward."

"You know I'm eighteen, right? You can't legally force me to go anywhere."

"Then I'm *asking* you. Whatever your problem is with Arabella, it ends now. Elena is trying very hard. I know she's had problems. I didn't go into this marriage with my eyes closed, Son. No matter what you may think. I know her history, just as she knows mine. Just answer me one question."

"And that is?"

"Where did you get the photographs of Arabella?"

"I don't have any photographs of her."

"You're telling me you didn't upload a half-naked photograph of her today?"

"A *what?*" I reach for my cell and swipe the screen.

I've had it on silent all day. There are a multitude of notifications sitting in the top left corner, and a list of missed call alerts from Kellan. I tap on one of the notifications, and it opens onto Churchill Bradley's social media app.

"Oh fuck." I lift my eyes to search out my dad. "It wasn't me."

"Eli. It's on your account."

"It *wasn't* fucking me." I aim for the door again and my dad blocks it. "I need to speak to Arabella. I didn't do this. I *swear* to you, this wasn't me."

"All the evidence points to you. I'm sorry, Son, but I don't see how it could be anyone else. Arabella, for obvious reasons, doesn't want to see you. I promised Elena I'd send you to Edward's until her daughter goes back to school. She doesn't want you anywhere near her."

"Elena believed I didn't upload the videos."

"And she regrets that now. She *defended* you, Eli. Spent days arguing with the school on your behalf, and *this* is how you thank her?"

"And you have no doubt at all that I'm behind this?"

"You're my son and I love you dearly, but I'm not blind to your flaws. I know what they call you. How you behave."

And there it was.

"You're talking about the nickname they have for me." My voice is flat.

"People don't get names like that for no reason."

"And based on that, you believe I did this." It wasn't a question, but he nods.

"What if I say it was me? What if I admit to it?"

"Churchill Bradley is willing to reconsider their decision if you write a letter admitting your guilt, agree to attend therapy sessions once a week, *and* stay away from Arabella."

My jaw clenches, and my fingers curl into fists. Fury boils under my skin, but I know nothing of it shows on my face.

The Monster of Churchill Bradley is firmly in the ascendant.

If I don't go back to school, there's no way I can find out who the fuck is targeting me.

"Fine. Okay. I did it."

90

Arabella

"We're here," Elena cheerfully announces as she drives the car through the gates of Churchill Bradley Academy.

I hunch further down in my seat, while she lowers her window to talk to the security guard before he waves us through. A four-hour drive listening to songs on the radio has done nothing for my anxiety levels.

Eli was sent to his uncle's place on Christmas Day after he uploaded the photo of me to the school's social media app. All those lies about how he hadn't shared the video, only for him to do it again. This time on his own account for all to see.

My heart beats so fast with my hate for Eli that it roars in my ears.

I will never trust him again. *Ever*. Whatever softness remained toward him shattered the second I saw the photo.

The car travels along the long drive of the sprawling campus, already alive with students arriving back from the Christmas break. I don't say a word when she finds a parking spot. I don't move when she cuts the engine.

She swivels in her seat, her smile bright. "Come on, Bella, let's get your bags out. I'll help you take them up to your room."

Toying with the stalk of the red rose I'm holding, I pout. "I still don't know why you're making me come back here."

"Because you need to graduate. I never did, and you'll thank me for it."

I roll my eyes. "Yeah, sure."

My mother sighs. "Churchill Bradley Academy will open doors to your future. The school is as prestigious as Harvard—"

"When have you ever given a fuck about my future?"

"I don't want to fight with you, Arabella. Let's just get your things to your room." She climbs out of the driver's side before I can say another word.

I huff out a breath, pull my hood up to cover my head, then open the car door. My long black coat swirls around my boots when I move.

Elena already has the rear of the car open and is hauling out my four suitcases. A lot more than I left with, but with a whole new wardrobe, I needed them. I tuck the flower carefully in my shoulder bag, so it won't get crushed, then grab the handles of two of the cases.

My mother locks up the car. "That rose you bought with you will brighten up your room."

"Yeah." I'd taken it on a whim from the vase in the hallway.

She pockets the key and takes the other two cases. "Lead the way."

Walking across the campus, I'm aware of people staring at me as I pass. I lead my mother to the dorm building and up to my floor. Students whisper when they see me, but I ignore them.

I'm made of stone, just like the gargoyles sitting on the roof of the school. I can't feel anything. Let them stare. Let them whisper. It doesn't matter. I don't need them.

Thankfully, the hallway is empty when we reach my room. I unlock the door and push it open. My side of the room is just how I'd left it, but Lacy's is empty.

"This is nice." Elena closes the door behind us. "Looks like you have a room to yourself."

I place my bag on my bed. "Because no one wants to share with me."

The Whore of Churchill Bradley Academy.

My jaw tightens at the nickname I've been christened. I've been tagged in enough photos to know what everyone thinks of me.

"That's not so bad." Elena continues to sound upbeat and positive. "You get to do whatever you want with it. Where do you want these?"

I gesture to my left. "Over there by the wall."

She wheels the cases over and lowers the handles. "There we go."

"Thanks for driving me."

"You're welcome, sweetheart." She glances around the half-empty room. "Do you have everything you need?"

"I think so." I wrap my arms around myself, and stare forlornly around.

"The school has assigned you a counselor, who I'm sure you'll get to meet soon."

"Great." I can't muster up the energy to pretend to be happy about it.

She pulls her phone out and unlocks the screen. "I'm sure your friends are excited to have you back."

"What friends?" I reply.

"I should get going. Remember, we're only a phone call away. Text me any time and take care of yourself."

My stomach is tight with nerves. "Okay."

The months ahead look bleak, and all I want to do is run back to the car. The one light in the dark is that Eli isn't coming back. From what my mother has said, the principal is refusing to readmit him.

He can stay in Rhode Island and burn.

Elena pauses in the doorway, and I wonder if she's waiting for me to offer to walk back to the car with her. When I don't say anything, she pulls the door closed behind her as she leaves. I unpack my bags, using the spare closet for all my new clothes. I'm halfway done when I'm hit with the need to get out of the small space.

I put my earbuds in, and press play on my phone. Avril Lavigne's voice fills my ears, singing the lyrics to 'I'm With You.'

I leave my room, rose clutched between my fingers, keeping my head down, and stride along the hallway, making my way past other students and pretending they aren't there. I can't shake the anxiousness that swamps me.

The cold nips at my skin as I exit the dorm building. I huddle beneath the warmth of my coat and set off across the grass. My anxiety doesn't ease until I hit the path that winds through the woods. Pace steady, I follow it until the bench and cemetery come into sight. The familiar sight eases a little of the tension in my shoulders. I walk through the arched gateway, tug out my earbuds and weave my way through the gravestones.

My footsteps take me to Churchill Bradley's tomb. I curl my fingers around the solid metal padlock and pull, but it doesn't give.

Has Sin been back?

It feels like a lifetime ago since I was here last. I place my palm on the metal door and lower my head until my forehead is resting against the cold surface.

Does he know I'm back? Will he contact me?

I'd do anything for the strength he'd given me before. It's something I'm going to need for the weeks ahead. His words made me strong, and I need that right now.

I push away from the tomb and move toward a short column of stone beside one of the headstones.

"Hey. I brought you something." I kneel and place the rose below the plaque that says Zoey Rivers, the red petals bright against the dirt. "I'm back, and I didn't forget you."

"You know, talking to a bunch of graves is kinda creepy."

I twist my head around. Kellan leaning against a tree, watching me. "I was talking to Zoey."

"She's not buried here." His voice is soft, his smile sad.

"I know."

We stare at each other for a moment.

"What do you want?" I finally ask.

He pushes away from the tree and strolls toward me, hands shoved deep in his jeans pockets. "I'm just out here stalking girls brave enough to come into the woods." His lips tip up. "You looked lonely."

I rise slowly from the ground and brush the dirt off the knees of my black jeans.

"If you're trying to take photos of me doing something nefarious, you're going to be disappointed. Eli can fuck right off, and you can be a good little minion and go with him."

I expect a mocking comeback, but his expression turns serious.

"Watch yourself around Jace. He's still pissed over what Eli did."

I toss my head. "And why the hell should I care?"

Kellan stills, tilting his head to study my expression and purses his lips. "You don't know, do you? Jace sent Eli the photograph of you with your tits out when you came home for Thanksgiving."

I recall the accusations Eli had thrown at me over the photo. "I know—"

"Eli beat the shit out of him."

My heart jolts with shock. "What? Eli beat Jace up?"

Kellan nods. "For forcing you into that situation."

I absorb the knowledge in silence.

Why the fuck would Eli care? He's been sharing naked photos and videos of me with the entire goddamn world. Was he pissed that someone else had one of me? Does Kellan know that Eli and I had sex? Is that why he's lurking to keep tabs on me?

I give Zoey's plaque one last look. "I should get back to my room."

"I'll walk with you."

"I don't need an escort, especially from *you*." I eye him with suspicion as I make my way toward the path.

Kellan falls into step beside me. "I'm just trying to be a nice guy here."

I snort. "Yeah, right."

"Believe it or not, I actually like you."

Pressing a hand to my chest, I widen my eyes in fake surprise. "Gasp, the horror."

"You're different." He laughs and waves a hand from my head to my toes. "I also like the whole Queen of the Damned thing you've got going on."

I ignore the compliment. "I've grown up a lot. I'm not the same as before."

"I can see that." His look seems thoughtful. "Have you seen Miles yet?"

The question burrows under my skin, reminding me of the one friend I'd had in this place. "No, he dumped me."

"I know," he replies softly.

"No scathing comeback?"

"It's tempting, but *that* particular Prince Charming wasn't for you, Princess."

I grit my teeth. "Don't call me that."

Silence laps over us. Kellan escorts me to the edge of the tree line and stops before the expanse of grass.

I halt beside him and pull the sides of my coat more securely around me to keep out the bite of the icy cold. "Let me guess. The stalking only counts if I'm in the woods?"

He shoves his hands deeper into the pockets of his jeans. "That's where the monsters usually do their lurking."

"You're such a fucking weirdo."

He gives me a wink. "Weirdos are cool."

I roll my eyes at him before walking away toward the dorm.

Eli

I bring my car to a stop outside the house. It's been two weeks since I've been home and yet it feels like a lifetime. My dad is leaning against the doorframe, face expressionless, as he watches me climb out and walk around to the trunk to take out my suitcases.

He doesn't offer to help, and I don't ask him. While he looks healthier than he did the first few days after his heart attack, he still needs to take it easy. It's one of the reasons I didn't argue overly hard about him sending me away for the rest of the Christmas break. That, and the knowledge I would not have been able to stop myself from forcing Arabella to face me and listen to what I had to say. It would have caused far too much tension, and I didn't want to be responsible for him having another heart attack.

When I reach the top step, he moves to one side so I can drag my suitcases through the door.

"How was the drive?"

"Barely any traffic, so I made good time." I look around, noting that the Christmas tree is gone, and the entrance hall is back to its original state. "Where's Elena?"

"She should be home soon. She took Arabella back to Churchill Bradley this morning."

The school reference tightens my nerves. "Has a decision been made?"

"Not yet. Arabella doesn't want you there, obviously."

I glance over at him. There's a note in his voice that I can't read.

"Once the initial shock of what happened wore off, Elena is still quite adamant that you're not behind the video or photograph."

I turn to face him. "Why? The comment with the photograph makes it clear it was me."

"That's her argument. You're not stupid, Eli. Why would you attach your name to it and tell everyone you're the one responsible? And where did you get those images from?"

"I stole her cell phone, remember." My voice is bitter.

"And left it in your locker. Elena's right. It doesn't add up. I was too angry and upset to think straight, but over the past two weeks … she's convinced me you're not the person behind it."

"But not Arabella." I laugh softly, but there's no humor in the sound.

"No." He gives a quiet sigh. "I don't know what happened between the two of you, but something clearly did. I'm not a complete idiot, Son. It's obvious that the pair of you have history, and that's dictating how you're both behaving with each other. Did you know each other before I married Elena? Is that why you reacted the way you did?"

"No. I reacted the way I did because you married a woman after knowing her for only a week." I drag a hand through my hair. "Do we have to do this now? I was up early to avoid traffic. I'm tired. I just want to go upstairs, unpack and crash for a few hours."

"I'd like for us to have dinner together tonight."

I grab the handles on both my suitcases and move toward the stairs. "Sure. Whatever."

***

"I spoke to Principal Warren after I dropped Arabella off," Elena says into the silence.

The three of us are sitting around the table—Dad at the head and us either side of him at one end.

I don't look up, pushing the food around my plate. My appetite has been minimal since Christmas, my focus elsewhere.

"He wants to see how Arabella settles back in for a couple of weeks before making a final decision on whether you will be allowed back."

I nod. I've already spoken to Kellan, who told me he saw Arabella in the cemetery.

"I think, if you would just tell us what's going on, that would help." Her voice softens, turns cajoling. "Eli, I know you're not behind that awful video and photograph, but you must have some idea of what's going on. You were at school with her. What was she *thinking*? Arabella has never done things like that. She works hard and has always been focused on her goals. She's a good girl. "

The phrase makes my lips twitch. Yes, Arabella wants to be a good girl, just not in the way her mom thinks. That's one of the things that got us into this situation in the first place.

"Eli, please don't ignore me."

I lift my gaze to find her looking at me through blue eyes so similar to Arabella's it makes my stomach ache.

"Did she fall in with the wrong crowd?"

I laugh at that. "She was on the cheer squad and hung out with them, as well as the jocks. Her boyfriend is captain of the swim team."

"But he wasn't one of the boys in the video, was he?"

I shake my head. "No."

"Do you think they drugged her? Spiked a drink, maybe?"

"She wasn't drugged *or* drunk." Just eager to please and horny as fuck.

"You must know *something*!"

I'm surprised by the hitch to her voice, the tears filling her eyes. "From everything Arabella told me, *when* she was talking to me anyway, I didn't think you gave much of a fuck about her."

She flinches but collects herself quickly. "I've made a lot of mistakes. I know that. And I want to do better. I'm *trying* to be better. To be the mom Arabella needs."

"I think it's a bit late for that. She's eighteen. Officially an adult."

My barbed comment hits home, and her face drains of color.

"Eli," my dad warns softly and my gaze swings to him.

"It's no surprise the pair of you found each other really. You're both fucking useless parents." I shove to my feet. "I'm not hungry. I think I'll go to bed."

"Sit down!" Dad snaps, but Elena touches his wrist.

"No. Elliot, let him go. He's right. We've both messed up so much. We need to listen to what they want and learn from that."

I throw my head back and laugh, the sound bouncing off the walls. "Listen to yourself. It's too fucking late, don't you get that? Arabella needed a mother when she was fucking growing up, but you were too busy running after rich guys in the hopes they'd put a ring on your finger and make your life easy." My gaze touches my dad and back to her. "Guess you found one in the end."

"That's not what happened."

"Of course, it's not. Most people meet, fall in love, and get married within a week, all the fucking time." I stalk toward the door.

"I signed the post-nup you wanted, just before Christmas."

Her words stop me, but I don't turn back.

"I know you don't believe me, Eli. I *know* you think I married your dad for his money. Maybe you were right at first. Maybe I loved what he had more than who he was. But did you ever consider that your dad didn't marry me out of love either? Maybe *he* just needed someone in his life, someone to hold him at night."

"I don't want to know about what happens in your bedroom, thanks."

"You know that's not the point I'm making. Have you ever considered the fact that just maybe your dad was lonely?"

I hate that her words make sense. Hate that I've been so angry, so *blinded* by the fact I was convinced it was about his money, that I haven't considered what his life has been like since Mom died.

But I was fourteen years old. I shouldn't have had to take control of everything when I was mourning the loss of a parent.

I walk out without replying.

92

Arabella

"Bella."

I'm halfway across campus on my way to breakfast when I hear my name being called. I turn to find Miles coming toward me, with Lacy, Brad, and the others behind him. Jace is glaring at me, one arm in a white cast.

Kellan told me that Eli beat him up at Thanksgiving.

My stomach drops at the sight of them. Yesterday I managed to get out of seeing anyone. Instead of going to the cafeteria, I ate the sandwiches that I had packed from home and stayed in my room.

Miles' green eyes are pinned to my face. "I want to talk to you."

"No thanks." I keep on walking, aware of our audience hanging back.

He grabs my arm, and pulls me across the grass, to put distance between us and the others. "Hi." The softness of his voice is the opposite of how he's acting.

This is not how I expected to see him. I yank my arm free, and cross my arms. "What do you want, Miles?"

"I'm sorry I didn't get to slip away and see you last night."

I shrug. "I wasn't expecting to see you at all."

"I *told* you we're still friends."

"Friends don't sneak around. Friends don't lie. Friends don't pretend to hate each other."

Guilt ripples over his expression. "Please try and understand."

The anger that never leaves me simmers, just beneath the surface, with all my resentment and bitterness. "You don't want to be seen with Churchill Bradley's Academy Whore."

Miles rakes a hand through his hair and looks away from me. "I don't believe you're a whore."

Doesn't he?

"I don't know why you're talking to me at all. Won't it tarnish your reputation?"

"I'm worried about you."

I snort. "Really? You came with an audience?"

Miles keeps his attention on my face. "They won't leave me alone."

"Uh huh."

"No, seriously. I've become a sun they gravitate around since they all got back from Christmas break."

"They just want drama."

He nods. "And gossip."

"I don't want to be the center of attention."

"I know."

My brows knit together at the softness of his voice. "Why can't they just leave me alone?"

"You still have me."

"No, I don't."

He starts to reach for me but stops himself. "I meant what I said, Bella. I'm still your friend. I swear I am."

"I'm not sure what to believe anymore."

"Trust me, please."

"You're so annoying," I mutter.

The corners of his mouth curve faintly up. "Endearingly annoying."

My attention shifts to the others, who are avidly watching us. "Your *friends* are waiting for you."

Miles takes a step closer to me. "Slap me."

"Seriously?"

"Please."

I don't even have to pretend to be angry. My hand lifts, and I swing it hard. The blow to his cheek leaves my palm aching. He staggers sideways. While the jocks jeer and laugh, Lacy, Tina, Maggie, and Linda are wearing matching expressions of disgust. I ignore them all and stalk off toward the cafeteria.

Students glance my way, a surge of whispers flowing through the room, when I step inside. Ominous thoughts form in my head, and my steps falter.

I am brave.

I am fearless.

There's nowhere to run from this. I keep up the litany of words, bolstering my courage, and cross to the line for the serving counter. The two girls in front of me stop talking when I step behind them.

A quick scan of the tables around me and I see Kellan sitting in his usual place. He's playing with his phone, seemingly oblivious to everything around him. Miles enters the cafeteria with the others, and they head to the same tables they always use.

I grab a tray and give my order to the woman behind the counter. A few moments later, I'm handed a plate. I add a cup of coffee to it and break away from the line and find an empty table far away from Lacy and the jocks. I prod at the plate of scrambled eggs in front of me. I feel like I'm on a stage, with people watching every move I make, waiting for me to put on a show.

I catch someone nearby saying my name, followed by rough masculine laughter and the scrape of chair against tile.

Oh god, is someone coming over?

Did you really think you were going *to survive this unscathed?*

"You should eat that before it gets cold. Breakfast is the most important meal of the day." Kellan flops down in the chair beside me.

My head snaps around, and I frown at him. "What do you want?"

"Don't flatter yourself. I'm not here for you. This table has a better position to watch Miles from."

I dart a look toward the boy in question. Kellan is right. I've picked a table with a perfect line of sight to the jocks. Jocks who have retaken their seats and are glaring in our direction.

"Seriously?"

Kellan smirks. "Uh-huh. I bet that slap you gave him earlier was gloriously satisfying. The poor baby looked so shocked. Kinda makes me want to go and kiss his boo-boo better."

"What is it with you and Miles?"

"I like seeing him blush." He eyes my plate. "Eat. Don't mind me."

"I'm not hungry." My stomach chooses that second to rumble.

Kellan laughs. "Sure, you're not. Put the food in your mouth, Princess."

My fingers clench around the handle of the fork. "Stop calling me that."

"Are you going to stab me?"

"Are you going to keep calling me Princess?"

His gray eyes sparkle with unholy amusement. “Eat your breakfast, and I won’t call you it again today.”

“How about ever?” I scoop some eggs up, shove them into my mouth, and chew.

“Where would the fun be in that?” Kellan’s attention returns to Miles. “Jace has been telling everyone he was in a car accident to cover why he’s wearing that cast. The little prick doesn’t want anyone to know what really happened.”

“If what you told me is true, I’m surprised he hasn’t used it to get Eli in trouble.” I eat another mouthful. “That was assault. Not that I care.”

Kellan laughs softly. “He won’t do that.”

“Why not?”

“Because he’ll then have two broken arms, silly.” He bumps me with his shoulder.

We fall into silence.

Although I’m wary and a little paranoid about why he’s joined me, I’m also a little grateful for his presence. It acts as a shield, keeping other students at bay. I manage to finish half of the food on my plate before I push it away and sip my coffee instead.

The first bell rings. Chairs scrape on the floor, and everyone around us rises to rush to class.

Kellan leaves me without a word. He walks toward the door behind the rest of the crowd, whistling softly. I take one more gulp of my coffee, savoring the taste. I have the feeling I’m going to need the caffeine hit to get me through the day. I pull on my coat, snatch up my bag, and follow everyone out.

Once I reach the main building, I navigate through the throng of jostling students moving toward the lockers. I have my first appointment with Counselor Clarke today, and I'm not looking forward to it. I have no idea what I'm supposed to talk about, and the idea of opening up to someone I don't know feels daunting. I can't exactly tell him that I've been sleeping with my stepbrother—the boy who also bullied me and released photographs and videos of me to the entire school. That just makes me sound insane.

I laugh quietly, bitterly.

Maybe it won't be so bad. I'll just act antisocial, and everyone will leave me the fuck alone.

My locker door swings open, and I jump back with a surprised gasp when a sea of foiled packages floods out onto the floor. Laughter erupts around me, the condoms in a pile at my feet. People crowd around me, phones out and recording. My heart sinks.

Guess I was wrong.

Eli

"So, yeah, it rained condoms when she opened her locker." Kellan's voice echoes around the room. I have him on speaker, so I don't have to hold the cell to my ear while I sketch.

"How many did you grab?"

"A handful. Not sure I'll trust them though. Someone could have pierced them. I just helped pick them up. That's not the only thing, though."

"Oh?"

"When we walked into math, someone had left a dildo on her seat. You know the ones with the suction cups that you can stick to the wall? There was a note hanging from it saying it was to give her something to ride on during the class."

"How did she react to that?"

"Threw it in the trash. I told her it was a waste of a good pretend dick, and that she should disinfect it and keep it because she wasn't going to see any real dicks in school that big any time soon. She wasn't amused."

I snort a laugh.

"Seriously though, you need to come back. I can only watch her for so many hours a day before someone arrests me." He pauses to chuckle. "Or she stabs me. I'm pretty sure she's considering it. She gets this weird look in her eyes whenever I sit down."

"Elena is working on it." It's weird how hard she's fighting to get me reinstated at school. She's adamant that she believes I'm innocent. I don't even know why. "She has another meeting with Warren today."

"That reminds me. Whoever took Arabella's cell and logged into the cloud to get the footage and photographs knows what they're doing. There's no trace of them anywhere, so I have no way of tracking where they logged in from. Although, to be honest, it was probably from the school grounds, so even if I could trace the IP address, it wouldn't tell me much."

"I think we both know where to look."

"We know the general direction. We just don't know which specific person we need to focus on."

"They'll show their hand soon enough. We just need to push them."

"And how do you plan to achieve that?"

"Not sure. I need to get back to school first. Keep watching Arabella. That might drive them to do something. What about Miles?"

"Ohhhh." Kellan's laugh is low and wicked. "That boy … He dumped Arabella, and yet is surprised that she's angry with him. He doesn't understand why it's a big deal. He told her he wants to be friends in secret. So, now he has two dirty little secrets to keep."

"You're still fucking him?"

He sighs. "No. He still hasn't let me. I think he's a virgin."

"Are you corrupting the poor boy, Kellan?"

"I'm *trying* to. He won't even look at me in class. It's hilarious."

"*Eli*!" My name is accompanied by a tap on the door.

"Elena is calling me. Let me know if anything else happens." I end the call and set my sketchbook to one side. "Door's open," I call out.

The door swings open, and Arabella's mom walks in. She's dressed in clothes that, for her, are subdued. Dark jeans, a pink blouse, knee-high leather boots, and a chiffon scarf draped across her shoulders. Her blonde hair is in some complicated style that holds it off her face. She's actually quite stunning without all the thick makeup she'd been caked in when I first met her.

"I've just got back from my meeting." She crosses the room and perches on the end of my bed. "Principal Warren has agreed to let you go back, with a few stipulations."

"Oh?"

"The weekly therapy sessions like originally discussed. While he accepts that you can't completely avoid Arabella, he expects you not to interact with her at any time. He still doesn't believe you're innocent but is willing to concede that there is a small possibility that someone else is trying to put the blame on you. But until there is proof either way, he wants to limit your contact with her."

"Why are you helping me and not her?"

She doesn't answer for a few seconds, plucking at the sheet on the bed, then she turns her head to look at me. "I *am* helping her. When you came back from Christmas shopping, she was different. Whenever you looked at her, she lit up. I don't know what happened between you, and I don't *want* to know. But something did. Something *good.*" She bites her lip, and it's so reminiscent of Arabella that it hits me right in the gut.

"She's alone in that place right now, Eli. And I remember how cruel kids were at school. God knows, I was the focus of their nastiness a lot of the time. I was called names, mocked, and bullied. I've sent her back to a place where everyone is out to get her. I've messed up being her mom, so I'm doing what I can now."

She rises to her feet and walks to the door. "And I know one thing for certain, Eli. You'll protect her, even when she doesn't want you to." She turns and leans her shoulder against the doorframe. "You're to stay home for one more week, and then you can go back. You can go back on Saturday, so you have the weekend to settle back in."

She steps out into the hallway, then turns back. "Oh, and Eli?"

"Yeah?"

Her smile is brittle and cold. "I want you to find who *did* release those images of my daughter and deal with them."

My smile is as cool as hers. "You got it."

99

Arabella

My breath is visible in the cold wintry air every time I exhale. Huddled in the warmth of my coat, I keep on walking to stop the chill from seeping into my bones. I passed the cemetery a while ago and veered off the path to the left of it, weaving my way through the trees. It's Saturday, and nearly everyone has kept to the warmth of the dorms and common areas. I'm bored of being stuck in my room, and instead decided to face the freezing weather beyond the walls of the dorm, just to get a change of scenery.

It's been six days since I returned to school. Miles hasn't spoken to me since that first day, but I can't seem to get rid of Kellan. Everywhere I turn, he's nearby. Not always watching me, but there. It's like he's become my permanent shadow. It makes me uneasy. I'm sure Eli is using him to watch me.

Hasn't he done enough to me already? Hasn't he taken enough from me?

I feel like I'm trapped in an alternate universe where everything is upside down. I've gone from being a princess to a villain in everyone's eyes. I no longer know who to trust.

The condoms in my locker were only the start of the pranks. I've found lurid notes left on my desk, a dildo, and dick pics have been sent to my phone. I came back from classes on Wednesday to find a crude dick spray painted on the door to my room. Whoever is behind it is out to humiliate me. They don't want me to forget what has happened. I wonder if it's Kellan following Eli's instructions, but the idea of him sneaking around doesn't seem to fit. Kellan doesn't hide who he is or the things he does. If he was going to torment me, like Eli, he'd do it where I can see.

I scan the trees around me, and my attention latches onto dark gray stone further up ahead. My feet move in the direction before I give it any thought. I've not been out this far into the woods before, always stuck to the path around the cemetery. The gothic-looking structure that comes into view looks like it hasn't been in use for a long time. It's surrounded by wild, tangled bushes, and the path is overgrown with roots. Two steps lead up to a solid wooden door, which has a column either side of it with angels carved into the stone. They stand, frozen in time, guarding whatever lies within.

Another tomb?

The door opens easily under my touch, and I peek inside. The interior is dipped in gloom but broken up by pools of sunlight pouring in through stained-glass windows. It's discolored, distorted, and gorgeous. Spiderwebs shimmer in the light like silver threads draped across wooden pews. Right at the front, there's a stone altar, that looks worn and weathered with time.

A chapel.

It's musty and dry inside, the air stale. Nothing an open door can't solve, so I leave it ajar, and venture past the first set of pews, soaking in the silence. The walls stand firm, and none of the windows show damage. Raising my head, I check the roof, but that's just as untouched as the rest of the chapel.

When I run my fingers along the wood of a pew, it comes

away coated in a thick layer of dust. The place looks like it's been abandoned. I wonder how many people know that it's here.

I make my way up to the altar, then spin in a circle, absorbing the beauty of the stained-glass windows. Angels are in all the designs. Some are covering their faces with their hands while they weep. Others have their arms raised, holding swords. Below them, red flames lick upwards, grotesque demons clawing upward from the fire.

"Stunning, isn't it?"

My heart slams against my ribs and I jump. Kellan is leaning against the doorframe.

"Old Churchill commissioned a famous artisan to make the piece for him. Eli could probably give you their name." His attention doesn't move from the stained glass. "Zoey used to like coming here a lot."

I swallow nervously, aware that he's blocked the only exit. "You used to stalk her, too?"

His gaze shifts my way, and he scratches his jaw. "Yeah. Sure. We can call it stalking if you like."

"Why do you keep following me?"

"I wasn't."

I snort. "You just happened to come here at the same time as I am?"

Kellan smiles. "Complete coincidence."

"Uh-huh."

"Here." He straightens away from the door, and holds out a bag.

"What is it?" I don't move to take it.

"A sandwich. You weren't at breakfast again this morning, and you can't keep skipping meals."

"What are you? My mother?"

"From what I've heard, your mother wouldn't have noticed that you weren't eating." He waves the bag at me again.

"I already got some food from the vending machines." I don't trust that he hasn't poisoned whatever is in the bag.

. "You can't live on candy bars, Arabella." He takes a step closer. "I can take a bite out of everything if you don't trust me. But, honestly, I'd rather not. It's kinda gross. I don't generally share body fluids with someone unless I'm fucking them."

"Or Eli?"

His mouth tilts up. "He doesn't count. We're basically the same person."

"You're nothing like him."

"Sure, I am. I'm all the nice parts that he's missing. He's all the nasty parts I don't have. Together, we make one reasonably sane person." He lifts the bag. "I promise. Nothing in here is going to hurt you."

There's something in his voice, a tone that makes me believe him, and I *am* hungry. I take the bag from him and open it to find a wrapped packet of sandwiches, a Hershey's chocolate bar, and a drink. "How do I know I can trust you?"

Kellan's burst of laughter bounces off the walls. "Paranoid much? Fine, don't eat it."

"I don't trust this." I gesture between us.

"This?" One eyebrow lifts.

I nod. "What are we supposed to be now? Frenemies? I don't believe you're being nice to me out of the goodness of your heart."

"Didn't I just get finished telling you that I'm the nice one?" He takes a slow walk around the altar. "Do you really believe Eli posted the video and the photograph?"

"Yes."

"I get that you believe he has plenty of motive." Kellan passes me and does another circuit of the altar. "I know how it looks, but do you *really* think he would be stupid enough to incriminate himself? Eli is an act-as-soon-as-the-mood-takes-him kind of guy, but he's not stupid. Besides, with the computer skills I have, I'd be more the likely culprit."

"You're his minion." I point out tightly. "You could have done it for him."

"So suspicious." He doesn't sound upset, though, only amused.

"After what he did to me, why are you so surprised?" I turn away, clutch the bag, and stride for the door. "Thanks for the food."

I leave the chapel and take off through the trees in the direction of the school. I'm not about to let Kellan mess with my head. Eli's done enough of that.

I've almost reached the tree line when my phone pings. I tug it out of my pocket to check my messages.

`Unknown number: Travers is coming back to school in a week. You are going to make his life miserable.`

Eli is coming back to school?

My body goes cold, and I stop to lean against a tree. I've spent the last week convincing myself the school wouldn't allow it.

My lips press together at the words on the screen.

Is this some stupid joke? Kellan trying to prank me?

Me: Whoever this is, I'm not going to play your stupid games. Just leave me alone.

Unknown number: Wrong answer, Arabella.

95

Eli

"I haven't seen you out here in a long time."

I finish my lap of the pool, then tread water near to where my dad stands by the ladder. "I spend more time at school than I do at home, so why would you? Is there something in particular you wanted?"

"I thought we could go and pick up a new car before you go back. You've had the Bugatti since you got your license, and *I* had it for a year before that."

I tilt my head, staring at him. "*Pick up* a new car? Not buy one?"

He smiles. "I've already paid for it. I had it on back order. I hoped it would arrive for Christmas, but there was a delay."

"I *like* the Bugatti." I haul my body out of the water and reach for a towel to dry off.

"You'll like the Lamborghini more."

"You bought me a Lamborghini?" I wrap the towel around my hips, pull a t-shirt over my head, and walk toward the house.

"An Aventador. In black, of course. They delivered it to the dealership this morning. Go and get dressed, then I'll drive you over there to get it."

"What about the Bugatti?"

"Maybe Arabella can have it. Can she drive?"

"I have no idea. Not sure a Bugatti is the car to learn in, though."

We part company at the staircase, and I go up to my bedroom to dress. He's waiting for me when I go back down.

"What happened to punishing me for what happened to Arabella?"

He glances at me as he drives through the gates leading out onto the road. "I'll be honest, Eli. I have no doubt you're capable of doing all of that to someone if they did something to inspire your hatred. But Elena is right. If you did, you wouldn't broadcast your name all over it."

"So, you believe me?"

"I do. I'm sorry I thought otherwise."

***

The stereo is on low, more like background noise than being played to enjoy the music. The streetlights flash through the window as we drive down the highway. I'm focused on my phone, arranging where to meet Kellan when I get to school. We've left early, before sunrise, because Mom and Dad are flying out to Bermuda for a week to celebrate their twentieth wedding anniversary, and she wants to get back and not have to rush around before their flight leaves tonight.

"Are you sure you don't want to come with us, honey?" Mom's voice sounds over the music.

I shake my head. "I don't really want to spend a week watching you and Dad playing kissy face."

"If we had never played kissy face, you wouldn't be here."

"Yeah, don't need to think about that."

Her laughter is light. "Open the glove compartment. I left something in there for you."

I drop my cell onto my lap and lean forward to open the glovebox. There's a small box with my name in silver writing across the top.

Lifting it out, I settle back into the seat and pull off the lid.

There's a thick silver chain inside. I hook a finger around it and pick it up. A padlock hangs from it, holding the two ends of the chain together.

"I miss you when you're at school, but I want you to have the best education for your life ahead. I know school can be difficult sometimes, but you're strong, clever, and talented. And I love you. We love you. I saw this necklace and it made me think of you." She dashes a hand across her eyes. "Look at me, getting emotional."

I laugh softly. "Like you do every new school year."

"Anyway, the padlock signifies security and protection—"

Screeching fills my ears, lights flare, and the world turns red. My mom screams my name, throwing out a hand, and then pain explodes across my body.

"Fuck!" The shout is torn from my mouth as my eyes snap open.

My heart is racing. The smell of burning still fills my nose. The sound of sirens, shouts, and screams echo inside my head. There's something digging into my palm, and it takes a minute or two for me to reorient myself.

I'm in my bedroom, in my *bed*, and I'm clutching the padlock around my throat. I force my grip to loosen and release the metal, then push into a seated position. The scars on my back are burning, like fire licking at my skin. I know it's in my head. They haven't hurt for years.

Three years, seven months, and twenty-four days, in fact.

"Fuck." I repeat the curse softly, rubbing at my face.

I haven't dreamed of that day in a long time.

So why now?

Arabella

My shoulders sag in relief when the bell sounds to signify the end of the last class of the day. The week has passed in a blur, and it's already Thursday. Just a few more days, and Eli will be back at school. I feel sick at the thought. Not even focusing on studying has been able to distract me.

Elena has been calling me every few days. When I asked her about him returning, she didn't deny it. The way she speaks about him leaves me angry and hurt. I don't know what crap Eli has fed her, but she seems to believe it.

Counselor Clarke keeps trying to reassure me that everything will be fine when my stepbrother returns, but I don't believe him. He's been asking continuous questions about the man behind the video. It's left me defensive and closed. I'm pretty sure the school just wants to know who it is. Maybe that's why he's been assigned to me. There's no way I'm going to tell him about Sin, the dares and what we did in the dark. It has made our session tense and uncomfortable.

Gathering my books, I shove them into my bag and rise from my chair.

"Hey, slut. Suck any cocks lately? I bet your stepdad loves having you on your knees." Tina's catty voice comes from my right.

"When she doesn't have Eli's dick in her mouth." Linda snickers.

"Maybe she does them both at once," Lacy adds, and all three girls descend into laughter.

I paste a smile on my face and meet their stares. "What's the matter? Eli never gave you attention? From what I've heard, he's had half the female population of the school. Including most of the cheer squad."

Lacy's smile turns malicious. "So, you admit that you had sex with your brother?"

"Stepbrother," I correct her through gritted teeth. "And I'd rather fuck a cactus than Eli."

"Or maybe a corpse." Tina's eyes crawl over my ripped black jeans and the velvety blood-red shirt before settling on the leather choker around my neck. "You look like the kind of freak who'd do it. Is the collar so he can clip a leash on and walk you around like the stupid bitch you are?"

"I'd rather be me than fake like you. Haven't you been on your knees for Eli, Lacy? What would Brad think of that?"

My ex-roommate flushes red.

I walk past them, with my head held high. Satisfaction at the way I stood up to them makes me smile.

I'm *done* cowering and backing down. If I have to strike back at them to get through the rest of the year, then that's what I need to do.

"Look out."

I turn at the sound of Miles' voice, just as something wet drenches half my face and hair. I let out a shriek, and wipe frantically at my cheek. My hand comes away red.

Is it blood?

Laughter explodes from around me. I catch sight of Bret running along the corridor away from me with a bucket in his hand.

"Get it off." Panic swallows me whole, and I claw at my skin.

"Get it off."

Hands grab my wrists. "It's food dye."

My eyes brim with frightened tears. Miles' face blurs in front of me. "Get it off!"

"Arabella, it's food dye," he repeats slowly, like he's talking to a child.

His words eventually penetrate through my fright, and the tears spill free. I jerk out of his grip, and run along the hallway sobbing, while everyone around me laughs. I don't stop until I reach the dorm, fighting to breathe through my tears.

So much for not cowering and backing down.

The second I'm in my room, I slam the door shut and lock it and run into the bathroom. I strip off, leaving my ruined clothes in a pile on the floor. Red dye stains one shoulder and arm.

Under the shower, I scrub and scrub, until my skin turns red and it's hard to figure out what is the dye and what isn't. I slump forward, head resting against the tiles, arms loose at my sides and just stand there, letting the water wash over me. The water turns from red to pink to clear and my arm and shoulder is *still* covered in dye. Defeated and exhausted, I turn off the shower and step out. Avoiding my reflection, I wrap my body in a towel and go back into the bedroom.

What the hell am I supposed to do now? Is there anyone I can ask for help?

I'm giving serious thought to calling Elena when my cell chimes with an incoming message.

`Miles: I've left a bag outside your door. It has foam shaving cream inside. It will help get the dye off your skin.`

***

Miles' foam did the trick to help remove the dye from my body. It took me ages to get to it all. I missed dinner, and curfew has already crawled around. With the strict rules in place, I can't even go to one of the vending machines to get food.

How much of today was planned? There's no way Bret was just hanging around in the corridor outside class with that bucket. *Had Tina and the others been a distraction?*

I flop down onto the bed and shoot off a text to Miles.

`Me: Thank you. I've managed to get it all out. Bret is a little prick for what he did today.`

I'm exhausted, stressed, and on edge. I don't want to think about what other cruel pranks they have in store for me. My stomach churns, a mixture of hunger and fear at what might be coming.

A message notification flashes up on my cell, and I tap it, expecting it to be a reply from Miles, but it's not. It's an unknown number.

I debate whether to open the message or not, but a sick sense of curiosity wins out and I tap on it. It's a video with no text attached. My fingers seem to move of their own accord, hitting play.

A couple is moaning and groaning on the screen… having sex. The image pans out, bringing the stone angel they are writhing up again into focus. It takes me a second to recognize it. The statue from the Country Club. The stone angel. I lay frozen in place, watching Eli as he fucks me. My face is clearly visible over his shoulder, lips parted, a look of extreme pleasure etched onto my features. The entire thing has been recorded, right up to where I slap him and storm away. Our faces and voices are both clear. There's no way either of us could deny that we're the couple.

Unknown number: Do you want us to tell your stepdad you're fucking his son? What do you think he'll say when he finds out the Churchill Bradley Academy Whore has her claws deep into the Travers heir? Or should that be the Travers' heir has his cock deep inside of you? He might not survive the next heart attack you give him. You're going to do exactly as we say, Arabella, and play our game.

Eli

I don't go straight to school. Instead, I arrange to meet Kellan in the town nearby, and we go for coffee. He whistles softly when I climb out of the car.

"An Aventador?" He circles it, stroking his fingers over the paint.

"Christmas present from Dad." My dad has been a car freak for as long as I can remember. He has a garage at home with over fifty different sports cars, all of which he takes out at least once a year. It's a passion I've definitely inherited from him. My love of cars is beaten only by my love of art.

"The school is alive with rumors about your return," he tells me once we're settled at a table with drinks.

"What kind of rumors?"

"Your dad had to pay a million dollars for the school to let you return. Your stepmom sucked Principal Warren's dick to secure his agreement. There's a restraining order keeping you two hundred feet away from Arabella at all times."

"I don't think any of them are true. Pretty sure Elena wouldn't have sucked dick on my behalf." I take a sip of coffee. "Does Arabella know?"

"Not sure. She hasn't said anything. Not that we have conversations. Our interactions mostly consist of her telling me to stop stalking her and me claiming it's just a happy coincidence I'm wherever she is. I think she has other things on her mind right now, anyway."

"Like what?"

He taps around on his cell and turns it toward me. A photograph of a blonde covered from head to toe in red … What is that? Paint? Blood? Something must show on my face because Kellan sighs.

"It's food dye. Bret threw a bucket of the stuff over her head. Miles got to her before I did."

"Did she report it?"

He shakes his head. "Don't think so. Just disappeared to her room and stayed there. Silver lining. No one can blame you."

"I need to talk to her."

His eyes widen. "Eli, you *can't* talk to her. Isn't that the whole basis of the agreement for you to return to school?"

I scowl. "Like anyone gives a fuck about that."

"The *principal* does. And he's the only thing between you and getting thrown out for good before you graduate."

I rub the back of my neck. "She's blocked my number, so you'll have to be the go-between to work out the fine details. I can't meet her somewhere public, not until I know for sure she'll listen to me."

His eyes are troubled as he stares at me. "Okay, but I want it on record that I think it's a really bad idea."

"Noted." I drain my coffee and stand up. "Let's go."

Since Kellan drove to town to meet me in his own car, we have to travel to the school separately. He's ahead of me when we reach the gates, and he waves his lanyard at security as he drives through. Because I'm in a new car, I pull up and let the window slide down.

"Eli Travers." The security guard smiles at me. "New car?"

"Lamborghini body kit. It's really just a Chevy Spark."

He laughs, hands me back my ID and waves me through. I close the window, sealing myself inside behind the tinted glass.

There are students everywhere. Some of them stop to stare as I drive through toward the parking lot. Logically I know they can't see me through the tinted windows, but it doesn't stop my mind from whispering about how they're watching, judging, waiting to see what I do.

Kellan is out of his car and leaning against the side when I pull into the space beside him.

"Ready to go to war?" he asks when I climb out.

"Born ready."

18

Arabella

Unknown number: Travers has arrived. Intercept him on the way to the dorms. Give everyone a good show. If you don't, we'll send the video to your stepdad. He already thinks you're a whore. The video will confirm it.

My hands shake as I read the message.

Eli is here?

I want to bolt back to my room, and it takes everything in me not to.

What would Elliot say if he sees that video? Will he be disgusted with me? Will he think I've seduced his son?

After the other video of me he's seen, it's possible. Elliot Travers has been nothing but kind to me, I don't want him to think badly of me.

Me: Why are you doing this to me?

Unknown number: We thought you liked to play games. They get you hot. Make you horny.

Another photo appears. This time of me kissing Eli under the mistletoe in the department store in the Americana Mall just before Christmas.

Has someone been following me?

Everything inside me withers with shock.

Me: Have you been stalking me?

Unknown number: We're always watching. Tick tock time's ticking. Don't ignore us, Arabella. You won't `like the consequences if you do.`

I search the faces of the students clustered nearby uneasily. Lacy, Brad, Miles, Kevin, Garrett, Jace, Evan, Bret, Tina, Maggie and Linda are standing with the other cheerleaders and jocks. All eyes are focused on the driveway which circles past the main buildings and out to the parking lot.

Word has gotten out of Eli's return, and many have gathered to see the Monster of Churchill Bradley Academy return to school.

"Here he comes."

The whispered words are to my left, and I turn to look in the direction everyone else is focused. Eli and Kellan are making their way toward the dorms. A dark lock of hair is tumbling over Eli's forehead, and his expression is closed-off and broody.

Don't ignore us, Arabella. You won't like the consequences if you do.

I push off the wall I've been leaning against and shove my phone into a pocket. The grip on the Styrofoam cup I'm holding tightens.

Eli sees me first and the whole world stops when he meets my gaze. For one heartbeat, I'm lost in the heat I see flashing in their depths. Kellan is talking to him, and he doesn't notice me until I'm right on top of the pair of them.

I move without thinking. If I stop to think about it, I won't do it. The contents of my cup hits Eli in the face. Orange juice douses his hair and drips off his eyelashes. Shock covers his and Kellan's faces, quickly concealed behind blank masks.

Remorse fills me but I push it down. I can't afford to feel guilty.

You won't like the consequences ...

"I don't know how you wormed your way back here, but I hope

to hell it doesn't last." I spit the words at him.

Eli wipes a hand over his face. "What the fuck—"

"You disgust me."

"Ari—"

"Don't fucking call me that," I scream. "I *hate* you, Eli Travers. You're nothing but the monster everyone says you are."

I spin away from him, take off across the grass away from the gathered crowd, and aim for the trees. The phone vibrates in my pocket, but I ignore it. I don't stop running until I reach the safety of the bench near the cemetery. I heave in breath after breath as I sink down onto it. The flicker of confusion, followed by anger on Eli's face is burned into my mind. Fishing the phone out of my pocket, I unlock the screen.

`Unknown number: You didn't put much effort into that. You could have done so much better.`

My heart feels like it's going to explode, it's beating so fast.

`Me: I did what you wanted. Now leave me alone.`

`Unknown number: That's not how this works. We'll contact you again with further instructions.`

Further instructions?

No, no, no.

`Me: I don't want to play your game.`

`Unknown number: Don't you want to get him back for everything he's done to you? All the humiliation and the pain? How he used and discarded you? You don't mean anything to him. You were just another hole for his cock to fill. Now that he's returned,` he'll only carry on hurting you.

I search around, paranoia clawing through me.

Who the hell is this? Someone who's been watching me closely.

The thought leaves me sick to my stomach.

Me: No, I just want to be left alone.

Unknown number: Arabella, we've only just gotten started.

Eli

My first instinct is to take off after her, but Kellan's grip on my arm stops me.

"How you respond right now is going to dictate what everyone else does." His voice is low. "Control the narrative, Eli."

His words remind me that we have an audience, that I'm not at home, and that what just happened is not Arabella's idea of foreplay. I dig deep inside myself and plaster a cocky grin across my face, throw my head back and wipe my fingers over my cheek. Catching the eyes of the watching cheerleaders, I lift it to my mouth, lick it clean, then wink.

"Guess she *really* wanted to be the first to get my attention." I pitch my voice loud enough to be heard by those closest to us.

There's muted laughter and comments about how the *Whore of Churchill Bradley* is so desperate for dick, she will even settle for her stepbrother's. I grit my teeth against the desire to defend her. Right now, she still believes that I've done this to her. I understand her anger, and I need to figure out a way to prove that it's not me.

"She made me all sticky, and not in a good way. Whoever she's been fucking needs to explain that's *not* how you get someone wet." There's more laughter in response to my dry words.

We weave through the crowd, ignoring the calls of my name. Everyone wants to speak to me, ask about the leaked footage, make it clear that they are on my side, for fear of me turning my attention to them next. Everyone here has secrets they don't want spilling out for all to see.

Which reminds me …

I stop, looking over the faces of the students gathered around.

"Eli?" Kellan's voice is curious.

When I finally find what I'm looking for, I smile. Miles' face turns white.

"I suggest you fuck him out of your system quickly," I tell Kellan, my attention not leaving Miles.

Kellan follows the direction of my gaze. "Why?"

"Because if he doesn't out himself soon, I'm going to do it for him."

"What's he done to you?"

"Nothing. But he doesn't even have the balls to support Arabella, because he's so fucking scared of his so-called friends finding out he's gay."

"You did hear what she just said to you, right?"

"She thinks I'm the bad guy who put her in this situation. I understand her anger with me. His betrayal of someone who's kept his secret?" I nod toward Miles. "That I don't get." I step toward the swim team captain. "Hey, Cavanagh." I raise my voice.

"Travers." His voice is calm, but his eyes dart around as he looks for an escape route.

"Sucked any dicks lately?"

Kellan snorts beside me. "Only one." His words are for my ears only, but Miles sees his lips move and turns even whiter. It's clear he's waiting for Kellan to out him.

"Little bird tells me you like nothing more than getting your face covered in cum. Tell me, do you spit or swallow?"

"Fuck you, Travers."

"From what I've heard, you prefer to be the one getting fucked. Is that why you dumped your girlfriend when the video was leaked? So, people wouldn't question why she's looking for dick somewhere other than you? Because it's clearly *not* you in the video, is it?"

There are two red spots on his cheeks, and his eyes are blazing with futile anger as he glares at me. But he can't respond. If he denies my words, people will question whether he's the masked guy Arabella is sucking off. But if he agrees with me and says it's *not* him, they'll wonder if I'm right.

I smirk and start walking again, then pause when I reach Miles and reach out to pat his cheek. "Maybe next time you'll think of someone other than yourself when shit goes down." My words are soft, but his eyes widen, and I know they've hit their target.

***

"I heard about what happened with Ms. Gray yesterday." Counselor Clarke waves a hand to the seat opposite him. "You didn't retaliate, which is a great start."

"Terms of my parole. Do not engage with the enemy." I stroll across the room, hands shoved deep into the pockets of my jeans.

"Her reacting to your presence is going to be expected. Seeing you after everything that happened is going to be difficult for her. I don't think it'll be the last time she confronts you."

"Even though I *didn't* actually do anything." I sit down, eyeing the counselor. "For the record, I didn't retaliate because I'm aware of how she feels, but don't take that to mean I will let her do something like that again without taking suitable action. I agreed to keep my distance. I did not agree to roll over and let her kick me. I'm not going to allow someone to treat me like shit for something I didn't do."

"But *she* believes you did, and all the evidence points toward you. The cell was found in *your* locker and the latest photograph was posted from your account."

"How stupid do you think I am? Why the fuck would I post something like that from my own account? Do you have any idea how many people have been wrongfully imprisoned because the *evidence* says they did it? Do you know that more than four percent of death row inmates are potentially innocent? That's a fucking lot of people."

"You're not under a death sentence, Eli." The half-smile on his face makes me want to punch him.

"You have no idea what being at school is like, do you?" Nothing of my irritation sounds in my voice. "My reputation here will carry over to the *real* world later. It might not be a death sentence in the strictest sense of the term, but it's a form of it, all the same."

"I think that's a little extreme."

I lean forward on my seat. "How much do you earn, Counselor? Sixty thousand a year? Let's say you get a higher rate because of where you work. Eighty thousand? Did you go to a private school for your education? Come from money?"

"What does that have to do with anything?"

"I can spend eighty thousand dollars in an afternoon and not put a dent in my bank balance. My dad makes eighty thousand dollars while he's sleeping. For the average Joe, you work in a job and get paid. For the elite, those of us *born* to money, the people you connect with can make or break you. If people in the circles we frequent don't want to network with you, you're dead in the water. If they can't *trust* your word, you might as well not even bother."

"I don't—"

"If me saying that I didn't have anything to do with the video and photograph being leaked isn't believed, if my *word* can't be trusted on it, then what about when I need to make contracts or network with people later in life? My word will always be doubted. I'll always be *that bastard who ruined a girl's life.* You see my problem?"

"If that's true, then how do you think Ms. Gray feels?"

"Oh, don't get me wrong. There will always be people whispering behind her back about that one time in school when she had a threesome, and it was caught on video. But most women will be jealous, and most men will want to search it out and watch it for themselves. Believe me, if I wanted to ruin Arabella's life, I'd have come up with something far more creative."

I ignore the whisper in my head that reminds me how my original plan had been to do exactly what has happened to her. That was before I had a taste of her, discovered who she was, felt her body around mine.

That changed everything.

50

Arabella

It's Sunday morning, and the cafeteria is fuller than usual. I'm aware of eyes on me from where I sit at my table alone. After what happened yesterday between me and Eli, there's a tense anticipation in the air among the rest of the students.

I'm not even sure why I'm sitting here. I should have taken my breakfast back up to my room.

Because I crave human contact like everyone else. There's only so much a person can take of being isolated and alone.

My food is untouched on the plate on the table in front of me. My focus is on the caffeine in the coffee, which is all I've been living on lately. Occasionally, I look around me, checking to see where everyone is.

Lacy and Brad are sitting close together. Tina is with Garrett, but the others are missing, including Miles. Kellan and Eli are at their usual spot. Eli's eyes are boring a hole in my head, and I can almost feel him mentally demanding I look at him properly.

I don't.

Instead, I keep my head down. Icy fingers of dread slide down my spine when my cell vibrates.

`Unknown number: Go to your locker and open it.`

The words chill me. I've barely been able to sleep, waiting for them to contact me.

Maybe I can call their bluff. Would they really send the video to

Elliot? How would they even have his phone number or contact details?

I suck in a deep breath.

`Me: No.`

`Unknown number: Your stepdad will divorce your mom, and you'll be back in poverty. Do you think she'll ever forgive you for that?`

Would Elena really hate me if that happened?

My thoughts go back to how happy she'd been at Christmas, and my heart sinks. Yes, she would.

`Me: You can't predict the future. You don't know what's going to happen.`

`Unknown number: True, but we know your dreams. Do you think any fashion house with a prestigious name will want to hire you? One video of you is out there for all to see. Do you want to risk a second? Your hopes of being a fashion designer will all come crashing down. We have the power to destroy your future with just a single click of a button.`

I shift uneasily in my chair, glance around and then back down at the cell in my hand. Although I haven't kept what I want to do in the future a secret, it's creepy that they know so much about me.

What other things do they have on me? Do they know about Sin? Did they follow me and Eli to the hotel? Why are they targeting me? It could be anyone.

`Unknown number: Go to your locker and open it.`

Like a puppet on a string, I rise from my chair. Someone calls me a whore as I pass the tables, and I can't hold back a flinch. Head bowed, I leave the cafeteria and walk toward the main building.

There's no one in the hallway when I reach the row of lockers. I open mine, and stare down at a box of eggs beside a screwdriver.

My phone vibrates.

`Unknown number: You have a choice. Egg Eli's car or carve your initials into the paint. One will get you a reward. The other … won't.`

It takes a second for the words to sink in, and I reread them slowly in growing horror.

`Me: I can't. That car is more expensive than everything I own.`

`Unknown number: Tick tock, Arabella. Choose now.`

`Me: He'll kill me.`

`Unknown number: Eli isn't allowed to come near you. It's part of the agreement to his return. You're wasting time.`

Whoever is sending the texts is forcing me onto a collision course with Eli, and I can't avoid the impact that's coming. I snatch up both items, and I stuff them into my bag. I close my locker, hurry along the hallway and back out into the cold air. The wind picks up as I wind a path toward the parking lot, lashing my hair against my cheeks. When I reach the vehicles, there is no one around, and relief floods through me when I don't see Eli's Bugatti.

`Me: His car isn't here.`

`Unknown number: He has a new one. The black Aventador.`

I stare out over the cars before responding to the message.

Me: I don't know what that is.

Unknown number: Guess we shouldn't be surprised you're so fucking clueless. It's obvious you don't belong here.

The insult stings. A second later, a photo appears on my screen. Studying it, I match it against the cars in the parking lot and find the Aventador. I run my fingertips over the paint when I reach it, admiring the sleek lines.

It's got to be worth a fortune.

Another message hit my phone.

Unknown number: DO IT NOW. CHOOSE.

I push my hair out of my face, and scan the area for other students, but no one is around.

How can they be watching me?

This isn't who I am. I'm not a bully, and guilt at what I'm about to do is already eating me up inside. I feel for the items in my bag. My fingers close around the screwdriver, but I release it immediately and take out the box of eggs. I flip open the box.

Do it. Don't think. Just do it.

The first egg splats against the windshield. I take another and toss it against the driver's side door. Four more follow at different angles around the car. There's no satisfaction in my actions, just a sick dread instead of a thrill.

At least Eli can get it off.

My phone chimes.

Unknown number: You disappoint us with your choice, but we're not surprised by how much of a coward you are. Carve your initials into the paint of the hood.

I shake my head.

Me: No.

A new video flashes up on my screen. This time it's of me inside the tomb. I'm naked on top of the coffin. Sin's dark head is between my legs, and his friend's hands are groping my breasts.

Unknown number: Travers wasn't the only one with access to that cloud. Do as we say, and we won't share it. Take a photograph as proof once you're done. Make your initials nice and clear, big enough for everyone to see.

My stomach churns.

They have all the videos and photos. All the ones I sent to Sin. Everything he took of me.

Is he behind all this? Is he the one doing this to me? But what if it's not?

Indecision holds me back from asking.

How secure was the link Sin sent me all those months ago? Why did I ever believe it was safe?

I reach into my bag, and my shaking fingers close around the solid handle of the screwdriver.

51

Eli

Kellan is waiting for me when I exit the counselor's office. His expression is grim, and he pushes away from the wall the second I appear.

"Do not lose your shit."

Not the greeting I expected, and I'm immediately on edge. "Why?"

"I'm going to tell you something. Do not fucking react. Get your game face on. People are watching to see what you do."

I stop at a vending machine, and Kellan rummages in his pocket for coins and punches the numbers to release two bottles of water. He waits until the machine grumbles into life before speaking.

"*Someone* has keyed your car."

"*What*?"

"Watch your fucking face," he snaps.

Schooling my expression, I lean down and snatch up each of the bottles as they are released. I hand one to Kellan and pop open the other.

"How bad?"

"Bad."

I turn without another word and head down to the parking lot. There's a small cluster of students around my car, and they part silently to allow me through. Dried egg yolk covers the windows and roof, but my main focus is on the hood. Two large letters are scratched into the black paint, and it doesn't take a rocket scientist to figure out what they stand for.

A.G.

Arabella Gray.

Internally, I thank Kellan for preparing me for this. I'm not sure I could have stopped myself from reacting without the warning. She's scored the letters so deeply into the paint they stand out in stark white contrast to the black of the hood. Part of me is curious about how long it took. This wasn't a quick keying or a slight scratch. She's used something else to make sure the lines of the letters are thick and deep.

The message is clear. The line in the sand clearly marked out. Whatever we had before Christmas is over. Gone.

We are officially at war.

Without removing my gaze from the car, I take out my cell and hand it to Kellan. "The number for my dad's mechanic is listed. Call them and arrange for someone to collect the car. Tell them what needs to be fixed."

I turn away, casting my eyes over the crowd standing a few feet away.

"Where is she?" My voice is soft.

"I saw her go back to the dorm," one voice calls.

"No, she went out into the woods," another shouts.

"Eli. You can't go near her." Kellan breaks off from his call to remind me.

I grunt in acknowledgment, and stride over to the first one who spoke. "When did you see her go back to her room?"

"About an hour ago."

I swing to the second person. "And you?"

"No more than twenty minutes ago."

"Good enough." I set off for the dorm building.

Kellan jogs to catch up to me. "What are you going to do?"

"She's gone out of her way to make her intention clear. Now it's my turn."

Fury bubbles under my skin. There is no need for her to behave like this. But she's making it clear that the time for talking is over. And I've received her message. She doesn't want to hear my truth. She thinks I'm a monster.

She wants the Monster of Churchill Bradley?

Don't let anyone say I won't live up to people's expectations.

It's a role I've been playing for years. It fits like a glove. She thinks she knows what it's like to be the focus of my attention. She's about to learn that, so far, I've just been toying with her.

Now though... *Now* I'm really going to show her what the Monster of Churchill Bradley is capable of.

My strides take me back to the dorm building and up to the floor which houses the senior girls' rooms. Tina and Lacy are coming out of a room a few doors down from Arabella's when I walk out of the stairwell.

"Eli! What are you doing up here?" Lacy asks.

"Are you looking for me?" Tina flutters her eyelashes.

I frown at them both. "Which room is Arabella's?"

Their eyes widen at the ice in my voice.

"3B." Lacy points to a door mid-way down the hallway.

I hold out my hand. "Key."

"We don't have a key to each other's rooms."

My hand doesn't move. I stare at Lacy. Her tongue snakes out to wet her lips.

"Are you going to make me take it from you?"

She blows out a breath. "Fine!" She pulls a key from her pocket. "I'm supposed to give it back to reception."

I flash her a smile. "Allow me to do it for you." I pluck the key from her fingers. "Now fuck off and find somewhere else to be."

"What are you going to do?" Tina whispers.

"None of your fucking business. Get out." I walk along the hallway and stop outside Arabella's door, before turning to look back at the two girls.

Kellan steps forward, presses his palms to both the girls' backs and ushers them toward the stairwell. "Come along, ladies. Nothing to see here."

I wait until he's escorted them through the door and out of sight before shoving the key in the lock and twisting. There's a soft click as it unlocks. I push down on the handle, open the door and step inside.

The room is neat and tidy, and I take a slow walk around. There are photographs and postcards stuck to the wall. The photographs are of Arabella and another girl. I assume it's her old friend. The one who barely speaks to her now. The postcards are of various places around the world—Paris, Milan, Rome, London.

Turning away from those, I walk over to the closet and throw it open. Dresses, skirts, and long-sleeved tops adorn the hangers, and I flick through them, then crouch to pull out the suitcases. They're all empty. The dresser is my next target. I go through each drawer. Underwear—mostly black instead of the white she'd had when she first joined Churchill Bradley, and lacy instead of cotton—fills one drawer. The second is jeans and sweatpants. T-shirts are neatly folded in the third.

I smile when I open the bottom one. Her diary is there, tucked safely inside the box I'd given her. I could take it, and read it, but I won't. Not yet. Not unless she forces me to. Beside it is a little pink taser. I pick that up and pocket it. Further digging reveals a screwdriver tucked at the back, black paint coating the tip.

Bingo.

I take that as well and walk back to the door. Kellan straightens when I pull it open. I hand him both items.

"Take these to our room."

"What are you going to do?"

My smile is tight. "I'm going to remind Churchill Bradley's Whore the reality of her position at this school."

52

Arabella

H*as he seen the car yet? Has someone told him what I've done?*

I gnaw on a thumbnail while I continue my path around and around the outside of the chapel. The constant movement keeps my edginess from brimming over. My thoughts are in turmoil, and I'm choking on despair. Guilt festers away inside me, merging with my doubts and fears.

Eli has plenty of money. He'll just get it fixed.

And what about the message it leaves?

Who is the real enemy? Who can I trust?

Slicing a glance around, I check I'm alone. My paranoia is high, my nerves on red alert.

Are they watching me now? Are they going to release the videos anyway? They have a chokehold on me, and I don't know what to do.

Whoever is messaging me is using me as a tool. That's clear.

Are they getting some sick kind of entertainment from what they're making me do? Do they hate me that much, or do they have a grudge against my stepbrother?

I round the side of the chapel and stop dead in my tracks. Eli is standing there. For a moment, I question what I'm seeing. Is he a hallucination, summoned out of my thoughts?

His green eyes are cold, lips pressed together in a thin white line, and his slashing cheekbones add to the air of menace that's clinging to him.

This is no hallucination.

Our eyes lock and hold.

This is not the boy I grew to know over Christmas.

The one who held my hand. The one who teased me and fucked me until I came.

The darkness swirling in his gaze is a blackhole of destruction threatening to suck me in.

His nostrils flare.

Everything inside me shrinks back at the sight.

This isn't just another student standing in front of me.

This is a predator.

This is the Monster of Churchill Bradley Academy.

And I'm his chosen prey.

I take off through the trees, my heart in my throat and adrenaline flooding through my limbs, but I don't get far. Arms wrap around my waist and haul me backward. He picks me up, my struggles futile against his strength. He tosses me over his shoulder, ignoring my pleas to let me go. My arms flail against his back as he turns and carries me back toward the chapel.

"Stop fucking fighting." His hand comes down on my backside hard.

I cry out. "Put me down!"

His palm connects with my ass a second time. "You wanted my attention, and now you have it."

He's going to kill me.

I pound my fists against his back, but I might as well not bother for all the notice he takes. The steps of the chapel appear beneath us. He doesn't stop moving until we're inside.

One second, I'm over his shoulder, and the next, the world spins and my feet are on the stone floor.

He strips me out of my coat, spins me around and presses a hand against my spine to bend me over the dusty pew, to pin my flailing hands behind my back with an ease that scares me.

The hard length of his cock beneath denim digs into my ass.

"You're going to pay for what you did to my car." His voice is low and dangerous. He reaches around and pops the button on my jeans.

I try to wiggle free of his grip. "I'm sorry." My voice shakes.

"What's the matter, Hellcat? Are you scared of what I'm going to do to you?"

He steps back, and wraps a hand around both my wrists, while he drags the denim down my thighs with his other one. "Did you think there weren't going to be any consequences for your actions? That I was going to sit there and let you disrespect me?"

"Eli—" A hand comes down on my ass in a stinging slap, and I yelp.

He holds me in place effortlessly and spanks me, over and over, until I lose count and there are tears in my eyes. There's nothing sexual about the act. He's breaking me down, ripping me open until I am raw and exposed. When he finally lets go of me, I'm shaking with rage and humiliation.

"You want a war. Congratulations. Now you've got one," he growls.

I twist and lunge at him, clawing at his shoulders, neck, and face, my only thought to escape the threat in his voice. He rears back before my nails scratch out his eyes and grabs my wrists. The fire in his eyes burns through the remnants of my control.

I don't know which one of us moves first, but our lips meet in a fiery clash. We writhe against each other, and somehow end up on the stone floor.

He kisses his way down my neck, his tongue gliding across my hot skin. I tangle my fingers in his hair and yank his head back up so I can claim his mouth. His tongue duels with mine, both of us silently battling for supremacy until he breaks away.

With rough hands, he pulls off my sneakers and untangles my jeans and panties from my legs, leaving me in my sweater and bra. He parts my legs with his knee, unbuttons his jeans, and shoves them down to free his cock.

I glare up at him but don't move. A perverse part of me needs what he can give me. "I hate you."

Pulling a foil packet out of his pocket, he rips it open and sheathes himself in the condom.

"Don't worry, I'll fuck you like I hate you." His teeth flash in a snarl. "Because I don't have to fucking pretend."

He runs his cock over my clit. I pant, arching up toward him, and spread my legs wider.

"Look at how desperate you are." His laugh is dark, and his eyes watch me with unbridled fury.

I should be scared. But I'm not. This thing between us is animalistic and visceral. I want to feel him skin to skin. I'm desperate for the intensity of his need for me.

His hand wraps around my throat, and he squeezes, thrusting into me at the same time—*hard.* My pussy wraps around him, *welcomes him,* tightening around his cock as he sinks deep inside me. We both groan.

He catches my wrists, one at a time, and pins my arms above my head.

"You can't get enough of me, can you? The Whore of Churchill Bradley Academy is addicted to the Monster's dick."

Oxygen and coherent thought desert me at the same time, and I screw my eyes shut at his taunt. Over and over, he slams into me until I'm shaking beneath him as he fucks me into the stone floor.

"Say it." The fingers on my throat flex, and I shake my head. "Tell me you want me."

I press my lips together and curl my fingers. I want to touch him badly, but I can't with them pinned above my head.

He slows his thrusts. "Beg me to fuck you."

A whine rips from my throat. "Eli, please."

I'm at his whim, and there's a part of me that *wants* to be punished for the bad things I'm doing to him.

The tension builds and builds. I climb higher, clawing my way to the edge of release. I'm almost there. I can *taste* it, but then Eli shudders on top of me. Writhing against him, trying to find my own fulfillment, I'm not prepared when he stills inside me, then pulls out.

He climbs to his feet and rakes a hard look over me.

"You shouldn't play games with people who know how to play them better."

Stunned, panting, I watch him remove the used condom, tuck his cock away and stroll for the door, as he whistles beneath his breath.

He leaves me there. Wet, aching, trembling in torment. Cold and alone.

Tears crest my eyes, and flow silently down my cheeks. I lay there, curled into a ball, half-naked, knees hugged to my chest, shame and despair closing in on me.

53

Eli

I don't stop until I'm inside the tomb with the doors closed. Spinning, I bury a fist into the wall, relishing the pain that radiates through my knuckles and up my arm. I do it again … and again until blood is dripping down my fingers.

"For an artist, you don't take very good care of your hands." Kellan's voice is a dry drawl.

"How long have you been standing there?" I drop my fists and stand there … panting.

"Long enough. I take it your little chat didn't go well."

There's nothing in his voice to indicate he knows what happened. I turn slowly. He's leaning against the opposite wall, arms folded, and legs crossed at the ankles. "I saw her running over the grass." He tuts. "You made her cry, Eli."

"She should be glad I didn't make her fucking bleed." I spit the words out from between clenched teeth.

"It looks like you're bleeding enough for both of you. You're going to need to go to the nurse for that." He reaches out and grabs my wrist so he can twist my hand around to examine my knuckles. "That was a stupid thing to do."

"It's fine."

"Only because I distracted you."

"Why are you here?"

"I'm feeling the love right now." He pushes away from the wall.

"One. Because I'm your friend. Two. Because you're a fucking liability when you're in this kind of mood. And three. Because it's dinner time."

"I'm not hungry."

"And yet we're going to go to the cafeteria, and we're going to sit down and eat food. We're going to talk and laugh and make everyone around us question why the fuck you haven't gone postal over the state of your car."

"Did you get through to the mechanic?"

"Yes. He's picking it up tomorrow." He walks toward the door, then turns back, waving a hand toward my jeans. "Your fly is down. I'm guessing not a whole lot of talking was done at all." He pushes the door open and walks out.

I tug up my zipper and follow him.

The cafeteria is full when we arrive, but a quick scan of the interior shows no sign of Arabella. I walk over to our usual table, while Kellan joins the line, and settle onto my seat. I place my cell on the table and tap the app for the school's social media. Photographs of the damage Arabella has done to my car are all over it, and my anger flares higher with every one I see.

Laughter, loud and raucous, brings my head up just in time to see Kellan trip over something and lose his grip on the tray, which crashes to the ground splashing food and drink everywhere. My gaze drifts to the table of jocks close by and then down to the floor where one of them has his leg stuck out.

I lean back on my seat, the damage to my car forgotten for the moment.

Oh, this is going to be good.

Kellan's eyes follow the same path as mine. His gaze sweeps across the two guys closest to the edge of the table, then down to where one leg is stretched out just far enough to have clipped his foot and made him stumble.

Oh, Bret, you fucking idiot.

Kellan straightens, his easy smile unwavering, as he turns to the jocks nudging each other and laughing. Laughter which cuts off abruptly when, almost too quick to follow, Kellan grabs the back of Bret's head and slams his face into the table *twice*. Blood explodes outward. Bret howls. Kellan introduces his face to the table once more, then leans forward, fingers still tangled in his hair.

"If you *ever* make me drop my food again, it won't be your fucking nose I break."

He releases his grip, takes one of the trays littering the table, and turns back to the food counter, whistling cheerfully.

The entire cafeteria is silent. No one speaks while Kellan refills his tray and strolls back to me. He slides the tray onto the table and sits down.

"There's blood on your sleeve." I flick a finger toward the dark red splash as I reach for my coffee.

"I'll send the asshole my dry-cleaning bill."

59

Arabella

My hand moves the paintbrush over the canvas in front of me, as I bring the painting to life.

A cemetery sits in darkness, touched by the silver light of a full moon. Twisted trees surround the tombstones encircling a fragmented doorway at the back. A figure is in the dark, dressed in red.

"Wow, Miss Gray, I'm impressed."

I find Mr. McIntyre just behind me. "Thanks."

"It really evokes death and loneliness. I hope that's what you were going for."

"I just painted what was in my head."

Despair, seclusion, my life as I know it.

"Keep it up, Miss Gray."

His praise sends warmth tingling through me from head to toe. It seems like forever since anyone said anything positive to me.

I step back from my easel, stretch, and glance nervously around the classroom at the rest of the students. We're spaced out around the room. Eli is to my right, absorbed in his painting.

Three days have passed since I ruined his car. Three days since *he* ruined *me*. The long-sleeved top I'm wearing hides the purple bruises he's left around my wrists from when he pinned me down.

My body still pulses with frustration, empty of the release I was denied. No matter how many times I've used my fingers in my bed at night, I haven't been able to find satisfaction. His rejection still lingers with me. A sharp thorn in my insecurity and pride.

Eli hasn't approached me since it happened, but I haven't been able to avoid his hostile stares whenever we're in the same room. The hate that dissipated over Christmas is now back in full force.

Did he really post the video and the photo of me?

The quiet question niggles at the back of my mind.

I don't know what to do. I want to confide in someone, to tell them what's happening, but who do I turn to? I don't trust the counselor not to share what I say with the principal. If someone can get the private videos and photographs I sent Sin, they can get anything recorded by the counselor.

Miles is keeping his distance, and I have no other friends here.

Amanda?

I haven't spoken to her since I ran away to Mrs. Goldmann's, but she's always been the one person I have been able to confide in. And I really need someone to tell me I'm not going crazy.

I'll call her tonight.

My cell vibrates in my pocket, and I'm plunged into panic. Every time a notification goes off, I'm scared to check it. So far, my blackmailer has been silent, but I know that won't last forever.

I take a peek at my phone when Mr. McIntyre isn't looking and break out into a cold sweat.

`Unknown number: Destroy his painting.`

They have to be joking. Not now.

`Me: But it's the middle of class.`

`Unknown number: Use your imagination. You have ten minutes to do as ordered, or we'll upload the video` of you getting eaten out on old Churchill's coffin.

No.

This is going to end in a confrontation I've been desperate to avoid. This is so fucked up, but I have no choice but to comply with the instructions.

My gaze darts around the room, and I search for a way to complete my order.

In the far corner, clay sculptures are drying on a shelf above a couple of pottery wheels. There are drawing tables and workbenches. The studio has it all. My eyes settle on the paint that's been left out on a table.

With a shaky breath and fear slithering through my veins like poison, I cross the room. Tension burns through my limbs, and I'm sure that everybody is watching me. I fill the free spaces in the palette I'm holding with bright colors—red, orange, blue, and purple.

Out of the corner of my eye, I catch Linda watching me, so I linger at the table until she looks away. Then, palette clutched between my fingers, I walk back across the room. Just as I reach Eli, I make a show of stumbling. Throwing my hands forward, I slam right into him. The palette full of paint hits the back of his hoodie with a wet splat.

He recoils, head snapping up. "What the fuck?"

"I'm sorry. I tripped."

I reach for the palette, peel it off and grimace at the bright paint streaks staining the dark material.

"Bullshit. You did that on purpose." Eli twists to scowl at the mess over his shoulder. "This is my favorite fucking hoodie, and *you* know it. I didn't think you were such a fucking spiteful little bitch."

If looks could kill, I'd be dead right now from the way Eli's eyes are boring into me. The expression on his face sends chills down my spine. His fingers curl into the front of my top and he hauls me toward him.

Mr. McIntyre appears between us.

"Mr. Travers, that's enough." He taps Eli's wrist with his fingers. "Let her go."

"I-I'm so-sorry." I back away.

The teacher frowns. "Return to your easel, Miss Gray, and stay there, please."

"Yes, sir." I lower my head and scuttle back to my place. My heart bangs against my ribs like a trapped bird. Guilt and dread for what Eli will do in response makes me nauseous.

My phone vibrates. I have to wait until the teacher isn't watching before I can read the message.

`Unknown number: You failed. Strike one against you, Arabella. You know what that means, don't you? Bad girls get punished.`

55

Eli

I peel the hoodie over my head and toss it onto the bench behind me. Arabella is back behind her easel, brush strokes moving over whatever she's painting. Her eyes are on me, though, and every time I move, she flinches.

She's expecting me to retaliate. And I *will*. But not in any way she's expecting.

When the class is over, I take my painting off the easel and walk over to where Arabella is cleaning her brushes. Leaning past her, I prop it on the shelf above the sink in front of her.

"Really should have aimed for the painting instead of my hoodie," I whisper and walk away, grabbing my hoodie as I pass it.

The outraged gasp reaches me as I step through the door, and I smile to myself.

The painting I've spent the class working on is of Arabella bent over the pew in the old chapel, jeans around her ankles and red handprints covering her ass. I've written the title in bold red paint across the top.

The Whore's Prayer.

I'm down by the lockers before she catches up to me. Her fingers curl around my arm and I let her pull me around to face her.

"Eli, I—"

I twist free of her grip, grab her shoulders, and slam her back against the lockers. She hits them with a thud.

"Careful, Princess. *Someone* might think you're trying to get me thrown out of school."

"Please, just—"

"Oh, so you're *begging* now?" Movement out of the corner of my eye tells me students are starting to fill up the hallway. I drop my hands and step back.

"Go on, then. Fucking *beg*. On your knees. Like the good little cock-sucking bitch you are." My lip curls when her cheeks turn red. "No? But isn't that your favorite position? On the floor, with your mouth open and tongue out. Eager to have it filled by a dick? Like a *good girl*?"

The shock in her eyes fades away, and anger replaces it, burning like a fire I can feel over every inch of my skin. I let my gaze move over her face, down her throat, over the swell of her breasts.

"Do you get off on being degraded, Princess? Is that it? Are your nipples hard right now? Is your pussy wet? If I pushed a finger into your panties, would you soak it?"

She pushes away from the lockers and bolts down the hallway.

"There's nowhere you can run, Hellcat," I call after her. "You woke up the monster, and now he's fucking hungry."

***

I spend the evening with my sculpture. Kellan drops food off outside the door but doesn't disturb me, and my alarm has gone off warning me that it's close to curfew when I finally lock up and go back to the dorm building. The path connecting the two buildings is dark and I wonder if the lights, which usually illuminate it, are broken. If that's the case, it's unusual for them to not be fixed already.

"Hey, Monster." The female voice, muffled by … something … comes from my left. "Catch!"

My hands automatically lift to catch the white ball that hurtles toward me. It's soft, warm, and wet when it hits my hand, and I frown down at it.

"Maybe this wet pussy is more to your liking …"

The lights flare back to life, and I find myself staring down at a …

"What the fuck?"

For a second, I think it's an animal and I drop it. Closer inspection tells me it's not real. It's a stuffed animal. A white cat … partially soaked in what looks like blood, but I *think* is red paint.

I turn in a slow circle but can't see anyone. Whoever it was—and I've got a good idea who that is, because there's only one person who's going out of her way to antagonize me right now—has taken advantage of my distraction to bolt.

Unfortunately for her, I know where she fucking lives … and now it's after curfew, there will be no one around to witness my retaliation. I crouch to pick up the stuffed animal and set off for the dorm building.

It's silent when I enter, and the lights are low. I take the stairs two at a time, bypass the exit for my floor and walk out on the third. When I reach room 3B, I don't knock. Most people don't lock their doors once they're inside. I turn the handle and throw the door open.

It bangs off the wall and slams shut behind me. My palm hits the light switch, flooding the room with a bright artificial light and my gaze searches out the girl pretending to have been startled awake beneath the blankets on the bed.

"Are you fucking twelve?" I throw the stuffed animal at her. "Was this supposed to scare me? Is there something fucking *wrong* with you?" I stalk closer to the bed as she scrambles up, eyes landing on the sticky wet mess the toy has made on her sheets and widening.

"What is that? Is it an animal? Did you *kill* an animal, Eli? Oh my *god!"* Her voice rises in pitch with each word.

"Stop fucking pretending you didn't throw that at me."

"But I—"

"What was supposed to happen? Was security supposed to arrive and find me with it? Are they supposed to think I'm just out there in the dark slaughtering fucking kittens when everyone's asleep?"

"No, I—"

I'm next to the bed, my fingers around her throat before she finishes speaking. I use my grip on her throat to hold her down on the mattress and lower my face, so it's close to hers.

"Listen carefully, Hellcat, because this is the last time I'm going to say this. You. Will. Not. Win. This. War."

I squeeze, cutting off her air supply and keep my attention on her face until the fear seeps back into her eyes and she claws at my wrist, lips parting as she desperately tries to take a breath.

"Stop fucking with me. Next time I won't be so nice, and this …" I smear my red-painted hand across her cheek. "This won't be fucking paint."

I shove her back against the mattress and walk out.

56

Arabella

I sit with my back against the stone wall, phone cradled in my hands, while I stare at the pretty colors and patterns the light from the stained-glass windows cast on the floor. Snow fell during the night, to leave a blanket of pure white over the whole campus. Although it's cold, I'm out of the icy bite of the wind, hidden away inside the chapel.

It's Friday lunchtime. I'm still shaken up after Eli burst into my room a few nights ago and accused me of something I hadn't done. The days are crawling by at a snail's pace, and each hour that passes turns me into more of a nervous wreck than before.

I'm waiting for the next blow to fall. The next text to arrive. The next video or photograph to be leaked. The next explosion from Eli.

I've tried to call Amanda, but so far, she hasn't picked up.

Please be there. I need someone to talk to. Someone to confide in before I lose my mind.

I swipe my finger over my phone screen and hit her number. It rings and rings but finally my persistence is rewarded, and the call connects.

"Hi, Amanda. Are you busy?" I speak quickly.

"Oh, hi." Her voice sounds odd. "I'm on my lunch break."

My grip tightens on my phone, and I press it closer to my ear. "I could really use someone to talk to right now."

"Is this to do with why you ran away before Christmas?"

"Things have gotten worse." Everything rushes out of me in a fast mess of words. "I'm being blackmailed into doing things. I don't know who to talk to—"

Amanda cuts me off with a sigh. "*Really*? Blackmail now?"

I frown at the disbelief in her tone. "It's true."

"First, it was the evil stepbrother. Now, this. Can you *be* any more dramatic? Are you seeking attention again, like you always do? Your mom's not there, so you're making up a new story."

"No, it's not like that—"

She hums. "The more I think about it, you had never-ending drama."

Hurt and shocked, I blink back tears. "I thought you were my friend."

"You're in your fancy school surrounded by rich kids. I guess things change, and people move on."

"Amanda—"

"I have to eat my lunch. Good luck with the blackmail." The line goes dead.

She doesn't believe me. Has she always thought that I made things up about my mother? All the times I confided in her, did she think it was all a lie?

Something soft and delicate dies inside me as I go through everything she's said.

Big, fat tears roll down my cheeks. I drop the phone and cradle my face while I sob into my hands. All my pent-up emotions and fears pour out.

I'm desperate to have someone put their arms around me. To feel the solid warmth of comfort. For someone to tell me that everything is going to be okay.

I cry until my chest hurts and my head feels heavy and dull, and then I curl up on the floor, my cheek pressed to the hard chilly stone. A numbness creeps over my body.

I don't want to go back to school. I'm too wound up to eat. I can't sleep. The thought of walking into my next class, not knowing who's watching me or what will happen, makes my stomach twist in painful knots.

I'm waiting for the threatened punishment. It hangs over my head, but nothing has happened so far.

Eli won't listen to me if I try to tell him what's happening. He doesn't believe that the fake animal wasn't me. There's too much emotion between us, and it's all toxic.

Churchill Bradley Academy has become my prison.

My gaze moves aimlessly through the chapel, and finally settles on something tucked beneath one of the pews. I shift up onto my hands and knees and crawl toward it. Reaching out, I curl my fingers into the soft brown leather and pull it out from its hiding place.

A bag.

Has it been here the whole time or is someone else using the chapel when I'm not here?

I unzip it slowly, expecting to find someone's stash of alcohol or drugs. But that's not what greets me, and I remove the items one at a time, lining them up in front of me.

A heavy silver lighter, a round compact mirror, a comb, and a pink pen with a sparkly top. But it's the thick book with a red cover that holds my attention. I run my fingertips over the front and open the first page.

My heart stops.

The thoughts and life of Zoey Rivers.

I glance around the chapel, uneasily.

Why is her diary here? Did she hide it?

I turn to the first page and start to read.

First day back at school, and Lacy has been giving me hell. I've already told her I'm done with the cheerleading squad, but she doesn't want to hear it. She's still trying to rule my life. She might think she's Queen of the school, but I'm not her minion. Thank God I have Eli and Kellan. Life would suck without them. I can't even imagine what it would be like to have no one here.

I do. Sadness shrouds me, but I keep on reading.

Bret asked me out after lunch, and I politely declined. Even if I liked boys, he wouldn't be my first choice. None of the jocks would be. Brad acts all sweet, but I've seen what he can do when he's angry. I'm pretty sure Bret is secretly hot for his roommate Garrett. Miles lights up my gaydar like a Christmas tree. Kellan thinks he's in denial. Jace is impulsive and doesn't know when to stop, while Evan follows him around like a puppy on a leash. Like Eli says, we all have secrets, even the popular crowd.

My phone pings.

"Fuck." Torn between the desire to read more and the nauseating need to see who the message is from, I shuffle back to where I left my cell.

Please don't let it be from my blackmailer.

Miles: You're not in class. Where are you?

I check the time on the screen. Where did the hour go?

Me: I'm not feeling well. Can you let the teacher know, please?

Miles: The others are going to give me shit over it.

I don't fucking care.

Me: I don't have anyone else to ask.

Miles: Ok, I'll do it.

Me: Thanks.

My attention returns to the diary. I close it and hug it to my chest.

Zoey.

I already feel a connection with her. Seeing her thoughts and feelings written on the page only deepens the sensation.

I should turn it in to the principal.

No, not yet. Maybe I'm being selfish, but I want to read to the end. She had a friendship with Eli and Kellan. One I don't understand. But she became an outcast because of it, and I need to know what it was like for her to be here at the academy.

Maybe it will stop me from feeling so alone.

57

Eli

I dump my bag at my feet and drop heavily onto the chair opposite Kellan. His eyes lift from the magazine he's reading, and one eyebrow quirks up.

"I didn't expect to see you here today."

"Why not?"

"You haven't shown your face anywhere other than classes for days."

"Only because I didn't want to be arrested for murder. I'm over it now."

His shoulders move as he laughs. "Sure, you are."

"Shut up and get me a coffee."

He flips his magazine closed and stands, presses his palms together and bows. "Yes, sir. Right away, sir."

I shake my head, laughing, and he winks at me before he steps away from the table, only to stop. "Oh, look. My favorite chew toy has come for lunch."

I follow the direction of his gaze to see Miles Cavanagh walking through the doors. He's scowling down at his cell and doesn't see Kellan glide out from between the tables to block his path.

"Well, hello there, pretty boy. What can I do to turn that frown of yours upside down?"

Miles' reaction is comical. He comes to an abrupt stop, his cell falling from his fingers to hit the ground. His face turns red, then white, before settling on a shade of puce I don't think I've ever seen on a person before.

"Fuck off, Fraser." Jace unfurls himself from his chair and stands.

I do the same and move to stand beside Kellan. My eyes flick down to the garish red cast the football captain still has on his arm.

"Aren't you due to get that removed next week? I'd hate for you to make a decision that means you'll lose one cast only to gain another two."

The cafeteria slowly falls silent as other students notice the stand-off. One by one, the rest of Jace's friends stand to join him. Except Bret, who stays where he is with his black eyes and taped-up nose. I toss him a smile and touch the side of my nose. He ducks his head and looks away.

No one reported Kellan as the culprit. Bret claimed it was an accident during football practice. Not that Kellan would have cared if he had been hauled in front of the principal for it.

Jace, Evan, Brad, and Kevin fan out behind Miles. I prop my hip against the edge of a table and fold my arms. Kellan is smiling, his gaze still on Miles.

"Is this what you want to do, pretty boy?" His voice is silky, rich with amusement.

Miles shakes his head. "No one needs to get into a fight. Kellan is just being an ass, as usual." He shoots a glare at my friend and pushes past him.

Kellan laughs. "You guys are so uptight. You need to get laid more often." He turns to me. "Coffee, you said, right?"

"That's right." I don't move from my position.

Kellan is about to turn his back on five people, and I'm not going to let that turn into a mistake. Jace looks at me, then Kellan, and finally Miles.

"Leave Miles alone, Fraser. This is your only warning."

Kellan gives him a two-fingered salute, smirks, and walks toward the food counter. I stay where I am and watch as the five of them walk out of the cafeteria before going back to my seat. When Kellan returns with food and coffee, I nail him with a glare.

"Why do you keep trying to force Miles to acknowledge you in public? You know he's never going to do it."

Instead of the flippant response I'm expecting, he sighs. "He's fucking obsessed with the idea that if he comes out as gay, he'll be kicked off the swim team."

"Pretty sure no one gives a fuck about his sexuality."

"His so-called friends might. I think he's scared of how they'll look at him. Especially after he claimed to be dating Arabella."

"The girl he abandoned, you mean?"

"You don't really have any right to be annoyed by that, Eli. Not with the way *you're* treating her."

His mild words hit their target.

"If she would quit provoking me, I'd leave her alone."

"Would you, though?" He takes a sip of coffee. "See, I'm not sure you would. If she hadn't started this … this *thing* between the two of you, then you would have done something to get her attention. There's no way you'd have allowed her to ignore you. You don't like the fact she won't believe you didn't leak that video. I know you, Eli. You wouldn't be able to leave that alone."

I'm about to reply, to *argue*, when a scream rips through the room. A second one follows almost immediately, and everyone surges up and runs for the doors.

"What the fuck was that?"

We trade glances, then move as one, following everyone else out and along the hallway to where the lockers are. Shocked whispers are rippling through the crowd when we get there, and then the students part to allow a white-faced Arabella through.

She comes right up to me, blue eyes blazing in her pale features, and slaps me.

"*Why?*" The demand is high-pitched. "*Why,* Eli? I told you it wasn't me! What kind of fucking monster are you?"

She goes to hit me again, but Kellan grabs her from behind and pulls her away before she makes contact.

My gaze shifts over her shoulder. I walk around her and through the still-whispering students. A couple of the girls have their hands pressed to their mouths, tears in their eyes, and I follow the direction of their gaze.

There's a dead rat, its entrails pulled out, pinned to the front of her locker.

Whore is painted below it in blood.

58

Arabella

"Calm down." Kellan's arms tighten around me to stop me from attacking Eli again. I'm shaking. Sick to my stomach. He must have left the dead rat as some kind of macabre trophy.

Is this to get back at me for what he thinks I did with a stuffed toy?

Do you really think he would kill a defenseless animal?

I'm too horrified and angry to listen to the voice inside my head.

"What the fuck is wrong with you?" I spit.

"It wasn't me." Eli's voice is flat. "Just like the last dead animal wasn't me." He raises his voice. "You need to get more original with your pranks."

I struggle in Kellan's arms and try to break free. "Bullshit. It's not funny, Eli. You need to get your head examined."

"What is going on?"

Mrs. Winters appears, pushing her way through the crowd. Her attention jumps from my face to the bloodied rat pinned to my locker. I watch in morbid fascination as she goes pale, and horror takes over her expression.

"Mr. Travers." Her voice is low and unsteady. "Report to the principal's office immediately."

Anger ripples over Eli's expression. "It *wasn't* me."

"Don't argue with me, young man. Miss Gray, go back to your dorm room."

Kellan loosens his hold on me, and I step away from him. Not able to voice another word without losing my shit, I glare at my stepbrother before walking away. Miles gives me a worried look but says nothing. I'm still shaking with shock, unable to process fully what I'd just found.

I shove my earbuds in and hit play, the lyrics of 'Reaper' by Silverberg flooding my brain. I let it drown out the noise around me. The music blurs out the things I don't want to think about. A coping mechanism I use as armor. It's the only way I've been able to survive these last few weeks.

I walk fast, not stopping until I reach my room and slip inside. As much as I hate being alone, I'm grateful there is no one here to torment me.

An image of the rat flashes through my head, its entrails hanging like red ribbons from the jagged cut in its body. Shivering, I remove my earbuds and drop my bag on the bed. The thought of using my locker again leaves me feeling cold. Even though I didn't touch the dead rat, I feel dirty and tainted. I can't strip out of my clothes fast enough, leaving them in a trail across the floor as I pad into the bathroom and turn on the shower. Once it's hot enough, I step under the spray, tip my face up under the cascading water and close my eyes. The heat relaxes my muscles and slowly calms the chaos in my mind.

We found a chick today out by the cemetery. It was chirping so loud. Kellan found the nest it had fallen from, and Eli climbed the tree to put it back. I hope the momma bird doesn't get scared off because we helped it. I'd hate for our good deed to cause it more harm. Eli was as worried as me, but Kellan was convinced we did the right thing.

The words from the latest chapter of Zoey's diary whisper through my head. Her version of Eli clashes with the one I know. How can he be the same person? He's so different from what she describes. All I see is the monster everyone talks about.

But I liked the boy I glimpsed at that hotel before Christmas. The playful Eli with a smile that lit up his face, and the husky mischievous voice when he whispered dirty things in my ear and heated my blood.

The memory messes with my emotions even more. He showed me another side to himself, the closest I've seen to what the dead girl describes.

A thud disturbs my thoughts, and I freeze, listening. When I don't hear it again, I cut off the shower, step out, and dry myself. Wrapping a towel around my body, I go back into the empty bedroom, and stop beside the bed. There's a thump against the wall, followed by muffled laughter from the room next door. I can't help but roll my eyes at whoever is messing around. But it relaxes me a little, knowing people are around me, even if they aren't in the same room.

I drop the towel and dig fresh clothes out of my closet. I'm just pulling my top on when a knock sounds on my door. When I open the door, I discover one of the security guards on the other side.

He gives me a polite smile. "Miss Gray, I'm here to escort you to the principal's office."

"Okay."

This has to be about Eli.

Nerves hike up my anxiety levels, but I slip into shoes and follow him out of the dorm. By the time we reach the principal's office, I've got my anxiety mostly under control.

The security guard leaves me in the office, where the secretary peers at me from over her spectacles. "Go right in. He's expecting you."

I offer her a weak smile of thanks and do as I'm instructed.

"Ah, Miss Gray." Principal Warren gestures at me with one hand. "Come in, shut the door and take a seat."

I take the seat on the other side of his desk, sinking down into the soft leather. "You wanted to see me, sir?"

He rests his elbows on his desk, his expression stern. "I know you've had a bumpy start coming back to school since Christmas, but vandalism of another student's property is unacceptable."

My stomach dips. He *must* be talking about Eli's car, but that was days ago. Why is he bringing it up now? I thought this was about the dead rat on my locker.

"Yes, Miss Gray. I know what you did to his vehicle. I was prepared to turn a blind eye, but I can't do that anymore." Principal Warren's voice is deep and calm. "When Mr. Travers came back to the academy, I understood and expected that you would want to lash out, but the lengths this is going to is not acceptable. I've had multiple reports of you trying to provoke him while he has made every effort to stay out of your way. If this continues, I'm going to have to notify your parents."

The disappointment in his voice makes me squirm in my seat. "But he left a dead rat on my locker."

"Eli denies playing any part in that."

"*Who* else would do that?"

"It could merely be a distasteful prank trying to fuel the aggression between you both. I assure you; we are looking into it." He sighs and his expression softens. "You have good grades, Arabella. I would hate to see you ruin your future here. Your mother fought hard to get Eli back into this school, and your stepbrother has assured me what went on earlier was nothing to do with him. What do you think she would say if she learned you were sabotaging his education out of petty retaliation?"

"Of course, she did! Because he's so fucking perfect in her eyes." My words are bitter.

"This needs to stop now, Miss Gray. I won't warn you again."

Anger sears through my usual caution, and I take the chance in front of me. "I'm being blackmailed."

"Blackmailed?" He frowns.

I nod. "Into doing those things to Eli. It's not me. I'm being forced to do them."

"Really, Miss Gray?" His tone of voice makes it clear he doesn't believe me. "Do you have any proof?"

"Yes! There are texts on my phone." I take my cell phone out of my pocket, searching for the messages. The messages app is empty. Not a single text to or from anyone. "Wait, they were right here." My voice trails off in confusion.

Am I losing my mind? Where did they go? This can't be happening. How is it even possible for them to vanish into thin air?

Principal Warren is staring at me, pity in his eyes. "If this is some kind of cry for attention or help, then you need to speak up. Counselor Clarke has said that you refuse to talk to him. If you need help, you have to tell us, Arabella."

I shake my head wildly. "I'm not lying!"

"Then where are these text messages you claim you have?"

"They're gone, but—"

"I think that will be all, Miss Gray. You may go."

He's not listening. I'm already dismissed. He doesn't believe a single word of what I've said, and if I don't have evidence, he never will.

A sudden thought strikes me.

"I want my phone back." I blurt out. "The one you found in Eli's locker."

He frowns. "I'm not sure that's a good idea—"

"It's my property. I didn't break any laws sending photographs to someone."

His frown deepening, Principal Warren studies me for a moment before he opens the drawer of his desk. He takes out the familiar phone and slides it toward me.

I snatch it up, stand and walk out of his office without a backward glance. The second I'm out in the hallway, I switch it on.

Part of me hoped there would be a text waiting for me. *Something.* Anything to say Sin was thinking about me. But no messages arrive, and I have to blink fast against the tears that sting my eyes. I release a long shuddering breath and type out a text.

`Me: Sin, please talk to me. Everything has turned upside down, and I don't have anyone else. I need you.`

I wait for a reply, but nothing comes.

Disappointment is a bitter lump in my throat. I shove the phone into a pocket and find my earbuds. I slot them into my ears, 'Crawling Back To You' by Daughtry playing through the speakers.

59

Eli

I spend Saturday locked away with my sculpture. It's starting to take shape, and while part of me regrets the design I decided on before Christmas, it's too late to change it now. But it looks amazing, and I can't deny that the concept I had is coming together better than I thought it would.

This past week has been tougher than I expected, especially the latest run-in over the dead rat yesterday. Thankfully, Principal Warren believed me when I denied having any part in it, which is a step in the right direction after the dead rabbit incident a couple of months ago. He hadn't believed me when I claimed my innocence over leaving that in Arabella's locker.

I lock up earlier than usual, instead of working until curfew. I want to go for a run and try and work out some of the stress that has my muscles aching and my head throbbing.

My name being called by a familiar voice the second I step out of the building snaps my spine taut. I consider ignoring her, but my body has other ideas and turns to face her before I even register the move.

My gaze sweeps over her. She's clutching a travel mug in one hand, and her steps are cautious as she comes toward me, eyes on the thin layer of snow on the ground.

"What do you want?"

"I'm sorry for blaming you yesterday. I thought that …" She bites her lip and holds out the travel mug. "Peace offering?"

"What is it?"

"Coffee. The cafeteria closed earlier than usual because of the snow, and I know you usually like to get a drink before curfew." The hand holding the travel mug trembles. "I'm really sorry."

The sound of footsteps on the snow behind me heralds Kellan's arrival.

"What are you two doing? Do I need to call a referee?"

"No." I start to turn, and she catches my sleeve.

"Please, Eli."

I don't know why my name on her lips makes me take the coffee from her, but it does, and my fingers curl around the heated mug. I lift it to my lips and take a sip, then point it at her.

"This does not mean we're friends."

"I know." Her voice is quiet. She turns and walks away.

I take another mouthful of the coffee, my eyes on her until she disappears around a corner.

"What was that about?"

Kellan's question drags my attention away from her and I look at him.

"Not sure. Maybe Warren gave her a warning." I start walking again, Kellan beside me. "I'm going to change and go for a run. You coming?"

"Fuck, no. Why do you keep asking me that?"

"One day you might say yes."

"Only if there are zombies chasing me."

He's *still* listing all the reasons why he'll never come running with me when we reach our room. I drain the rest of the coffee and change into sweats and a t-shirt.

"Last chance to change your mind."

He flaps his hands at me. "Go. Run. I'm going to find a movie to watch."

I'm still laughing when I exit the building and jog toward the woods, pressing play on my music.

***

Twenty minutes into the run, 'Papercuts' by Machine Gun Kelly is loud in my ears, and I have to stop. I feel weird. My heart is hammering against my ribs at a frenzied pace, and my head is spinning. I feel off-balance, *woozy*, so when I reach the bench, I sink down onto it and try to steady my racing pulse.

A minute passes, then another, and what feels like the threat of an impending heart attack seems to fade. I stand, a little cautiously, and walk a few feet. When I don't keel over, I set off again, slowing as the chapel comes into view on my left.

The last time I'd been here was after Arabella keyed my car. The thought of her bent over the pew while I spanked her ass heats my blood.

Is she in there?

Curfew can't be far away. She probably isn't, but I'm outside the doors and pushing them open before I can stop myself. Stepping inside, the first thing I notice is the lack of snow.

I shouldn't be surprised by that. The building is secure, other than the doors being unlocked. Aside from the other day, I haven't been here in over a year. In my head, I can hear Zoey's laughter as she dances around the altar, Kellan's dry sarcasm as he teases her, and the soft sound of pencil on paper as I sketch the both of them.

I move deeper inside, my fingers trailing across the back of the pews and my gaze trained on the altar ahead of me. There's a figure perched on top of it. Shadows from the windows fall over its back, making it look like they have wings, and my fingers twitch. I wish I had something at hand to capture the beauty of the pose.

My steps are silent as I move closer until I'm right behind her. Her perfume surrounds me, drawing me in, and a surge of something … a *need* so fucking strong I can't deny it … takes over. I reach out and stroke my fingers down her neck.

She jerks away, jumps to her feet and spins, blue eyes widening. "*Eli?*"

My head tilts. Her voice is like music, a physical caress over my skin, and I want to hear her speak again. My hand reaches out to touch her and she takes a step backward.

"What are you doing?"

A tiny voice inside my head echoes the question, but I ignore it. Squash it down. I don't need to answer it. It's not important.

"You're so pretty." I skirt around the altar, and she does the same, keeping distance between us.

"You look like an angel." My lips twitch into a smile. "With hair like silk and eyes so blue, I think I could drown in them."

She frowns. "Is this another one of your games?"

"No game." That inner voice screams at me from a distance. I shake my head, dislodging it. "Don't run from me, Ari."

Her eyes widen at my words, but she doesn't move when I close the gap between us and take her hands. My thumbs rub over her wrists as I lift them to place against my chest. Her fingers curl into my shirt.

"What are you doing?"

"How are you so warm?" I run my knuckles down her cheek. "So fucking soft." I cup her chin and tilt her head up. "So sweet." My head lowers and I brush my lips over hers.

She doesn't respond, so I do it again, flicking my tongue out to lick over her bottom lip.

"I miss you, Ari."

60

Arabella

I miss you, Ari.

Those four words echo through my head, making me feel even more wretched than I already am. I've been torturing myself over giving Eli the coffee, knowing it was a curse in disguise. I threw up this morning when I'd found a new text from my stalker. It had been a warning about what would happen if I went to Principal Warren again. Then the next instruction came at lunchtime to pick up the drink and give it to Eli.

I should have said no. Whatever is in it is affecting him. He's acting … weird.

What if it's dangerous?

He curls his hand around the back of my neck and crushes his lips to mine. Deep, hard possessive, a forceful demand which leaves me trembling. Stress and desire twist me up inside. I'm playing with him because I have no choice. I'm pushing him to get the reaction my blackmailers want.

I want to keep him at arm's length.

I want to hold him close.

Eli smiles against my mouth. "I think you like it; you know. All the fighting and the hate. The more it hurts, the hotter it feels, doesn't it? You want me to fuck you again. You want me to punish you with the way it burns between us, don't you?"

I cradle his face gently in my hands. "Eli, I'm sorry—"

He silences me with his kisses and backs me up until I hit the altar. His hands are everywhere, roaming restlessly over my body.

"You're so fucking beautiful." He nips my lip and tugs my coat down my arms. I don't stop him.

"Eli, you're not yourself."

He ignores me. His fingers slip under my top and unclip my bra. Shoving my sweater up, he lowers his head and takes one of my nipples into his hot, hungry mouth. I can't stop a moan at the contact and tangle my fingers in his hair, head tipped back.

I've been starving for this. The intimacy between us. Even if the sex doesn't mean anything, I still crave it. I've become addicted to what Eli can give me.

He's a dirty addiction that makes me feel good when I need it the most.

With his mouth on my body, I can pretend I'm not being blackmailed. That the videos don't exist. That there's no hate between us.

"I need to be inside you so bad, Ari." My name leaves him with a tortured groan, his mouth trailing a wet path between my breasts.

He'll hate you even more for this.

I squeeze my eyes closed in an attempt to blot out the little voice.

"We can't do this. Eli, you have to …" I moan when his lips close around my other nipple, sucking on it roughly.

He reaches for the button on my jeans. "Yes, we can."

I grab his wrist, torn between wanting him inside me and knowing this is wrong. How he's behaving is unnatural.

"Eli, there was something in the coffee. Please, are you listening to me?"

He licks a path along my neck. "Let me fuck you, Ari."

I pull his head up and press my forehead to his. "I'm sorry, Eli. I'm so, so sorry."

His entire body goes rigid, and for one second, I think my words have penetrated through the fog of whatever drug I've given him. He tears himself free from my embrace, and staggers away, across the chapel to the door.

"Eli?" Fear courses through me. Not sure what's happening, I pull down my sweater and dash after him.

He makes it down two steps before his chest heaves, and he vomits into the snow. Swaying, he collapses sideways and hits the snow, face-first.

"Eli!" I scramble across the snow, drop to my knees, and roll him over onto his side. His face is pale, and his eyes are closed. I press my fingers against his throat, checking for his pulse, and I sag with relief when I feel his heart still beating.

What was in the coffee?

The question repeats over and over in my head.

I can't leave him like this. Not out here in the snow and dark. Whoever is behind the texts wants to hurt him, and as much as we dislike each other, I don't want to see him dead. I dig my fingers into my pocket and pull out my cell and send a text to the one person I can think of for help.

`Me: Miles, please, I need your help. Eli is really sick.`

Eli mumbles something I don't catch.

"It's okay." I stroke his shoulder. "Everything is going to be okay."

My cell pings.

`Miles: Where are you?`

`Me: The old chapel.`

`Miles: Ok, don't move. Help's on the way.`

Tangled emotions clog my throat, and tears burn the backs of my eyes.

Thank you, Miles.

"Help is coming," I say into the dark. I'm not sure if Eli can hear me, but I hope the sound of my voice tells him he's not alone.

His body rocks in a shiver beneath my palm. He's in sweats and a t-shirt. They're both soaked through from the snow. He must be freezing.

I glance back toward the chapel, chewing my lip while I think. I need to keep him warm until someone gets here.

My coat!

I dash back inside and snatch it up, then run back to where I left him. I tuck the coat around him as best I can, then kneel at his side, shivering.

It's so fucking cold. My hands feel numb, and I can't stop shaking. I tuck my fingers under my armpits.

Where are you, Miles?

"What the fuck happened?"

I stiffen at the voice. Kellan strides toward us through the trees, expression grim.

"Where's Miles?"

"Not coming," he growls.

"How—"

"He told me that you'd texted him. What happened?"

"Eli was acting weird, and then he threw up and collapsed."

He drops to a crouch in the snow. "Define weird."

My fingers brush Eli's hair away from his forehead. "He kissed me, said he missed me, and then tried to have sex with me."

Kellan examines his friend, and frowns when Eli mumbles incoherently. "He's out of it."

"I'm sorry." I choke the words out.

Kellan goes rigid, his attention shifting to my face. "What did you do?" The question is delivered in a slow, measured tone.

"I'm so sorry. I didn't know what was going to happen. I didn't want to hurt him." The truth is ripped out of me. I keep my eyes on the snow in front of us, unable to meet his watchful gaze.

"Arabella, what the fuck did you do?" he repeats, and the edge to his voice hikes up my fear.

I shake my head and get to my feet. Terror drives me with the primitive need to escape, and I take off through the trees and away from both of them.

If anything happens to Eli, it's on me. This is all my fault. I won't be able to live with myself.

Lost in my torment, I'm not looking where I'm going and miss the figure who steps out in front of me.

A hand grabs my arm. "Bella?"

I throw my head up and find myself staring into Miles' worried face. "I did something stupid. Oh god, what have I done?"

"Slow down. What did you do?"

"Let me go. Please … you need to help Kellan."

"What's happening?"

"I-I can't."

I pull free of him and flee back in the direction of the school.

61

Eli

"Eli? Open your eyes."

"Kellan. Hey. What are you doing here?" Flopping onto my back, I smile up at my friend.

He doesn't smile back. "Can you sit up?"

"Sure." I try to prop myself up, fall back into the snow and laugh. "Guess not. Where's Ari? She's so pretty, isn't she? Like an angel … angel … hah … snow angels." I flatten my palms against the snow and swish my arms and legs back and forth.

"Oh, for fuck's sake." He wraps a hand around one of my arms and hauls me up into a seated position.

I sling an arm around his shoulder and pull him into the snow beside me and hug him. "I love you, Kell. You're my best friend. You know that, right?"

"If I wasn't so fucking worried you're about to die, I'd totally be recording this for blackmail purposes later."

"Do you need any help?" Another voice, one I should recognize but honestly don't give a single fuck about right now, intrudes.

"Grab an arm and help me to get him upright."

The world spins and then I'm on my feet, staring down at the snow. I throw my head back. "Hey, look. I can see the moon. It's so … *shiny*."

There's a sigh from my left … or maybe my right. I'm not really sure.

"What happened?" That voice I should know speaks again.

I turn my head to search it out and find the guy Kellan wants to fuck standing there. I squint at him. "You're …" I search my brain for the name, but my brain isn't working. Which is weird. I'm usually very good with names. "I think it begins with M?"

"Miles."

I snap my fingers, and the sound distracts me … so I do it again … and again.

"Eli! Concentrate."

"Why haven't you let Kellan fuck you yet? Are you scared?"

"What? No. We're not—"

I snicker. "He says you give great head."

"Stop talking." A hand slaps over my mouth, so I do the only reasonable thing.

I lick it. The hand is snatched away.

Kellan's fuckbuddy laughs. "Jesus fucking Christ. Is he *high*? What did he take?"

"He didn't *take* anything. His drink was spiked."

"Your hand tastes salty." I roll my head sideways to find Kellan.

"I'm not even going to touch *that* comment. Let's get you back to school before you die of hypothermia or something."

"Is he always like this?" That's Miles … I think.

"He's *never* like this. Now I know why I annoy the fuck out of him so much."

"What do you think happened?"

"Where's Ari?" I interrupt, twisting around to find her. "We were gonna fuck."

"No, you weren't. And she ran off after drugging you with

whatever the fuck was in that coffee." The usual light-hearted tone of Kellan's voice is missing.

"Pretty sure we were. I had her top off and everything." I twist to find Miles. "Maybe that's what you two should do. Find somewhere quiet like the chapel and just get it out of your system."

"We're not having sex." Miles keeps his attention on the trees ahead of us.

"I *know* that. Kellan complains about it all the time. So have sex. That way, he'll stop whining at me."

"You want to have sex with me?" Miles leans past me to look at Kellan.

"We've already talked about this." Kellan's voice is quiet. "You want to wait. So, I'm waiting."

"I thought you just wanted to fool around, hook up."

"I did … I *do* … but … you know, sometimes more would be nice."

"You guys should kiss." I think my suggestion is pretty helpful. The look Kellan gives me says it's not. "I kiss Ari when she's annoyed with me. It works out well."

"Yeah, that's why she's just tried to fucking kill you."

"Just a blip in the—" The world spins again, only this time it's not because Kellan is making me stand up.

I stop, sucking in a breath. That makes it worse. There's a buzzing in my ears, lights flashing in front of my eyes. My stomach twists, flips, and then I'm falling, the snow coming up to meet me at a rapid pace.

***

My head feels like someone took a hammer to it. My eyes seem to be sealed shut, and the inside of my mouth is drier than the Sahara Desert.

I part my lips, my intention to try and wet them with my tongue, only *that* appears to be stuck to the roof of my mouth and every time I swallow a foul taste burns my taste buds. I don't know if I make a noise or move because a hand touches my forehead.

I flinch from the coolness of it.

"Can you open your eyes for me, Eli?" A soft voice, female, unrecognizable.

I try, and the effort it takes is way more than it should be, but eventually, my lids part. The bright room beyond makes my eyes water and sends a stabbing pain through my temple.

"Let me close the curtains."

The hand leaves my head and then the lighting in the room changes, grows dimmer, and lessens the pain in my skull. I focus on the woman coming back toward me.

"How do you feel?"

I open my mouth to answer, and nothing comes out. I swallow, wincing at the bitter taste in my mouth.

"I'll get you a glass of water." A second later, a small plastic cup is placed to my lips. "Just a sip. Take it slow."

The water is refreshing. It's cool and soothes my throat. I let out a relieved sigh.

"What happened?" My voice sounds hoarse, rough to my own ears, like I've been shouting or screaming.

"We're not entirely sure. Your friends dragged you in from the woods last night. You were barely coherent, talking about someone called Harry, angels, and coffee."

Harry? Who the fuck is Harry?

Wait ... *friends ... plural?*

"Friends?"

"Kellan and Miles, they said their names were."

"Miles?" The second I say the name, there's a flash of memory. Of Kellan and Miles half-carrying me through the snow. Of me telling them they should fuck.

I groan.

"The doctor has taken some samples—blood, urine, and a swab from your mouth—and is testing them. So, if you want to admit to taking anything, now would be the time."

I let my head drop against the pillow, my eyes closing. "I don't take drugs." My eyes snap back open when the rest of her sentence sinks in. "The doctor? Where am I?"

"Hammonton Hospital." She names a place a couple of miles away from Churchill Bradley Academy.

"*Hospital?*" I sit up and immediately regret it when the room spins, and nausea threatens.

"The school medical staff were worried it was more serious than they could deal with on the site. They called for medical care, and we sent an EMT to bring you here. As it happens, it looks like it was a bad reaction to GHB, but the urine test should confirm that."

"GHB?"

"It's also called liquid ecstasy."

"What the fuck?"

62

Arabella

Eli is my strength, and Kellan is my shield. They bring sunshine to my day when there are only rain clouds around me. When I'm with them, I don't feel the pressure of fitting in. I don't have to pretend I'm someone else. Everyone around me is wearing a mask, but sometimes when they think others aren't looking, they let it slip.

"What are you reading?"

Slapping Zoey's diary shut, I find Kellan making himself comfortable in the chair beside me. I snatch up my bag and shove the book to the bottom of it. "Nothing."

The only thing I can lose myself in and take me out of this waking nightmare.

"Here's the coat you left at the chapel." He drops it on the floor beside me and eyes the book with interest. "Is that your diary?"

"No." Nerves dry my mouth and I lick my lips. "Is there any news on Eli?"

Sunday dragged, and I'd heard nothing from Miles, except that Eli had been taken to a local hospital. I spent most of the day a sobbing mess in my room, my mind spinning out of control with every potential outcome. Monday finally rolled around, and there's been no sign of Eli at breakfast.

His dad will never forgive me if anything happens. Elena will hate me. I'll be dubbed the Killer of Churchill Bradley Academy right before I'm arrested and dragged off to jail for murder.

"You don't look so well," Kellan murmurs, his razor-sharp gaze trained on my face. "Feeling guilty? What did you give Eli?"

My knuckles turn white where it's still clutching my bag. "I don't know."

"Who gave it to you?"

"I don't know."

"Bullshit. I can make you tell me."

The softly spoken threat hangs between us.

I remain silent.

Kellan's jaw clenches. "You need to stop fucking around."

A fracture cracks through the hard ball of unstable emotions I've been carrying around.

Tell him. Tell him. Tell him.

"I can't." My voice shakes. This is the worst pain I've ever felt.

"This is *not* how you get Eli's attention. You could have killed him."

"I know—"

You could have killed him. You could have killed him. You could have killed him.

The words repeat over and over in my head.

My heart screams inside my chest.

Tell him. Tell him. Tell him.

Kellan's voice is deathly calm when he continues to speak, oblivious of my inner turmoil.

"You've only had a small taste of what he can do. He's not even trying to hurt you right now. You understand that, don't you?"

The truth tumbles from my lips. "Kellan, I'm being—"

Before I can finish the sentence, the fire alarm screeches through the room. Chairs are scraped back, and students grab their bags and coats. Kellan jumps up and stalks for the door. I'm left hanging, the truth still on the tip of my tongue. I move slowly, to join the flow of people out of the building until we're standing out in the snow.

My phone vibrates, and I check it.

`Unknown number: You look a little too comfortable with Kellan. Don't let him sit with you again. We hope you weren't going to tell him about our game.`

Oh shit, no.

I twist my head from side to side, uneasiness almost drowning me under its weight.

`Me: No.`

`Unknown number: We don't believe you. Keep your mouth shut, or you'll regret opening it. This is your only warning.`

`Me: Eli got hurt. I don't want to play anymore.`

`Unknown number: You don't get to choose when you can stop. You play until we say you're done.`

A link pops up in the next message. I tap on it. It takes me straight to a video. Numbly I watch myself in the bathtub, immersed in the water, legs spread, my fingers playing with myself. A video I made for Sin.

Tears well in my eyes, but I blink them back.

***

`Me: Are you behind the videos?`

`Me: Please, are you there?`

`Me: I don't know who to talk to. They're watching`

`me all the time.`

`Me: I want to stop.`

I will Sin to answer, staring down at the screen of the cell in my hand until my eyesight blurs.

Where is he? Why hasn't he responded? Even if he tells me to go away, at least I'll know he's out there.

No one is going to believe me. Everyone will think I'm crazy. Whoever is doing this is careful and meticulous. It has to be Lacy. She was my roommate and knows most about me. It's the only thing that makes sense. But why?

My thoughts are interrupted by scratching at my door. The hair on the back of my neck rises, and I tense. A quick glance at my clock tells me it's midnight. The scraping continues, getting stronger.

"Arabella," a male voice calls through the door. "Open up."

Who is that? The voice is familiar.

Eli?

I crawl off the bed and inch my way across the room. The door is locked. I've made sure to keep it that way since the evening he burst in to accuse me of throwing a bloodied stuffed animal toy at him.

Someone knocks against the wood. "Come on. Don't be shy. We're here to stop you from getting lonely."

We?

My stomach knots in panic, and I press my ear to the door to listen.

"Garrett, knock again," a second voice says.

"Try the door," a third one demands.

The handle rattles, and I jump back away from it. "Go away, or I'll call security."

"Don't be like that," Garrett calls. "Just let us in. You got us all hot and bothered with that video posted earlier. It's only fair that you do something about it."

Bile rises up my throat at the thought of them touching me. The way they're openly standing outside my door, as they laugh and demand I let them in, is petrifying.

"I'm dialing the number right now." My hands tremble as I search out the number for the main office and press it. Someone picks up on the fourth ring.

"There are some boys outside my room trying to get in," I rush out and rattle off my room number. Instead of someone answering, the line goes dead.

What the fuck?

My phone pings. Heart still in my throat, I peer down at the message.

`Unknown number: No one is coming to help you. Next time, we will make sure you're asleep, and they have the key to the door. Bad things happen to those who don't obey. You don't quit until we say so.`

63

Eli

The drug tests they ran have come back inconclusive. The doctor explains that it's because there is such a small window where GHB stays in the system and is identifiable, so I didn't see the point in staying in the hospital any longer.

I'm fine and show no worrying symptoms or side-effects, but they *still* refuse to release me until Wednesday. And only then because I threaten to walk out if they don't sign my release papers.

Kellan picks me up in his car and drives me back to Churchill Bradley.

"How much do you remember?"

"Not a lot. I remember Arabella giving me the coffee, and then going for a run. Everything after that is a blur. I *think* I stopped near the chapel. Was Arabella there?"

"Oh, she was *definitely* there."

There's a note to his voice that has me twisting in my seat to look at him. "What do you know?"

"She spiked your drink. Wouldn't tell me what with but admitted there was something in the coffee she gave you. I'm guessing she was just trying to fuck with you, not fuck you over, and then when you reacted badly, she panicked."

"She *drugged* me?"

"Yep."

"*Arabella?*" I don't know why, but I find it hard to believe she'd do something like that. Fuck around with my car, throw drinks at me, accuse me of shit … but *drug* me?

"Don't forget the doctor said you need to take it easy for a few days. That means no hunting down the naughty girl to torment her."

"She's on the floor directly above us. I don't need to hunt her." My response is dry.

He slides a glance in my direction, then returns his attention to the road. "There's no way you're just going to let this go." He turns the wheel and pulls up on the side of the road. "Listen, Eli. This is getting fucking dangerous now. It's not funny anymore."

"Have you seen me laughing?"

"Actually, yes. You were finding the entire fucking thing hysterical the other night."

"When I was high, you mean? On the drug she spiked my coffee with. The one that could have killed me. That's when I was laughing." My voice is flat.

"I'm serious. You have to let this go. *Promise me*. No more retaliation. Someone is going to get killed."

"You know I can't make that promise."

"Eli!"

"I'm not going to lie to you, Kell. I don't know what's going to happen next. But she fucking *drugged* me. And you want me to just act like it didn't happen?"

"I want you to *think* about what might happen if you keep escalating this. Just fucking ignore her."

I tip my head back against the seat. "I can't do that."

He drums his fingers on the steering wheel. "Another video was released on Monday."

I close my eyes. "It wasn't me."

"I think that's pretty obvious at this point. My point is, maybe she'll finally realize that and leave you alone."

"And maybe it was never about those videos and photographs being released at all."

Kellan is silent for a minute or two.

"You think she's acting out to get your attention for another reason?"

"I think she's scared of her own sexuality because she's terrified she might end up like her mom, and she hates me because she wants me. But if she causes a fight with me and we fuck? Then it's clearly my fault and not hers." I crack open one eye. "Can you carry on driving now?"

He stares at me for a moment longer, then nods and pulls back onto the road.

***

I won't admit it to Kellan, but the drive from the hospital has exhausted me more than I thought it would. The doctor warned me it might take a few days for my body to recover, not just from the possible GHB in my drink but also from the vomiting and being out in the snow without adequate clothing. From what the nurse told me, by the time Kellan reached me, I was soaked through from lying in the snow, and then it took another forty minutes for him to get me back to the school.

I don't argue when Kellan insists on us going straight to our room, and I'm ready to crawl across the floor to my bed by the time we reach it. He says nothing as I stumble and fall onto the mattress, leaning against the wall with his arms folded as he watches me. I throw a hand over my face and close my eyes.

"I can feel you staring."

"Do you want help getting your shoes off?"

I grunt. I don't want to admit to the weakness I'm feeling. Kellan doesn't push, but a second or two later, he takes the sneakers off my feet.

"Are you hungry?"

"No."

"Thirsty?"

"I'd kill for an undrugged coffee."

He chuckles. "Coming right up. *Stay* here."

I don't think I could fucking move if I wanted to, so I just wave a hand at him. I'm pretty sure I fell asleep before he left the room because the next thing I remember is his hand on my shoulder as he shakes me.

"I'm awake." The words come out as a garbled yawn, and he laughs.

"There's coffee on the nightstand and I've put two cans of Coke in the mini refrigerator. I'm going down to get some food. Try and sleep some more. I'm locking the door and taking both our keys, so pray there isn't a fire."

"You don't need to do that."

"I *know* you, Eli. If you decide that it's time to confront Arabella, you'll do it even while you're half fucking dead on your feet. I'm not taking the chance. *Sleep*. I'll be back with food."

"Whatever."

In all honesty, I don't think I have the energy to face the stairs up to the next floor, let alone do a fight with Arabella any justice.

Anyway, I need to plan my next move, because she's not fucking getting away with what she did to me.

Kellan is right about one thing. It's not funny anymore.

69

Arabella

“Hey, Arabella, be a good girl and leave your door open tonight.” Garrett smirks as he passes my table.

“How long has it been since you last got fucked?” Jace comes up behind him. “That little pussy of yours must be getting hungry.”

Bret and Evan laugh, following in their wake as I pretend to ignore them and gather my books. The teacher has already rushed out of the class. The boys have been taunting me ever since the last video was released. Eli came back to school a couple of days later, but he hasn’t been in any classes, and I guess he’s resting in his room. Kellan and Miles have both been avoiding me, and I haven’t been brave enough to ask about him.

I’ve never felt more alone than I do right now. I’m drowning in public, and no one can see it. My phone pings, and my hand twitches at the sound. I don’t want to look at it, but I’m frightened of what might happen if I don’t. I stare down at the message.

Unknown number: Just a little reminder that we are everywhere. We rule this school, and no one is going to help you.

A photo appears beneath the words. It’s of me asleep in my bed, one hand tucked under my head, mouth slightly open. My heart drops, and I clutch the cell tightly. They’ve been in my room, standing over me while I slept. Anything could have happened. The knowledge turns me cold.

They were in my room.

I run from the classroom and barely make it into a stall in the restroom before I vomit. I empty my stomach of the few mouthfuls of food I managed to eat at breakfast. Shaking and panting, I flush the toilet and slide my back down the door until I'm sitting on the floor, spasms still rocking through me.

I don't know what to do.

I close my eyes and hug my knees to my chest. I'm positive now that Eli hasn't been behind any of the photographs or videos.

Has this been one long setup? Why are they doing this to me? Am I hated by everyone this much?

I don't know how much more I can take. I'm already breaking under the tension.

A crazed laugh leaves my lips.

Maybe that's what they want. To drive me over the edge.

I open my bag and find my other cell.

`Me: Sin, are you doing this? I'm so scared. I don't know how much more I can take.`

Tears try to break free from my eyes and I dash them away. I send a second message to him.

`Me: I'm not a bully. I don't know who I am anymore.`

No reply comes.

My guilt morphs into anger.

Why isn't he there? Why is he ignoring me?

I loved him, but maybe he hadn't felt anything for me at all. The dares had been a game. Maybe they had never been meant as something more.

Then why am I still messaging him?

The question twists my lips.

Because I don't have anyone else.

I climb unsteadily to my feet, push open the door and cross to the sink to rinse my mouth out. Washing my hands, I dry them and leave the restroom.

It's lunchtime. My appetite has been non-existent for weeks, but I still head toward the cafeteria. I crave human contact around me, just to feel a little bit normal. I'm almost there when a shoulder smashes into mine.

"Watch where you're going, freak." Tina spits, pushing past me.

Off-balance, I tumble sideways, landing in the snow.

"Did you hurt yourself?" Linda laughs, and kicks my bag along the path, out of my reach.

I keep my head down and wait for them to walk away. Hate seethes through me, but I don't act on it. Once they're out of view, I get back to my feet, dust the white powder off my coat and jeans, then collect my bag.

Miles is standing there, my bag in his hand.

"What's going on with you?" His voice is low. "Are you on drugs?"

I snatch my bag out of his grip and check to make sure all the contents are inside. "No."

"You don't smile anymore."

"I have no reason to." I resume my walk toward the cafeteria.

Miles falls into step beside me. "You watch everything like something is about to jump out and kill you."

"I just see this place for what it is now."

"And what's that?"

"Hell."

He hesitates, and I know he's waiting for me to go first, so we don't enter together. I shake my head a bitter laugh bubbling up, but don't comment. I've given up trying. What's the point? We're from different worlds, and there's an invisible wall between us. I'm an idiot for not realizing it's been there the whole time I've been at school. He's one of the popular kids, captain of the swim team, and I'm *nothing.* An unwanted nobody who doesn't belong here.

A few students look up as I pass, the cruel comments muttered my way making me flinch. I don't bother with food and go straight for the coffee instead, then pick an empty table in a corner away from everybody else.

The jocks all watch me, Evan, Jace, and Garrett make suggestive gestures at me. Lacy, Tina, Maggie, and Linda are sitting with their heads together, giggling as they shoot me malicious smiles. Whatever they are plotting, I'm sure it's just more torment to heap on top of me.

A familiar jolt goes through me, electricity dancing under my skin. I sense Eli before I see him. He's standing in the cafeteria doorway with Kellan, his narrowed-eyed gaze zeroing in on me. The cold rage I see just beneath the surface of his expression fills my veins with terror.

Dare To Take

65

Eli

"Get three coffees to go." I don't take my eyes off Arabella.

"Eli—"

"Two then, if you want to stay here."

He sighs and veers off toward the food counter. The cafeteria is silent as everyone watches me take a slow walk across the room. Instead of taking a seat at my usual table, where I can watch everyone, I turn right and go to the table Arabella is seated at.

The sound of me dragging the chair out is loud in the silence of the room. I sit and lean back, one leg crossed over the other and fold my arms. Her eyes are a shock of color in her white face as she stares at me.

"Here's what's going to happen. Kellan will join us in a minute, and you are going to leave the room with us." My voice is casual, with no hint of the anger burning me up from the inside.

"Eli, I—" Her voice, on the other hand, trembles.

"If you don't walk out with me, I'll drag you out by your hair." I deliver the words in a silky tone. "Your choice of how you want today to be remembered." I lean forward, bracing my hands on the edge of the table. "I know which option I'd prefer, so just give me a reason to do it."

I keep my gaze on her while hers darts around the room, desperately looking for an escape and finding none.

"The school said you can't come near me."

I throw back my head and laugh, long and loud. "You really think the school gives a single *fuck* about you after what you've done? You've proved to everyone that you're the problem, not me. I could strip you naked and fuck you on the table right here, and not a single person would stop me. Not now." I glance around, tapping my lips with one finger. "I wonder how long a line there would be if I bent you over and offered your ass to whoever wanted it."

"You can't do that."

"Can't I?"

"If you don't leave me alone, I'll scream."

My smirk drains the remaining color from her face. "Oh, Princess, by the time I'm done with you, your throat will be so fucking raw you won't be able to scream."

A shadow falls over the table, and I finally look away from her to find Kellan standing beside me, three takeaway coffee cups balanced in his hands. I shove to my feet.

"Let's go."

Her shoulders stiffen. "No."

I hike an eyebrow. "I'm sorry, I must have misheard."

"I'm not going with you."

I round the table and place my palms on the top so I can lean forward until my face is millimeters from hers. "And what exactly did I say or do to make you think I'm bluffing?"

"You won't—" She yelps when I tangle a hand into her hair and drag her to her feet.

"Won't I? I don't think you understand the situation here. No one is going to come to your rescue, Princess. There's no fucking white knight waiting to ride in and slay the big bad monster." I use my grip on her hair to pull her toward me. "Do you know why? Because *you* fucking *killed* him."

She stays silent, tears brimming in her eyes.

My smile is a baring of teeth. "I'd save up those tears, Princess. You're going to need them." I tip her head back and run my nose along hers, then lick the tear making its lonely way down her cheek. "I like the taste of your misery, Arabella," I whisper. "But your fear will taste even better." I release my grip and take a step back.

She staggers sideways and reaches out to balance herself against the table.

"Now, are you going to be a good girl and walk with me, or do I have to drive the point home?"

She's biting so hard into her bottom lip I'm surprised she isn't drawing blood. When she doesn't answer, I wrap a hand around the top of her arm and drag her along with me.

"Please!" She casts the word out. "Someone, please? I don't want to go with him!"

No one moves. Most of the students even look away. As we pass the table filled with the football players and cheerleaders, Miles starts to stand. I turn my head and nail him with a glare.

"Think very carefully about your next move," Kellan says, driving home the message in one sentence to the swim captain that our friendship will always trump their attraction. Miles drops back into his seat and lowers his eyes.

"Where are you taking her?" Evan calls as we move past.

I stop and glance back at him. "I've been sick for the past week.

She's going to make me feel better. Maybe there will be enough of her left when I'm done for the rest of you. Maybe there won't. We'll see."

She renews her struggles to escape at my words. I tighten my hold, my fingers biting into her arm, and haul her against me, her back against my front, and wrap my free arm around her waist.

"Kellan, put the drinks down for a second."

He glances around, and then places the three cups on the closest table.

"Take off her jeans."

Kellan doesn't even hesitate.

"What? No!" She twists in my grip, trying to evade Kellan's hands as they reach for her jeans. "Stop. Stop it!" He pops open the button and slides down the zipper. "No! Please! I'll go with you!"

She's panting, chest heaving, and I can almost taste the fear seeping out of her. I bite the lobe of her ear, and a small cry of pain leaves her lips. Smiling, I lick over the marks I've left. "Don't force my hand, Princess. I *always* keep my promises."

A few short weeks ago, I would have been bluffing.

Now, though? Now, she's killed everything I felt for her.

Now I just want her to bleed as much as I am.

"I'll go with you. Just don't … please, don't …" Her voice is shaking as hard as her body.

"Then fucking start walking." I swipe up one of the coffee cups, leaving Kellan to pick up the other two and wave a hand toward the doors. "*Move*, Arabella."

Her shoulders hunch and her head bows and I wonder if she'll try and bolt, but she sets off toward the doors without another word. I'm close on her heels, Kellan at my side. Once we're outside, she stops.

"Keep walking," I tell her, and press a hand to her back to urge her forward.

When we reach the spot where she gave me the drugged coffee, I curl my fingers into the back of her top and jerk her to a stop.

"Turn around."

She turns to face me.

I pop the lid off the coffee cup, reach into my pocket and pull out a small packet. Tearing it open with my teeth, I empty the contents into the cup, secure the lid back into place and swirl it, mixing the powder into the drink.

"Take it." I hold it out.

"What is it?" Her lips are quivering.

"Drink it." I ignore her question.

"Tell me what's in it."

"Drink it," I repeat, my voice flat.

"No."

"Kellan, hold her mouth open."

My friend moves up behind her and winds an arm around her waist. "I warned you, Bella," he says quietly. "I *warned* you not to fucking bait him."

"Don't do this." Her tears are flowing now, spilling down her cheeks. "Please, Eli. Don't make me drink it."

My hand doesn't move, the drink between us. "You either take it and down it, or I'll pour it down your throat until you fucking choke."

Kellan's hand wraps around her jaw, tipping her head back. I walk forward and pinch her nose closed. She throws out a hand, wildly trying to knock the cup from my hand. I lift it high above her head.

Kellan's hand slips down to her throat and he gives a gentle squeeze. "I'm sorry, Bella. But I warned you what would happen. You crossed a line, and there are consequences."

She tries to hold her breath, to keep her mouth closed, and she succeeds for all of a minute, but then her lips part on a gasp. Kellan moves fast, holding her mouth open, and I pour the cooling coffee into her mouth. She coughs, splutters, and gags, trying to spit it out, but I press my hand over her mouth, forcing her to swallow, then repeat the action until the entire cup is empty.

I pat her cheek. "Good girl. I hope you have a nice day." An alarm goes off on my cell. "You should hurry. You're going to be late for math."

Nodding to Kellan, he releases her, and we both walk away, leaving her crying and coughing on the path.

66

Arabella

I wipe a hand over my mouth, fighting to breathe through my panic.

What did Eli give me?

No one even tried to come to my rescue. They all watched as he ordered me out of the cafeteria. None of them lifted a hand to save me.

You really think the school gives a single fuck about you after what you've done? You've proved to everyone that you're the problem, not me. I could strip you naked and fuck you on the table right here and not a single person would stop me. Not now. I wonder how long a line there would be if I bent you over and offered your ass to whoever wanted it.

Eli's words taunt me. He's proved that no one cares what happens to me. Pain wells up inside my chest. I'm nothing to them. A *nobody*.

The bell sounds.

I wind my arms tight around my waist, and trudge toward the main building and the next class. People stop to stare at me as I pass. I hear their whispers. See their scornful looks. All I want is for the floor to open and swallow me down.

What did Eli give me? Maybe it was nothing? He's just trying to mess with my head.

The questions plague me as I enter the class.

"How's your pussy?" Bret asks as I pass. "Did Eli get you nice and wet for the rest of us to play with?"

Garrett grabs my wrist and jerks me sideways onto his lap.

"Ready for a ride?"

When I struggle against him, his dick hardens beneath my ass. "Let go of me."

"What's the matter, Arabella? I heard you like it rough."

The other jocks laugh.

A few other students look away uneasily while I fight to free myself, but no one moves to help.

Garrett secures my wrists in one hand and cups my breast through my sweater with his other. His teeth bite down on the side of my neck, and I whimper.

"You heard what Travers said. No one gives a fuck about you," Evan reminds me.

Jace chuckles. "No one is going to care if we pass you around."

Kellan walks into the room, Miles behind him.

"Please, stop," I beg, shame and humiliation colliding inside me.

"Mr. Drake is outside the door," Kellan warns Garrett as he strolls by.

Miles moves toward me but stops when Garrett releases me.

I scramble off his lap and fall onto my seat.

"We'll finish this later." Garrett blows me a kiss.

I can still feel the heat of his mouth on my neck. *Did he leave a mark? I claw* at the spot with my nails, trying to get rid of the sensation.

Mr. Drake walks into the room, and the class falls silent. I dart a peek around. Miles is looking at me, eyes dark with concern. The other jocks have hungry looks in their eyes. Kellan just stares at me.

I have to get through the rest of the afternoon before I can escape.

Hunching my shoulders, I pull out my books.

We're thirty minutes into the class when pain ripples through my abdomen. Pressing a hand to it, my eyes widen.

I throw my hand up. "Mr. Drake, I'm not feeling very well."

"You seem to be making a habit of this lately, Miss Gray."

Another wave of discomfort hits me, and I double up over my desk. "Please, sir. My stomach hurts."

He sighs. "Go back to your room. If it gets worse, report to the nurse."

I lurch up out of my chair and run for the door. Racing along the hallway, I dive for the girl's restroom, and make it into a stall seconds before my bowels let go.

***

Curled up on the bathroom floor in my room, I groan as cramps ravage my abdomen. It's clear now what Eli put in the coffee. I have no idea how long the laxatives are going to last. Nausea rolls through me, and I screw my eyes shut.

No one has come to check on me. No one has texted to see if I'm okay.

I've been waiting for Garrett and his friends to try and get into my room, but they've yet to turn up.

I deserve this after what I did to Eli. He has a right to be angry with me for what happened.

You could have killed him. You could have killed him. You could have killed him.

But it wasn't me. It was my blackmailers.

The tiny protest is drowned out by my guilt. My emotions are running wild, and I don't have the energy to get off the floor.

I must have drifted off to sleep because the next time I open my eyes, I'm shivering. I peel myself up off the floor and catch sight of my reflection in the mirror.

The girl staring back has hollow, empty eyes. She's lost weight in her face, her cheekbones sharper, and her skin pale. I tear my attention away, whimpering as another wave of discomfort washes through my body.

I'm sure dinner has come and gone, and the thought of eating anything leaves me queasy. I reach for Sin's phone, which is on my bed, and type him a message.

`Me: Everything is out of control. Someone is going to get hurt. I'm trapped on a runaway train, and there's no way to get off.`

He's just like everyone else. He doesn't give a fuck about me.

I fling the phone across the room in a frustrated burst of anger. It bounces on the mattress of the spare bed. Despair drags me down into a swirling maelstrom of guilt, hate, and shame.

Eli

I ditch classes all day in favor of working on my sculpture, claiming I'm still not one hundred percent healthy. The truth is I don't trust myself in the same room as Arabella right now. The fear in her eyes is imprinted on my mind and, instead of the satisfaction I expected to feel after forcing her to take the extra-strength laxative, I feel strangely hollow inside. I can't get the way her body shook when I held her against me out of my head, or how my hand had almost been able to wrap around her entire arm.

Has she always been that thin? That fragile looking? I don't think so, but I can't trust my memory. How much of what I thought she was had simply been my imagination or manipulation on her part?

I shake my head. It doesn't matter. None of it matters. I've paid her back for the spiked drink. She should be thankful I didn't use something worse than a laxative. Hopefully, I've put an end to it, and she'll think twice before coming at me again.

Kellan isn't happy with what I did. He hasn't said anything, but it's clear every time he looks at me. He wants me to just move on and ignore her. But if I do that, then someone else will try and bait me, and then another. What I've done is important to the rest of my school life. It sends a message to everyone.

I'm called the fucking Monster of Churchill Bradley for a reason.

Kellan turns up at some point with food and drink, and he leans against the wall watching as I work on a particularly intricate part of my design.

"I'm surprised you haven't changed it." He jerks his chin toward the half-finished face.

I shrug. "It works for the final piece."

"I suppose. It'll be interesting to see the reaction to it."

"I'm not doing it for a reaction."

"No, but if—" he shakes his head. "Doesn't matter."

"If you've got something to say, just say it." I put down the chisel and turn to face him.

"She looks sick, Eli."

"How could you tell underneath all the makeup?"

"What makeup? You know she wasn't wearing any."

"Does it fucking matter? I did what I needed to do. If she has any sense, she'll quit now."

"And what if she doesn't? Are you going to carry out your threat and fuck her in front of everyone?"

My smile is forced. "Maybe."

"No matter what twisted mess she's got going on in her head, you can't let her drive you to do something you won't be able to live with later."

I laugh, the sound hard and bitter. "She's nothing. I'll sleep perfectly well at night."

"Don't lie to me. You're not the fucking monster you pretend to be. I *know* you, Eli."

"Does it matter? I'm whatever they say I am. You know how it works, Kellan. Look at Miles. He's so fucking terrified of being cast out of his so-called group of friends if he admits he's gay. *Everyone* is molded by the beliefs of those around them.'

"I'm not." His voice is soft.

My smile is genuine this time. "You're the exception that proves the rule."

"Are you coming to English?"

"No. How long did Arabella last during math?"

"Ten minutes, maybe. Garrett was groping her when I arrived."

Tension stiffens my spine. "Groping her *how*?"

"Forced her to sit on his lap, had his hand on her tit. Bit her neck. Said he'd catch up with her later."

Fury heats my blood.

"It's your fault. You sent the message that she's available." There's no accusation in his voice, just fact. "You should be pleased. It means she'll be too distracted by them to annoy you."

He's not wrong. So why the fuck am I working out where Garrett might be tonight?

"Do they have practice tonight?"

"Miles does, so maybe?"

I nod.

"What are you thinking?"

"You're right. I did say she's available … but not until I'm finished with her."

"You *are* finished with her."

I pick up the chisel and walk over to the marble. "Am I?"

***

The cheerleaders are clustered just below where we sit on the bleachers. The coach is shouting instructions, and the football team is running around the field, throwing the ball to each other. Four of the team are on the bench, and I toss a stone at the ginger head of Garrett. He twists around, scowling. I smile. His glare falters.

"I hear you touched my little toy after lunch."

He smiles. "I've wanted a taste of her since she came to school."

Fucking idiot thinks I'm making idle conversation. When I don't smile back, he swallows.

"What did I say earlier today, Kellan?"

Kellan makes a show of thinking about it. "I believe you said that when you were done with her, there might be something left for the rest of them."

"And did I say I was done with her?"

He purses his lips. "Not anywhere I could hear you, no? Did you hear him say that, Garret?"

Garret's face pales, freckles standing out in stark relief against his white skin.

"She's *mine* to break. Get me? Touch her again before I say I'm done, and you won't play football again."

I shove to my feet and walk away before he can respond and make my way back to our dorm.

"I'm sneaking out to jump Miles once his swim practice is over," Kellan says once the door is closed, sealing us inside. "He's angry about lunchtime."

"What does he have to be angry about?"

"I threatened to out him if he ran to Arabella's defense."

"Like he was going to do anything, anyway. He's too much of a pussy. If he had any fucking backbone at all, he'd own who he is and stand by the girl he claims is his friend."

Kellan sits on the edge of his bed. "I've been thinking."

"Oh, for fuck's sake. That's dangerous."

He mock-growls at me. "I'm serious. Have you contacted her as Sin at all?"

"Why would I?" Everything we had in the dark has been tainted by the leaked video. "The last thing she'd want would be to hear from him … *me*. Anyway, the school took the cell phone I gave her."

"Oh … I forgot about that. Don't you have her other cell number? If you're set on this war with her, why don't you go back to your original plan? At least no one was going to end up in the hospital."

"You really want me to invite her into the woods in the middle of the night, knowing that the only thing I want to do right now is choke the fucking life out of her?"

"Hmmm. Good point. Forget I said anything." His cell chimes and he jumps to his feet. "That'll be Miles. Be good. Don't wait up." He blows me a kiss and saunters to the door.

After he's gone, I take a shower, then settle on my bed to watch a movie. But I can't settle. My eyes keep drifting to the closet, where I know the cell I used to message Arabella from sits at the bottom of a box.

When I have to restart the movie for the third time, I swing my legs off the bed and walk over to the closet and take out the box. Flipping it open, I stare down at the cell.

Maybe Kellan is right. Maybe I *should* try and contact her?

I reach into the box and take out the cell. My finger hovers over the power button.

What the fuck are you doing?

I toss it back into the box, close it up and shove it back into the closet.

Starting that up again would just add to the problem.

68

Arabella

"What's going on inside that head of yours?"

Arms crossed, I glance up at Counselor Clarke, then away again. "Nothing."

He sighs. "Arabella, if you don't talk to me, I can't help you. We've had weeks of you barely talking at all in our hourly sessions."

My throat feels tight with all the emotions I'm keeping bottled. I'm burning up with the guilt inside.

"Are those kids still giving you trouble?"

"Yes." I admit quietly.

"I'll have the principal talk to your class."

"That won't help."

Nothing will.

"Arabella—"

"I have nothing else to say."

"The videos weren't your fault. Whoever talked you into doing them is the villain here."

Sin. I don't say his name because it hurts too much.

"Lashing out at Eli is wrong, though," Counselor Clarke continues softly. "And I think deep down you know that, don't you? I don't think you really want to see your stepbrother injured or worse, do you?"

I press my lips together, and don't reply. I can't.

He sighs and glances at his wristwatch. "Our time is up. Let's pick this up next week. I'm not asking for much, Arabella, just for you to be willing to try."

"Sure." I leave his office without a backward glance.

The hallway is a blur in front of my eyes. Pushing the stairwell door open, I rush down the steps but don't make it far before I collapse into tears.

Hand pressed to my mouth to muffle my sobs; I huddle on the steps. The weekend had slipped past in a messy tangle of anguish and suffering. I kept to my room, only leaving to use the closest vending machines under the protection of my hoodie.

But now it's Monday lunchtime and afternoon classes are about to start. The first half of the day left me drained and stressed. Although Garrett hadn't tried to touch me again, he'd made plenty of suggestive comments with the rest of the jocks. Lacy and the other cheerleaders have been busy with decorations for the Valentine's Day Ball on Friday and ignoring me. Eli is back in class, aloof and frozen, watching me with remote indifference.

I want the world to stop. To go back in time to before all this started.

I don't want to feel his wrath anymore, but I know I'm just one text message away from unleashing all his fury on me again.

What will he do to me the next time? All the things he threatened? Fuck me in front of everyone. Let them fuck me while he holds me down?

So what if they share the video of me and Eli having sex? Is it really worth all this pain? Let them send it to his dad.

And give Elliot another heart attack? Have Elena hate me for destroying her happiness? Eli will blame me if it gets leaked. I'll be the criminal in everyone's eyes.

What about me? What about my happiness?

"Arabella?"

I startle at the soft voice. Wiping my eyes, I glance up the stairwell. Miles is standing a few steps up, watching me. His concerned expression only makes me sob harder. My shoulders shake with the force of my tears, and I drop my face and bury it into my hands.

"What happened?" An arm slides around my shoulders. "Did Eli do something to you?"

I clutch at the front of his sweater and burrow into it, searching for comfort.

It feels so good to be held again.

"I d-don't kn-know what to d-do." The words trip and tumble out of me.

Miles hugs me tight. "What's going on?"

"I c-can't br-breathe anymo-more."

"It's okay."

I swallow hard, dizzy with fear. "N-no, it's no-not."

"Bella—"

"No, don't ask me. They might be watching." I lift my head, searching around, half-expecting someone to jump out. Tears slid down my cheeks.

"Who?" Miles studies my expression. Whatever he sees in it deepens his frown. "*Who*, Arabella?"

"I can't—"

A door slams from above, voices filtering down, and footsteps heading our way. The bell rings, the sound bouncing off the walls, to grate on my frayed nerves.

He cups my face with warm, strong hands. "I'll come to your room tonight after curfew, and you can tell me what's going on."

"They tried to get into my room," I admit in a broken whisper. "They'll do it again."

The voices grow louder.

Miles glances up the stairs and then back at me. "I'll see you tonight."

He disentangles himself out of my arms, and hurries down the steps and away before we can be seen.

***

I pace back and forth, gnawing on a thumbnail, my stomach in knots of tension, and unable to stay still. Miles is coming, and I'm going to tell him everything. The secret is a poison that's slowly eating away at me, and this might be my only chance to tell someone without being seen.

It's an hour past curfew. *Where is he? Maybe he's waiting until security has done its sweep?*

Unable to wait any longer, I find his messages on my phone.

`Me: Miles, where are you?`

No response.

Could he be waiting for his roommate to fall asleep? Why isn't he answering?

I turn on the TV and let a random movie play, to keep my mind distracted. Another hour passes, and there's still no sign of him.

`Me: Are you ok?`

Still no reply.

I'm tempted to go to his room, but the thought of running into Garrett or one of the jocks holds me back.

My phone pings.

Relief floods me, and I check the message with shaking hands. A photo appears. Miles is lying on a bed, face pale and eyes closed. There's a bandage over his left temple, a red stain in the middle of the stark white.

The fear inside me blossoms, growing stronger at the image. My attention shifts to the message underneath.

`Unknown number: Next time, he won't come away breathing. We told you there would be consequences for breaking our rules. Keep your mouth shut. Be ready to play soon.`

Eli

My cell buzzing rouses me from sleep, and I grope around the floor for it. Lifting it to my face, I squint at the screen.

`Kellan: Miles slipped and banged his head, so I stayed in medical with him last night. I'm probably going to skip classes today and catch up on sleep. I'll meet you for breakfast first, though.`

`Me: Okay. Let me know if you need anything.`

He replies with a thumbs up. I toss my cell back to the floor. I debate on going back to sleep. . The problem is I'm awake now, so I roll out of bed and throw on a pair of sweats, and a t-shirt, grab a hoodie, shove my feet into sneakers and go out for an early morning run.

'I'm ok' by Call Me Karizma is playing when I reach the cemetery, and I pause by Zoey's plaque to catch my breath.

"Hey, ZoZo." I rest my palm against her name. "It's your favorite day on Friday. I'll bring you some chocolates. The ones Kellan hates. I never could decide if you decided you loved them most just because he doesn't." I tap pause on my music. "I'm sorry I haven't been by lately. Everything has been so fucked up since Christmas. You'd laugh your fucking ass off if I told you it all." I laugh softly. "Or maybe you wouldn't. You always said there was something weird about Churchill Bradley that messed with people's heads." I break off when I see movement on my right.

Turning my head slightly, I see a flash of color. Is it Arabella?

She spends as much time in the woods as Zoey used to. Part of me wants to follow her and see what she's doing, but the louder part—which oddly sounds like Kellan—convinces me it's a stupid idea and I need to go back to my room and get ready for class.

I turn back to Zoey and trace over her name. "I'll be back to see you on Friday, ZoZo." I tap my music back on and set off back through the woods.

Kellan is walking out of the medical building when I cross the grass and he waves to me.

"Do you want to grab breakfast now? I'm going to get something for Miles to eat and take it back for him. The nurse thinks he'll be able to go back to his room later today, but he's got to take it easy."

"What about his friends?" I fall into step beside him.

"None of them have been by. Not sure they know he hurt himself. He was alone. Good thing I said I'd meet him. He could have drowned." We walk into the cafeteria, and as usual, Kellan grabs the food and pays for it.

"Can we get it to go, please?" he asks the server, who smiles and bags everything up. "Where are you going now?" He hands me my drink and bag.

"Back to our room for a shower. I went for a run after you woke me up. I have art first, so I'll be working on my sculpture all morning."

"I'll come and get you for lunch." He waves the bag of food at me as we walk back out of the cafeteria. "I'm just going to drop this off to Miles, make sure he's okay, and then crawl into bed for a couple of hours. Those plastic chairs are just as uncomfortable in medical as they are in hospital rooms."

We part ways, and I push through the door that leads to the dorm rooms. When I reach our floor, it's to find a small crowd gathered in front of the door to my room.

"Eli's here," someone calls out, and the students part to let me through.

I frown at them as I walk through the path they've made until I'm standing in the doorway. My gaze moves over the room. The television is hanging off the wall. The mattress has been dragged off Kellan's bed, while mine has been ripped apart. Two of my blank sketchbooks have been torn into pieces and scattered around the room. Both our dressers have been opened, and the clothes and drawers thrown around, while the closet door is open, and the hoodies hanging up have been slashed.

But the thing that clenches my jaw and wipes all reason from my mind are the words spray painted on the wall.

You're just a fucking monster. You should have died alongside your mother.

70

Arabella

"Bella, please call me back. Stop ignoring me. We need to talk."

Miles sounds so fragile in the voicemail. I haven't answered any of his text messages. I don't dare. I'm too scared of what will happen if I do.

He got hurt because of me. I never should have tried to say anything to him.

I release a shaky breath, my eyelashes lifting, and I stare bleakly at the cemetery behind the wall, still covered in patches of snow. I'm sitting on the bench in the cold, numb inside and out. I haven't been able to sleep. After tossing and turning all night, I finally ventured to the one place I can lose myself. The woods.

I never meant for any of this to happen. Miles could have died, and from the threat my blackmailer made, they would have done it without a second thought. They're capable of anything. I see that now. This game they want me to play has become more dangerous than it was before.

"Arabella."

My head snaps up at the voice. Kellan stalks toward me along the path that leads from the school. His expression is harsh, his eyes pinned on me with a look that sends abject terror down my spine.

What do they want with me now?

I'm very aware of how alone we are, and it's enough to get self-preservation to kick in.

Scrambling up off the bench, I back away, hands held out to ward him off. "What do you want?"

"To talk." His gaze roams over my face.

I shake my head. "No. You stay the fuck away from me."

I take off along the path and veer into the trees. Memories roar through me. Kellan unbuttoning my jeans in the cafeteria. Kellan pinning me in place, his fingers forcing my jaw open while Eli made me drink the tainted coffee. His cruel and unfriendly words in my ear.

I run and run until my legs ache.

I don't look where I'm going, head down and breathing hard. When the primal urge to flee finally lets me go from its grip, and I glance over my shoulder, there's no sign of him.

Is he waiting for me back on the path?

The thought has me moving in a different direction, and I keep going until the chapel comes into sight. I check around anxiously, taking my time until I'm sure there's no one there. I slip inside, relief coursing through me when I discover it's empty. Tugging nervously on the cuff of my coat, I cross to the corner and lower myself down to sit with my back against the wall. It's the perfect angle to view the colors from the stained-glass windows as they dance across the stone floor. It's soothing. The longer I watch, the more my mind calms and my heart rate slows.

Classes will start soon, but I can't find the will to move.

I pull the red-bound diary out of my bag and weigh it in my hands. I'm hooked on Zoey's words, finding an odd sense of comfort in the pages. By reading it, I feel like I know who she was and how she felt. As if, somehow, I'm part of the life she lived.

I start to read.

There was a dare in my locker today. I know the whispers and the rumors surrounding them. Eli thinks it's just the faculty messing with us, but I'm not sure. This is the second one I've had. You're only supposed to get one, or so everyone says. I'm curious. Maybe it wasn't meant for me and was put in my locker by mistake.

Zoey got more than one dare. I reread the sentence, and frown. Could it have been from Sin? She'd been found in the cemetery.

Conflicting emotions roll through me. No, he couldn't be behind her death. He'd dared me, but he'd never hurt me physically.

As I turn to the next page, a noise disturbs me. I lift my eyes up from the words, and everything inside me turns to ice.

Eli is framed in the doorway. His lips are pressed together in a thin line, his eyes are blazing with an emotion I can't define. It's more terrifying than any other look he's ever given me.

He looks as though he's finally ready to kill me.

71

Eli

"Eli, what are you going to do?"

"Eli, do you think it was Arabella?"

Eli ... Eli ... Eli ...

The questions all merge together into a cacophony of noise, which I ignore by pushing my earbuds into my ears and hitting play. 'Johnny Wants To Fight' by Badflower replaces the voices, and I walk to the stairwell and head upstairs to the senior girls' floor.

Tina, Lacy, and Linda are standing in the hallway. They fall silent when I walk out of the stairwell.

Pausing my music, I pin each of them with a glare. "Where is she?"

"Who are you looking for?" Lacy sashays toward me and smooths her hand up my chest. "Whoever it is, you'll find me more interesting."

I push her away from me. "Where. Is. She?"

None of them reply.

"Is she in her room?"

"I think I saw her leave about an hour ago," Linda says before the other two hush her. "What? He's going to find out anyway!"

Tina rolls her eyes. "She took off around eight. She was in a hurry. Maybe she was going to meet someone."

I spin and walk back the way I came. Maintenance is coming up the stairs as I pass my floor, and I pause to tell them which room is mine and what needs doing. They nod and move past me, while I continue down to the exit. Three of the jocks are sitting on the low wall opposite the building—Brad, Kevin, and Evan. I veer toward them.

"Where did she go?"

Kevin frowns, while Brad and Evan exchange glances.

"Do not fucking test me right now."

"I saw her outside Miles' room earlier," Brad offers.

"So, she was on our floor."

"She had her coat, and that bag she carries everywhere. She seemed to be in a hurry."

"She disappeared into the woods about forty minutes ago," Evan adds. "Didn't see her come back and we've been out here since eight-fifteen. She was running and looking over her shoulder."

My head swings toward the woods. That means I know exactly where she is.

Kevin jumps to his feet. "Are you looking for her? Do you think she trashed your room? We can help you search if you like?"

"I *don't* like."

He keeps pace beside me as I walk across the grass. "Four of us searching will find her quicker than one."

"I don't need help."

His hand lands on my arm. I stare down at it, then slowly lift my gaze to his face. "One."

"What? Listen, we can look near the cemetery while you check the path that you jog along."

"Two."

"What are you counting for?"

"If I get to three and your fingers are still on my arm, I'm going to break them."

He snatches his fingers away and doesn't try to follow me when I continue toward the tree line. The first place I check is the cemetery, but it's as empty as always. There's no sign of her near the bench where I met her as Sin, which leaves the chapel.

I don't go inside straight away. There are footprints in the snow, which tell me she's here. They follow a path to the doors, but there isn't a set coming out. I rest my palm against the wood, then slowly push it open and step inside the dim interior. I intentionally let my foot scrape across the stone floor, and her head jerks up from where she's sitting in a corner near the altar.

"Get up."

The book she's reading drops to the floor, but she doesn't move.

"I said get up." My voice is soft, but she flinches and scrambles to her feet.

"What are you doing here?" Her fingers lift to her lips. "Oh god, is Miles okay?"

"I don't give a fuck about Miles." I take a step toward her. "I thought you learned your lesson. What the fuck is it going to take to get through to you that I'm not interested in playing these fucking games?"

"What games?"

"Stop it!" My roar echoes around the chapel, bounces off the walls, and repeats itself until it fades. "Just fucking stop it. Stop with the bullshit and lies. Are you so fucking desperate for attention that you'll do *anything?*"

"I don't know what you're talking about."

"Of course, you don't. Answer me *one* question. What the fuck do you want from me?"

"Nothing!"

"Nothing?" I reach out and curl my fingers into the front of her top. "Are you sure? Because for someone who doesn't fucking want anything from me, you're constantly putting yourself directly into my path."

I drag her toward me. She digs her heels in, and there's a slow scrape of shoe against stone as I pull her closer.

"Did losing your virginity unlock something? Is it like a high that you need to keep repeating? Is that it? Did it make you so fucking desperate that you'll resort to *anything* to get fucked?"

"No!" Her hands slam against my chest. "No."

"If that's what you want, Hellcat, you don't need to go to these lengths to get my dick." With one hand tangled into the front of her shirt, I wrap the other around her throat and tilt her head up with my thumb.

Her lips are trembling, eyes full of tears.

"Tell me you want me."

"No."

I flex my fingers. "Wrong answer. We both know the second my hand is in your pants, you'll soak my fingers. *Tell* me."

"No."

"Why do you fucking need to do it like this? Why do we have to fucking fight all the time?" I pull her closer, the hand in her shirt loosening to slide down over her stomach. "Is that what gets you off? Do you need to make me angry before it turns you on? Is that it?"

"No." A tear spills over her lashes and down her cheek. I release my grip on her throat to brush it away with one finger.

"Why do you keep doing this? Why do you fucking do this to

me?" My lips drift over her cheek.

"I'm sorry." The words are a choked whisper.

"Sorry for what?" I find the hem of her shirt and slide my fingers beneath them, the contact of her warm skin against my fingertips zapping like electricity through me. "Sorry for being caught again?" I kiss the corner of her mouth, lick a path along her jaw to her ear, and nip the lobe. "Tell me why. Do you hate me that much?"

"I don't hate you."

"Then why? Did you know the amount of GHB you put in my coffee could have killed me? Is that what you want? Me dead?"

A sob escapes her lips, and her fingers curl into the front of my hoodie.

"It's an easy question. Answer me, and I'll let you go. I'll walk away and leave you alone."

Her cell chimes somewhere behind her, and she stiffens.

"Just fuck me, if that's what you're here to do."

"Is that what you want?"

"Does it matter?" The emptiness in her voice rocks me backward.

"You think I'd fuck you if I didn't think you wanted it?"

She doesn't answer me. I release my hold on her and step back. "Do you really think I'm that much of a monster?"

Her silence is answer enough, and I'm not prepared for the pain that slices through me. I take another step away from her, fingers clenching into fists.

"I might be a monster, Ari, but I've *never* taken anything you weren't willing to give to me."

Spinning, I stalk toward the door and pull it open.

I don't look back.

Not even when I hear a soft thud and a choked sob.

72

Arabella

The tears come until I have no more to shed, and I kneel on the floor with my head bowed, strands of hair stuck to my wet cheeks.

The confrontation with Eli has cracked me wide open. A wave of pincer-like pain pummels my brain, dragging me down into an inky black ocean I can't claw my way out of. I'm choking on it.

Drowning.

I told him the truth. I don't hate *him*. I hate *myself* for being so weak.

Do you need to make me angry before it turns you on? Is that it?

Answer me, and I'll let you go. I'll walk away and leave you alone.

I might be a monster, Ari, but I've never taken anything you weren't willing to give to me.

His words circle in my head.

I wish I could stop. Walk away, but I'm trapped. I'd expected the lash of his anger, yet he'd walked away with a bleak look in his eyes.

For a second, I try to remember feeling anything other than this shrouding misery. I can't recall happiness, joy, or freedom. Do those emotions even exist anymore?

I climb up off the floor, swaying once I'm on my feet and walk to the diary where it's lying. I crouch and pick it up, sliding it carefully inside my bag, and take out my phone.

Another message from Miles is waiting to be read. The relief that washes over me makes me laugh, the hysterical sound bouncing off the chapel walls. It's only a matter of time before they contact me again. This is never going to end.

I walk out of the stone building and back toward the school. All I want to do is go back to my room and lose myself to sleep to escape the torture of being awake.

I'm almost at the dorm when my phone pings. My shoulders tense, pain throbbing in the back of my skull. My movements are wooden when I lift my cell and look down at the screen.

`Unknown number: Get back to class. You have no excuse to hide in your room.`

I scan the faces of the students hanging around the buildings, but don't see anyone familiar.

Are they watching me right now? Do they know what happened in the chapel?

Biting down hard on the inside of my cheek, I taste blood.

`Me: I don't feel well.`

`Unknown number: We don't fucking care. We will make you feel worse if you don't do as you're told.`

The hopelessness swelling inside me is like a heavy weight in my head. Despair has me locked inside its cage, and there's no key to escape.

Mr. Drake is already at the whiteboard, wiping it clean when I enter the room. I don't miss my name scribbled over it in bold black and a drawing of a dick. A few of the other students are already in their seats. Kellan is in his, but there's no sign of Eli.

I don't want to see him, but it's something I'm not going to be able to avoid.

The steel bands squeezing my chest don't lessen, and it's hard to breathe. I'm so tired. I'm not even sure how I'm going to get through today. Everything is raw and messy. My emotions are an open wound bleeding out all over the place.

"I can't believe you trashed Travers's room," Brad mutters as I pass him. "Do you have a death wish or something?"

"From the look on your face, I figure he found you earlier," Tina smirks.

Trashed Eli's room? *That's* why he came looking for me in the chapel? Denial rises in my throat, but it fades into nothing.

What's the point? No one is going to believe I didn't do it. Everything that happens is heaped on me. They've already judged and condemned me.

Ignoring her, I reach my desk and sit.

My phone buzzes in my bag. I fumble for it.

`Unknown number: Make sure you're where Eli can see you during lunch and dinner. We want to see you smiling at him.`

I glance around fretfully, my attention skimming over all the students playing with their cells. Others are flowing in, ready to start the class.

Who is doing this to me?

I just want them to stop. I'll beg if I have to.

They are throwing me into his orbit again, and he'll just perceive this as a taunt or challenge. I don't want to provoke him because it will only end with me in more pain.

`Me: Please don't make me do this.`

`Unknown number: Do it, or we'll pay a little`

`visit to Miles again. It would be a shame if he had complications from his head injury.`

I fight to stop the sickness in my stomach from rising up my throat. Miles is caught up in this because of me. He tried to help me and paid the price.

Another piece of me shatters, and I do the only thing that I can.

`Me: Ok, I'll do it. Please don't hurt him.`

Eli

After the clash with Arabella, I go back to my dorm and help maintenance clean up the room. Kellan takes one look through the door at the chaos and decides to go to class. I can't blame him. I don't want to be here, either, but one of us needs to oversee what's happening in case something gets thrown out that we need. At least, that's what I tell myself.

The spray paint has gone from the wall, the television and mattresses replaced, and eight trash bags full of destroyed books and clothes taken to the dumpsters before lunchtime rolls around. Eying the open closet, I take stock of what remains.

I have two hoodies, not including the one I'm wearing, that haven't been destroyed. Four t-shirts, another pair of sweats and one pair of jeans. Principal Warren has already given me permission to go into town and buy clothes, so that's the plan for this afternoon. First, I need to meet Kellan for lunch and give him his new key to our room.

I lock the door and head down to the cafeteria, where Kellan's already sitting at our usual table. He looks as tired as I feel, head resting on one hand, eyes closed, and the fingers of his other hand curled around a steaming mug of coffee.

I slip into the seat opposite him. "How's Miles?"

"I haven't spoken to him since this morning. His friends are there. How's our room?"

"Tidier than it was this morning. I need more clothes."

Kellan scratches his jaw. "I don't get it. What was the point?"

I blow out a breath. "I don't know. Maybe she's on drugs."

He nods slowly. "It would definitely explain why she looks so sick." His gaze shifts away from me. "She was on her cell during class this morning. From the look on her face, she was arguing with someone."

"Miles?"

"Maybe. I know he was texting her. I'll ask him later." A frown pulls his brows together, and I twist in my seat to see Arabella standing in the doorway.

Our gazes clash, and before I look away her lips curve up.

"Did she just *smile* at you?" Kellan's voice is incredulous.

I turn back to face him. "Maybe it wasn't meant for me." Her smiling at me makes no fucking sense, not after our face-off this morning. She'd been crying when I walked out.

"Sure as fuck wasn't meant for me. She was looking straight at you."

"Nervous tic? I confronted her about our room this morning."

"And how did that go?"

I shake my head. I don't want to think about what happened. The way she didn't deny she thought I was a monster who would force her to have sex with me. The pain of the memory is like a knife to my gut.

"I told her I was done with the games. I'm not playing anymore."

"Not playing as in …" He lifts an eyebrow.

"She can do what the fuck she wants. I'm done."

His eyes rove the room, and I know he's looking for her. "Probably for the best. Someone was going to end up dead."

"I think that's what she wants." My voice is soft. "I'm just not sure if she hates me or herself more." My gaze searches her out again, and she smiles for a second time, a quick curve of lips before they drop again. "I don't get it."

"She's on her cell again. I wonder who she's talking to? Could it be the friend she talked about in Michigan?"

I shrug and pull the second mug of coffee toward me.

"She's getting today's pasta concoction. I think that's the first time I've seen her eat in weeks. Now she's hovering over the desserts. Jell-O, it is. Weird choice. Green. Not my favorite." Kellan gives a running commentary as he watches Arabella. "Stopping now to check her cell again. Hot chocolate … no, she's put that back. Orange juice."

"Having fun?"

He pulls a face. "There's something wrong with this picture, Eli. It's bothering me. She's checking her messages again. Texting something this time. Hmmm. She's not happy with whatever she's reading."

"How can you tell? She's looked miserable as fuck since I got back to school."

"She's shaking her head and saying no. I can see her lips moving."

"You can lip read now?"

"It's a useful skill to have. Her cell's back on the tray and now she's looking for an empty table." His eyebrow hikes again. "She's walking this way. No, wait. She's changed her mind."

"Why are you telling me all this?"

"Because something about it doesn't make sense. She's on the move again. Her hands must be shaking. She's going to drop that tray if she doesn't steady her grip." A shadow falls over our table, and Kellan tips his head up. "Hi, Bella. What can we do for you?"

I frown, and slowly turn my head. Arabella is standing beside our table. Her blue eyes are focused on me, but it's like she's staring right through me.

"What?" At the sound of my voice, she jumps and blinks.

The plates and silverware on her tray are rattling, and her grip is white knuckled on the edges of the tray.

"Do you want something?"

Her lips press together, and she swallows. With careful movements, she sets the tray down and turns slightly, so she's facing me and picks up the bowl of pasta.

"I'm sorry." The words are low and shaky.

"For what?"

She upends the bowl on my head. Before I can react, the glass of juice joins it, dripping down my face. She twists away and flees. I surge to my feet, intending to chase her, only to be stopped by Kellan's grip on my arm.

"Let her go."

"What the actual fuck?" I snatch up a paper napkin and wipe my face.

"I need to speak to Miles. Go and get cleaned up and meet me at medical."

79

Arabella

I race past the students heading into the cafeteria and out of the door. The flash of rage on Eli's face when I dumped the food over him drives my fear. Adrenaline pumps through me, and I don't stop until I'm inside my room. Slamming the door shut, I dash for the bathroom, drop to my knees, and dry heave over the toilet, the spasms wracking my stomach.

What if he comes after me?

I scurry back into the bedroom and lock the door, then I stare at it, waiting for him to come. I'm braced for the lash of his fury, the cruel words which will rip what's left of me to shreds like the blade of the sharpest knife.

Time trickles by, and nothing happens.

Even if he doesn't retaliate now, he will in class tomorrow. I have no way to avoid him. I'll just leave. Pack a bag and run away again.

With jerky steps, I move to the closet and open it. Taking the first suitcase I see, I unzip it, move to the dresser, and stuff clothes into it.

Elena will just drag me back to school, and where am I going to go? They'll still have the videos. The one of me and Eli having sex. They could still hurt Miles.

The bitter truth stills my movements.

My attention jumps to my bedside table, and I dig Sin's phone out of the drawer.

`Me: I want to run. I want to run so bad, but`

I don't know what will happen if I do. I'm stuck. Churchill Bradley Academy is Hell, and I'm paying for crimes that are not mine.

Why am I still trying to contact him? I'm so fucking stupid.

I toss the cell on the bed, perch beside it and cradle my head in my hands.

My phone pings.

Peering slowly at it through my fingers, I'm quick to realize it's not Sin's phone that's made the noise.

My gaze slowly drops down to my bag, where I've dumped it on the floor. I don't want to look, but I'm scared of what will happen if I don't. I pull out my cell.

Unknown number: Well done, we liked the show. Tomorrow will be even better.

A video is attached, and I numbly watch as I dump the pasta covered in sauce over Eli's head. I see the shock ripple over his face and then harden with anger.

There's roaring in my ears, my hands shake as my vision blurs. I stumble back into the bathroom, I clutch at the sink, tremors wracking my body until I'm unsteady on my feet. My heart pounds faster and faster.

I try to calm myself, but my breath is shallow and sharp. My vision narrows, white dots dancing before my eyes. I sink downward and curl up on the floor.

I don't know how much time passes before I'm able to move and steady myself. It could have been thirty seconds or an hour, or even a week. It's not like anyone will come looking for me to see if I'm alive. I crawl over the floor, out of the bathroom, and over to the bed.

Exhaustion wraps itself around me. The need to sleep is strong, and I give myself up to it, taking refuge in dreamless oblivion.

75

Eli

Showered, clean, and dressed in fresh clothes, I walk down to the medical building to meet Kellan. He pushes away from the wall when he sees me.

"And why am I here?" My question comes out irritably. My day has been a fucking nightmare so far.

"Miles thinks you pushed him into the pool."

I tip my head up and stare at the sky, huffing out a breath. "What the fuck am I? The bogeyman who is responsible for every fucking thing that happens?"

"I told him it wasn't you, but he's convinced it wasn't an accident. I said I'd prove it to him."

"How?"

"By you coming here and telling him you didn't do it."

"Ever heard of lying?" My voice is dry.

"Did you do it?"

"No."

"Well, there we go. I know you didn't do it. You know you didn't do it. Now we just need to tell Miles."

I roll my eyes. "Whatever. Let's get this over with. I need to drive into town and buy clothes." I pause and glance at him. "Actually, *you* need to drive me into town for clothes. My car isn't back yet."

"Fine." He chuckles. "I'll take you shopping after we speak to Miles."

I follow him through the doors, and he pauses just before we enter the room Miles is in. “Could you do something for me?”

“What’s that?”

“Tone down the …” He waves a hand up and down in front of me, and smirks. “Tone down the whole ‘*I’m going to fucking eat you with a rusty spoon*’ vibe.”

I snort. “Didn’t realize I had that kind of vibe.”

He winks at me. “Eli, you have that monster vibe down so strong I’m pretty sure the bears in Wharton Forest would think twice about going up against you.” He rests his hand on the doorknob. “Seriously, though, Miles isn’t a bad guy.”

“And you like him,” I say softly.

Kellan smiles. “And I like him.” He pushes the door open and swaggers inside, a cocky grin firmly in place. “Hello, darling boy. Did you miss me?”

A groan comes from the bed. “Why are you always so … *upbeat*?”

“It’s part of my charm.” He rounds the bed and kisses Miles’ cheek. “Now, don’t freak out. I brought Eli to talk to you.”

“What? Kellan, no!”

“Oh, for fuck’s sake.” I stride inside and kick the door shut. “Contrary to popular belief, I’m not about to gut you and eat your liver for lunch.”

Kellan waggles a finger at me. “Play nice.”

“Kellan says you think I pushed you into the pool.”

Miles’ eyes dart from Kellan to me and away again. “Did you?”

“No. Why the fuck would I do that?”

“Because of Bella. She wanted to tell me something yesterday …

I'm sure it was about you and what you're doing to her."

"*Doing* to her? I'm not doing anything to her."

"Then why is she so scared all the time?"

"Because she's fucking insane?"

He shakes his head, then winces. "There's something going on with her. All this shit she's been doing. I thought it was retaliation for what you've done."

"And *what* have I done?" My voice is dangerously low.

"The videos. The photographs. The dead animals."

"None of that was me."

"You didn't deny it."

"I shouldn't have to. Especially to you."

He's silent for a long moment, and then he pushes up on the bed. "I was supposed to go and see her last night. I saw her in the stairwell yesterday. She was crying."

Tension stiffens my shoulders. "About what?"

"That's just it. She wouldn't tell me. Claimed *they* would know."

"They?" Both Kellan and I jump on the word.

"Tell me exactly what happened when you saw her yesterday?" I sit on the edge of the bed.

"I was heading down to swim practice, and she was sitting on the step crying. I sat with her and asked her what was wrong, whether *you* had done something to upset her. She said that she didn't know what to do, that they were watching her, and someone tried to get into her room a couple of nights ago. Then some of the girls hit the stairs, and she panicked. I promised I'd go and see her after practice." He touches his head. "Then this happened."

There's a heavy weight in the pit of my stomach. The words Miles is saying have a terrible familiarity to them. I've heard them before. My gaze searches out Kellan, and I can see my thoughts mirrored in his eyes.

"Zoey said she thought someone was watching her a few days before she died." It's Kellan who voices what we're both thinking. He looks at Miles. "Did you text her earlier … at lunchtime?"

"No. I took a nap. The nurse woke me up at one, with some painkillers."

"Did she mention talking to someone when you spoke to her?"

"I don't think so."

Kellan is chewing on the inside of his cheek, a sure sign that his brain is ticking over, compiling the information he has.

"At lunch … just before she dumped her lunch over your head—"

"She did *what*?" Miles said.

"Pasta, sauce, and juice. Just before she did that, she said she was sorry. Do you remember?"

"Hard to forget." She'd been white, shaking so hard I was surprised she could stand straight, and the emptiness in her eyes had torn my soul.

"What if she's following instructions?"

I laugh. "Seriously? Your go-to is a secret person giving her instructions?"

He looks at me. "Are you going to make me say it?"

"Say what?"

His lips compress into a line, and he shakes his head.

"It's not me."

"I *know* it's not you. But it *could* have been."

"What are you talking about?" Miles leans forward, eyes intent on Kellan.

"Nothing." I answer before my friend does. "It's not the same."

"Isn't it?" His eyes bore into mine. "Think about it, Eli. This was where you were heading before your plans changed. And where did *you* get the idea from? Someone else doing it. Is it such a stretch to think that you're not the only one who had the same idea?"

My jaw clenches. He's making sense. *Too much sense.* Has someone been behind the shit Arabella has been doing all this time? If that's true … I don't even want to finish that thought.

"How do we find out?"

"If I'm right, she'll get another text with instructions. We need to watch her. Look for a pattern. Although I think it's already there. She was getting messages in class this morning, and then she kept tossing you smiles." He pushes his hair off his face. "How did we not see this sooner?"

"We weren't looking for it." My voice is soft. "If someone is behind this, I want to know who, and I want to know why she hasn't told anyone."

"Then we need to behave like we haven't figured it out. If she does anything else, you keep control and don't fucking react. Do you think you can do that?"

76

Arabella

Bypassing the cafeteria, I give up on the pretense of going to have breakfast. There's no point when the thought of food just makes me sick. My eyes feel gritty, and I sleepwalk through the campus toward class. The little sleep I did have was full of nightmares that left me soaked in sweat and screaming.

I'm numb.

This cycle is never going to stop. I'm stuck in an endless loop of destruction.

I'd been late back to classes yesterday, waiting for Eli to strike out at me. Instead, he and Kellan had sat and glared at me all afternoon. By the time dinner rolled around, I'd been thankful to scurry back to my room.

At least on Friday, there won't be any classes as it's the Valentine's Day Ball, and we've all been given the day off. Just two more days of torture, and then I can stay buried in my room for three whole days.

I'm so lost in worry over what Eli might do that I'm not aware of someone beside me until a heavy arm drops around my shoulders.

"Are you looking forward to the Ball, Arabella?" Jace squeezes me tightly into his side. "We're going to make it real special for you."

Garrett leers at me from the other side of Jace. "I don't think we need flowers and chocolate to get her pussy wet."

I don't respond. There's no fight left in me to give.

Jace pulls me to a stop and swings me around. Bret and Evan

stand in front of me.

Bret licks his lips. "You'll spread your legs for us, won't you, Arabella."

"I bet she'll be able to handle the four of us." Evan joins in.

"Five. Brad said he wants a piece of this." Jace's grip on my arm tightens painfully. "What's the matter, Arabella? Got nothing to say?"

I keep my gaze down, pinned on the front of his jacket. "I need to get to class."

"Fuck, just look at her," Bret mutters. "I think Travers broke her."

"Are you the monster's whore?" Garrett questions with a sneer.

All I want is for them to leave me alone.

"Yes," I reply dully, giving them what they already believe.

Cruel fingers grip my chin, forcing my head up, and Jace pushes his finger between my lips. "Suck it."

Tears brim in my eyes, and I close them, doing as he orders. I suck on it, and almost gag when he pushes it to the back of my throat. He withdraws his finger from my mouth and shoves me away with a laugh. Eyelashes lifting, I meet their hungry gazes.

"I can't wait for you to be on your knees." Garrett's voice is husky, his hand at the front of his jeans as he readjusts himself. "With that pretty little mouth wrapped around my dick."

Bret smacks his shoulder. "You heard what Travers said. He's not done with her."

"He'll be sick of her soon enough," Evan snickers.

I duck my head and walk away. I should be frightened, but I'm hollow inside, empty. Head down, I don't stop until I'm in the classroom and at my desk. I blank out everything going on around me and dig out my math books.

"Stay away from my boyfriend, freak."

My bag is shoved onto the floor, the contents spilling out.

Lacy's lips are twisted in a sneer, her hand still outstretched. "You're nothing. A nobody. Trash that should never have been let into this school. Know your fucking place."

I'm motionless, her words barely scratch through my numbness. The second she moves for her desk, I get up and gather my stuff off the floor. No one helps me. No one says a word. When I have everything, I sit back down and check my phone.

`Unknown number: You and Eli will be called to the front of the class. Make sure he's the one who answers the math problem you're given.`

I wipe a hand across my eyes and wonder if I'm hallucinating.

Why is this so easy? Where's the hidden catch?

Just be happy it's nothing worse.

One question still bugs me.

`Me: How do you know I'll be chosen with Eli?`

`Unknown number: Drake has a list of people he's already paired for the class. He's predictable like everyone else.`

Mr. Drake is at the front of the room. When I turn my head, my gaze clashes with a pair of intense green ones. I expect to see hate. Instead, they are watchful. It's like he's daring me to do something.

My attention returns nervously to my desk, and I slip my phone into my hoodie pocket.

"Miss Gray and Mr. Travers, please come to the front of the class."

The writing in front of me swims before my vision, my mind empty of thought.

"Miss Gray!" The teacher's voice booms, making me jump. "Stop daydreaming and come to the front."

I scramble up, to see Eli already beside Mr. Drake by the board, his expression aloof and closed. Licking my lips nervously, I hurry to join them.

"Can you answer the multiplication question for me?" He offers me the pen.

Just do it. It's a simple task. They might leave me alone for the rest of the day. Get it over with. Eli isn't going to get upset over a math problem.

"I—" Tension coils through my muscles. "No, sir. Maybe Eli should answer this one."

77

Eli

Why the fuck is Drake calling me up to the front of the class. He *never* picks me for anything. When I take my place next to Arabella, he ducks his head and refuses to look in my direction.

My lip curls. Someone must have convinced him to do this. I prop my hip against his desk and look out over the room. When Arabella suggests I should answer the question, my head turns toward her. She's holding out the whiteboard pen in an unsteady hand.

Does she know about my issue with numbers? It's hard to tell.

"Mr. Travers, today would be good," Mr. Drake grumbles from beside us.

I reach out for the pen and let my thumb brush across her wrist before I curl my fingers over hers. In one quick move, I pull her into my body and turn her to face the whiteboard. I'm behind her, one arm wrapped around her waist, my palm flat against her stomach. I lift our combined fingers to the board.

"Maybe we should answer it together."

I make no effort to guide the pen across the board, letting her write the answer to the question. I'm more interested in how much she's shaking. This close, I can hear her teeth chattering. I *know* it's not due to the cold. The room is like a fucking furnace. When her hand drops, I let her go and step away.

"Nothing quite like teamwork." I wink at her and return to my desk.

Mr. Drake doesn't even look up. "Done? Good. Truman and Shaw, you next."

"What the fuck was that?" Kellan leans close to whisper. "Doesn't he have an agreement with you?"

I nod. I lean back in my seat and look around to where Arabella is lowering herself to her seat. My eyes narrow when I see Garrett leaning forward, his arm pushed through the slats on the backrest of her chair and his palm flat on the seat, waiting for her ass to sit on it.

He's so focused on Arabella that he doesn't see me stand. My foot connects with her chair, and Garrett howls as his arm is twisted by the momentum of the chair as it's shunted across the room. I have to force myself not to make a grab for her as she loses her balance.

She lands on her ass, much to the laughter of the room, but my attention is solely on Garrett. "What did I say to you?"

"Mr. Travers! You will not disrupt my class this way." Drake bellows before Garrett can respond. "Get out!"

I step over Arabella, who's still sitting on the floor, and grab my bag. "I'll meet you at lunchtime," I tell Kellan and walk out.

I don't really want to go back to my room, or work on my sculpture. My mind is too restless to concentrate, so I wander aimlessly for a while until I find myself standing in front of the tomb.

I haven't been inside since the last time I was with Arabella. The night I almost fucked her as Sin. It seems like a lifetime ago. Is it really only a couple of months? I don't have the key for the padlock with me, so I turn away. Kellan is leaning against a gravestone a few feet away.

"I need you to do something."

I raise an eyebrow.

"Come to lunch and I'll explain on the way."

***

"How is this going to help exactly?" I ask for the third time.

We're seated at our usual table, food and drink in front of us.

"It'll just confirm our theory." He jerks his chin toward the door. "Look, there she is."

She's like a fucking ghost, the way she moves between the tables. So pale, so silent. Her head lowered; cell clutched in her hand.

"Do it now." Kellan kicks my ankle under the table.

I scowl at him.

"Just do it, Eli."

I slip out of my seat and move to intercept her path. She's so intent on the floor that she doesn't see me and crashes into my chest. She stumbles backward and blinks up at me, eyes widening when they meet mine.

"Hit me."

"Wh-what?"

"Hit me." I repeat the words softly.

She shakes her head. I run my knuckles down her cheek, along her jaw, then wrap a hand around her throat. "*Hit* me."

"No."

I glance up at Kellan, who nods. I look like I'm threatening her, and my voice is too low to be heard by anyone around.

"Why not?"

"I don't want to."

My head tilts. "Tell me I'm a monster."

Something flickers behind her eyes. I flex my fingers.

"Say it."

She stays silent. Kellan nods again.

"I see you, Arabella."

When she turns white, I know she's taken it as a threat, a warning. It's neither, but I can't explain that to her. Not yet.

I drop my hand and walk back to the table.

"She didn't hit you."

"No."

"You'd think she would, considering the other shit she's done."

"So, you think your theory is proved? That she really is following someone's demands?"

"Certainly looks that way." A half-smile lifts his lips. "She has her cell in her hand. I guess that *someone* is in contact with her now. This should be interesting." He leans back on his seat. "Brace yourself. She's on her way over."

We both watch as she makes her slow way over to our table and stops just out of arm's reach.

Kellan props his chin on his hand. "You don't look well, Bella."

Her eyes jerk to him, then settle on me.

"Do it," I tell her. She stares at me. I smile. "It's okay, Ari. Whatever it is, just do it."

78

Arabella

My eyes burn, the phone clutched in my grasp. I raise my free hand, swing it, and slap him across the face with no real force behind it.

Eli takes the tap, his gaze still locked on mine. I'm shaking so hard I'm surprised pieces of me aren't falling off, or maybe that's just the inside.

"I'm the monster." The confession leaves me in a whisper.

My cell pings.

My eyes widen, and the tears spill free, and I turn away. I dart through the cafeteria and run blindly outside. My legs carry me across the campus and over the grass. The tree line comes up fast, and I rush along the path to the cemetery. I only stop when I reach the bench. Collapsing onto the dirt beside it, I suck in breath after breath. I'm dizzy from not eating properly, and it's stolen all the strength I once had.

I see you, Arabella.

The force behind those soft words chokes me.

What is he going to do?

Has he finally snapped?

Have they finally got what they wanted?

My phone pings again.

Glancing at it, I swipe the screen.

`Unknown number: Hit him harder.`

`Unknown number: Where the fuck are you going?`

`Unknown number: Get back here and punch him harder.`

`Me: You told me to hit him, and I did.`

`Unknown number: You need to do better. We want him to react.`

`Me: I'm doing exactly as you told me.`

`Unknown number: It's not good enough.`

I didn't have the strength or the will to hit Eli any harder.

`Me: I'm sorry.`

I sit there and shake, waiting for a reply, but nothing comes. Ten minutes pass, fifteen, thirty … and nothing.

Maybe they've given up?

I slowly get to my feet, and wander into the cemetery. Drifting between the gravestones, I wind my way toward Zoey's plaque. There's something placed at the base. Flowers. Delicate and white. They are wrapped in black paper.

Flowers from Kellan or Eli?

I've given up reading her diary, unable to lose myself in her words. I can't concentrate on anything, and I know it's only a matter of time before one of the teachers says something. My grades are already suffering. I'll be lucky to graduate at all.

The familiar numbness I'm becoming accustomed to settles over me. I embrace it, letting it take away my pain. I linger in the peaceful cemetery for a little while longer, before I go back to the school and toward the dorms. Lunch won't be over for a while, and I'd rather sit in my room than haunt the campus, waiting for the classes to restart.

When I reach my room, I let myself in and close the door behind me.

I sweep my gaze around the room and stop when it comes to the bed.

There's a rabbit lying on top of the mattress with its head bent at an odd angle. Its gray fur looks soft, while its black eyes stare sightlessly up. Pressing a hand to my mouth, I stare in horror at the dead animal.

My phone pings.

I slide it out of my pocket.

`Unknown number: Next time, it won't be a bunny. Everything you do wrong comes with consequences. Remember that next time. You belong to us. You will obey.`

79

Eli

"So, we agree someone is definitely watching and directing her actions." I lean my back against the headboard of my bed.

Kellan nods.

"That means they must have been in the cafeteria earlier."

"Most of the school was in there. It doesn't narrow it down," he points out.

"Wouldn't it need to be someone who was close enough to hear you?" Miles joins the conversation. He's sprawled out across the bed, with his head on Kellan's thigh.

"I wasn't paying that much attention to the surrounding tables."

"Me either," Kellan says. "I was watching to see how Arabella reacted to you."

"We're back at square one, with no fucking clue who it could be, other than it's *someone*." I throw myself off my bed and pace the room. "There must be some fucking way to figure it out."

"Who hates you?" The swim captain earns a glare from me.

Kellan snickers. "*Everyone* hates him, you know that."

"I'm serious," Miles says. He pushes up, away from Kellan and looks at me. "Look, Eli. I know you and Kellan are friends, but I've got to be honest. I've always wondered whether you were holding something over him to keep him close."

Kellan laughs, and Miles frowns at him.

"Oh. You mean it. The only thing Eli holds over me is his car keys when he wants me to drive."

"Stop joking." He takes out his cell and fiddles with it. "When the first video of Arabella was leaked, I got a text message telling me I should distance myself from her."

"You never told me that." Kellan sits up straight.

"Because I thought it was from Eli. I told her I couldn't continue pretending to be her boyfriend, but we could still be friends. But we had to be careful."

"I *knew* I wasn't broken!" Kellan crows.

"You were hiding the fact you were gay?" I turn to face him, and he nods.

"My parents … let's just say there's only one kind of relationship in their eyes, and it's not two guys together. Letting them think I had a girlfriend kept them off my back." He holds my gaze. "When you tried to call me out for being with Kellan, I was convinced the text telling me to keep away from Arabella was you. When I didn't stay away enough, I got another text with a video of me with Kellan, and a message that they'd send it to my dad if I didn't cut Arabella off."

"Why would I do that to Kellan?"

"Kellan doesn't give a fuck what people know about him. I knew that video getting out wouldn't bother him, but me? Eli, you have to understand that being on the swim team, being the *captain*, is all I have. My family would cut me off if they knew I was gay. I thought that you were using the fact I was sneaking around with Kellan as a way to control how much contact I had with Arabella."

"You have to admit, it's a good theory," Kellan says.

I can't argue. If I had carried on with my original plan to ruin

Arabella, I would have absolutely used Kellan's relationship with Miles as a means to get him away from her.

"Whoever is doing this is targeting *you*, and using Arabella as their weapon," Miles continues. "It's the only thing that makes sense. Could it be the guys she's with in the first video?"

Kellan chokes on the mouthful of Coke he's just taken. Miles slaps his back until he has control of himself.

"Are you okay?"

He shakes his head, but his shoulders are shaking with suppressed laughter. I sigh.

"It's me."

"What is?" Miles frowns.

"In the video." I rub a hand over my jaw. "It's me … and Kellan."

Miles' eyes widen. "*You* … *both* of you?"

Kellan shrugs. "I told you I'm a slut. But I was really just there as Eli's wingman, a distraction to stop her from focusing too much on Eli's voice."

"She was sucking your dick." Miles is gaping at me. "And she didn't *know* it was you?"

"She was a little distracted at the time." I rake a hand through my hair. "It doesn't matter. It means the people in the video aren't the ones doing this."

"Have you checked that cell phone at all?" Kellan straightens.

"I thought about it but, like I said the other day, what's the point? It was taken by the school."

"But if someone took that cell and put it in your locker, they might have sent something to the other phone."

We stare at each other. "You think all this is because I've ignored them?"

"Only if they know it's you on the videos. They *might* … if they've seen your dick before."

"Wait." Miles joins the conversation again. "What cell?"

I sigh, dropping onto the edge of my bed. "I gave her a cell phone when we started meeting, so I could contact her."

"Without her realizing it was Eli," Kellan adds. "He originally wanted to get her thrown out of the school." He smirks. "But then he caught feelings."

"Kellan." I growl his name.

"You *did* catch feelings. It's no lie."

"Jesus Christ, are you two always like this? Focus!" Miles stands up. "Where's the cell? Do you still have it?"

"Of course, I—" My eyes widen. "Fuck." I'm across the room and in the closet before I finish the sentence. The stab of relief that goes through me when I see the box in the corner makes me sag. "Thank fuck for that."

"You thought they took it when your room got trashed," Kellan says.

I nod, flipping open the lid of the box and taking out the cell. I stare at it. Now I'm thinking about turning it on, my heart is hammering.

What if there is a message? What if all the fucked up shit that's happened over the past few weeks could have been avoided? What if this all really is my fucking fault?

Sucking in a deep breath, I look at Kellan, then push the power button.

The silence after it powers up is anti-climactic. Nothing happens.

"I guess that—"

The phone in my hand vibrates, then dings with an incoming message, then another, followed by a string of them in quick succession.

The three of us stare at it as it chimes over and over. Once it falls silent, I glance up at Kellan and lick my lips.

"Well, someone really wanted to talk to you," he says softly. "You better see what they want."

`Kitten: Sin, please talk to me. Everything has turned upside down, and I don't have anyone else. I need you.`

`Kitten: Are you behind the videos?`

`Kitten: Please, are you there?`

`Kitten: I don't know who to talk to. They're watching me all the time.`

`Kitten: I want to stop.`

`Kitten: Sin, are you doing this? I'm so scared. I don't know how much more I can take.`

`Kitten: I'm not a bully. I don't know who I am anymore.`

`Kitten: Everything is out of control. Someone is going to get hurt. I'm trapped on a runaway train, and there's no way to get off.`

`Kitten: I want to run. I want to run so bad, but I don't know what will happen if I do. I'm stuck. Churchill Bradley Academy is Hell, and I'm paying for crimes that are not mine.`

My stomach churns, my eyesight blurs, and I rub a hand across my face. The pain in her texts is clear. The panic and despair. The fucking anguish.

The cell drops from my hand, and I bow my head, breathing deeply as I fight to contain the guilt flaying my soul.

"I'm going to fucking kill them." The sound of my own voice startles me. "I need to see her."

Kellan's hand on my arm stops me. "Not now. She says they're watching her. You need to get her somewhere they have no eyes."

"Where?"

"The tomb."

"How do I get her there?" My head is pounding. I can barely think straight.

"Eli, *concentrate*. You have a means of contact right in front of you. Those texts prove that she has the phone. Send her a message."

"A message … right." I scoop the cell back up and stare blankly down at it. "What do I say?"

"Fuck's sake. Give it to me." Kellan snatches the phone out of my hands and types rapidly, then hands it back to me.

`Me: I'm sorry, Kitten. Meet me at the bench. Usual time. Tomorrow night.`

80

Arabella

Curled up on the spare bed under a blanket, I stare at the TV fixed on the wall, but I'm not seeing the images of the movie playing on the screen. My thoughts are turned inward. I disposed of the rabbit in a plastic bag and stripped my bed down. After what happened, I'm not sure I can sleep on that mattress again. The whole thing has left me on edge.

If I got the locks changed, would it make any difference? What reason would I give to the school staff for why I want it done?

My attention snaps to the door and the chair I have wedged up against it. It's not enough to keep someone out, but it'll give me enough of a warning if they try.

And what do I do if they get in?

The taser Miles bought me is missing from my drawer. Whoever has been in my room went through my stuff. A shudder rolls through me at the thought of faceless strangers touching my things.

Not faceless. They're here in the school, but I just don't know who they are.

The chime of a message shatters my thoughts, and the noise locks up my throat.

I can't breathe.

I can't move.

A tremor rolls through my body, then another and another. Tears spring to my eyes.

Not tonight. Please God, don't let them make me do something tonight.

My hand shakes as I reach for my phone. When I look at the screen, there's no text waiting for me. I scrub at my damp cheeks with my free hand.

Am I going crazy? Was it in my head?

The sound has invaded my nightmares enough times over the last few weeks that just the ping triggers my anxiety.

A memory scratches at the back of my skull, and my messy thoughts have a hard time pinning it down. It takes me a few minutes to remember that I have two cells.

My gaze jerks to the other one, where it sits on my nightstand. I crawl toward it. I'd switched it on earlier to check for a response, but there had been nothing, as usual.

I tap the screen.

`Sin: I'm sorry, Kitten. Meet me at the bench. Usual time. Tomorrow night.`

I sit and just stare at the words.

Sin?

Sin has responded.

Am I dreaming?

This can't be real. He's left me hanging all this time.

Emotion thickens my throat, and a fresh wave of tears falls. I clutch the phone in both hands and bow my head over it in an agony of relief. Then anger stirs.

`Me: Where have you been? I've been texting you for weeks.`

Sin: I'll explain tomorrow.

Me: Can I trust you?

I watch the dots undulate, stop, and start again.

Sin: You trusted me with your body. Trust me again. I swear, Kitten, I want to help you.

My tears fall harder, building in momentum until they are pouring down my cheek.

Help me? I've been desperate for someone to say that for so long. I crave it with every fiber of my being. My thoughts turn to Miles and what happened to him.

Can I really take the chance? Do I dare risk it?

Me: The last person I tried to talk to got hurt.

More tears surge, and a sob wrecks my body. This isn't going to work. He can't help me. No one can.

The dots start their dance again.

Sin: Kitten, I promise nothing is going to happen to me.

He doesn't know that. I thought Miles had been safe, but it was just a lie.

What if something goes wrong? What if they find out?

Sin: Baby, I know you're scared, and I'm so fucking sorry for not replying sooner.

Sin: Kitten, are you there?

I'm torn between the need to answer and switching off the phone. I suck in a shaky breath but can't shake an impending sense of doom.

Next time, it won't be a bunny.

Sin: Kitten, please answer me.

The desperate desire to confide in someone wins, and I shoot off a text.

`Me: I'm here.`

`Sin: Meet me tomorrow night, it will be okay.`

My sobs quieten into sniffles.

`Me: You promise you will be there?`

`Sin: I swear on my life.`

I flop onto my side and cradle the cell in my hands.

`Me: I'm so tired.`

`Sin: I want you to try and sleep. Can you do that for me?`

My gaze shifts uneasily to the locked door and back.

`Me: I don't want to. I'm scared they might get in.`

`Sin: Who?`

`Me: The boys who won't leave me alone.`

A few minutes pass by, and he doesn't reply.

`Sin: Is your door locked?`

`Me: Yes.`

`Sin: Go to sleep. No one is going to touch you. Trust me. Remember, the bench. Usual time. Tomorrow night.`

`Me: Ok.`

I leave the cell switched on and turn off the TV. The light of my bedside lamp bathes everything in a warm, soft glow.

Sin has contacted me, and I don't know how to feel, but hope is a tiny ember in my chest.

81

Eli

I don't sleep at all. Miles slips back to his own room around three and drops a text to say no one was in the hallways. I think about walking up to the girls' floor, but Kellan talks me out of it.

His reasoning is sound. If someone *is* watching her, then my presence will raise questions. We spend the rest of the night talking about what we know of Arabella's movements since I returned to school. Neither of us can think of an occasion where she's targeted someone other than me.

"You know that means this is more about you than her, don't you?"

I blow out a breath. "You think she's just a useful pawn? When the first video was leaked, it had no connection to me."

"Unless whoever leaked it *knows* it's you." He taps around on his cell and pulls up the video.

"Why the fuck do you still have a copy?"

"I keep backups of everything, you know that. Anyway, I'm not interested in watching *her.*"

He fiddles with the screen, zooming in on me, then hits play. A couple of minutes in, he pauses.

"*There!* Look. I can see the tattoo on your arm." He points to where the sleeve of my hoodie has ridden up, and the tail of the snake tattoo on my arm can be seen.

My fingers are wrapped in her hair while her mouth slides up and down my dick. That part isn't on the screen, but I remember it. How her mouth felt, the way her tongue lapped at me. I bite back a groan.

"Do you need a moment to relive the experience?" Kellan's voice is dry.

I glare at him. "I should go and check on her."

"*No*, you shouldn't." He closes the video and tosses his cell onto the bed. "She's fine. If anyone was going to try and get into her room, they'd have done it by now. They're just trying to scare her to make sure she does what they want."

He settles back against his pillows. "You need to act normal tomorrow … *today* when you see her. No talking to her or acting like you don't want her dead. No rushing to her rescue when the assholes start their shit."

"I'm not sure I can do that."

"You have to. Otherwise, we'll never find out who's behind it. They need to believe you have no idea that she's not doing this for her own reasons."

My gaze drops to my hands, where they're curled into fists on my thighs. "I need to tell her who I am." I lift my gaze to find Kellan. "She's never going to fucking trust me again."

"It's trust you or keep on doing as she's told for the rest of the school year. And once we reach the end, then what?" His voice turns sad. "Zoey got a couple of text messages, do you remember, wanting her to play. She did the first two, then refused the third but never told us what she was asked to do."

"Three days before she died. I remember."

The unspoken thought that history could be about to repeat itself hangs between us.

***

I can't stop myself from searching her out when we walk into class. She's already at her desk, head resting on her arms, eyes squeezed closed as she tries to block out the catcalls and lewd comments from the guys surrounding her.

I clear my throat behind Garrett, making him jump, and he spins to look at me. When he realizes who it is, he raises his hands.

"We haven't touched her. Just making promises for when we can."

I lift an eyebrow and move around him until I'm in front of her desk. Kellan has told me I need to keep up the pretense that I'm furious about the things she's been doing and react accordingly.

I wrap a hand into her hair and tug her head up. "Wake up, Princess. It's a new day." I wait for her lashes to lift and grit my teeth against the bleak expression on her face. "Are we going to play today? Should I keep a change of clothes in my bag?"

She doesn't respond, just looks up at me through empty eyes. I release her hair and pat her cheek. "Alright then, you can make it a surprise. I'll be waiting with bated breath."

I move to my desk and sit down. With my bag on my lap, I reach in and tap out a quick text.

`Me: Smile, Kitten.`

I'm not sure if she has the cell with her, but if not, it'll be waiting for her when she checks.

The English class passes without incident, and as soon as the bell rings, everyone surges out of the room. I take my time, waiting for everyone to leave before standing. Art is next, and other than showing my face in the main art studio to Mr. McIntyre, my plan is to work on my sculpture until lunchtime.

Classes are ending early today, to give Lacy and her cronies time to prepare for the Valentine's Ball tomorrow. Kellan has arranged to sneak off somewhere with Miles, so I have nowhere else to be until I go to meet Arabella after curfew.

My mind turns to her.

How the fuck am I going to break it to her that I am Sin?

82

Arabella

Sin: Smile, Kitten.

I stare down at the message, and tug my lips up, but a smile feels unnatural on my face. There's nothing for me to be happy about, and not even his text can change that. The hours are crawling by. The day is dragging unbelievably slowly. All I want is to get to curfew so I can creep out to the cemetery.

And what if they see me? What if I'm caught? What will they do to me then?

I don't even want to think about it because it takes me deeper into the dark place I'm already struggling to survive. There's movement outside the stall, and I listen to the footsteps in the restroom. I'm supposed to be in art, but I'm hiding out instead. So far, my blackmailer hasn't noticed or contacted me to ask where I am. That gives me hope that maybe they can't watch me all the time.

Unless they're waiting to make me pay for my absence later.

My stomach flips at the thought.

I find my earbuds, push them into my ears, and press play. The lyrics of 'Numb' by Linkin Park drown out my thoughts. Eyes closed, head down, I lose myself in the words. Something drips off my chin. I touch my cheek and discover I'm crying.

I can't do this. I can't do this.

I send a message to Sin.

Me: I'm not sure I can do this.

The dots move immediately, bringing me comfort.

`Sin: Breathe, Kitten.`

`Me: You don't understand. I don't know what they'll do to me if they find out I'm going to meet you.`

`Sin: Did anyone find out about our meetings before?`

I sink down against the wall, and crouch, my whole focus on my phone.

`Me: No, I don't think so.`

`Sin: You know the place we go is safe.`

The tomb is locked, and he has the key. I blink away the tears. My chest aches remembering the last time I'd been there. He'd rejected me. Yet here I am, begging for his help. I'm still in love with him, and I shouldn't be.

`Me: Nowhere is safe anymore.`

`Sin: Please trust me. Come to me tonight. Don't change your mind.`

My courage wavers, and I don't reply. Two minutes pass, and the dots start jumping again.

`Sin: Kitten, I need to know you'll be there.`

`Sin: Arabella?`

Doubt circles in my mind, but I give him the answer I know he wants.

`Me: Ok.`

`Sin: Where are you? You're not in art class.`

`Me: I'm in the girl's restroom.`

`Sin: You need to act normal.`

My lips twist bitterly at his words.

Me: I don't have a normal anymore. Besides, if I'm in art, they'll make me do something to Eli. He's going to hurt me.

The dots stop, start, stop, and start again, and it feels like forever before the message comes through.

Sin: You're scared of him?

I answer him honestly.

Me: Yes. I don't want to provoke him. This isn't my fault, but he's going to take it out on me. I've seen what he can do. No one will stop him. I'm shaking just thinking about it.

Sin: Breathe, Kitten. Classes are finishing early. Go to art. He's not in the main studio. He's working on his project.

Eli isn't there. The knowledge eases a little of my anxiety.

Me: Ok, I'll go to class.

I hesitate for a moment, gratefulness making me smile.

Me: Thank you for helping me. Thank you for being there.

I slip my phone into my pocket and stand, unlocking the stall door. A flash of movement catches my eyes in the mirror a split second before pain spreads out across the side of my face. I stagger sideways, my legs give out, and I hit the floor. My hand covers my cheek, and I turn my head to find Tina lowering her arm, fist still clenched, and Lacy standing over me.

Tina smiles. "Oh, hi, Arabella. I didn't see you there."

Lacy flicks her hair over her shoulder. "I didn't realize you were so accident-prone."

My gaze bounces between them. "Shouldn't you be in class?"

My ex-roommate steps around me to move to the mirror. "The teacher let us out early, so we have plenty of time to make sure the ballroom is set up for tomorrow night." Opening her bag, she takes out her lip gloss and touches up her lips. "We also wanted to make sure it was clear that you're not welcome there."

I don't move from the floor. "I'm not going anyway."

Lacy puts the gloss away and pouts at her reflection. "Good. Not that anyone will be disappointed. No one is going to miss you."

She swivels on her heels, and trots toward the door.

"Come along, Tina. Linda will be waiting for us, and you know how she is if we aren't on time."

Tina moves to follow her. "See you around, loser."

I touch my throbbing cheek. Any thoughts of going into art withers and dies. I just want this day to be over with.

83

Eli

Do I wear a mask when I meet Arabella at the bench, or do I go as myself?

She's expecting Sin, so if I turn up, will she run?

My thoughts return to the text conversation earlier. She admitted she is scared of me. A few months ago, that would have brought me pleasure. Now, it just leaves me cold.

She'll definitely run if I show up, so I shove the ski mask into my pocket. If she's wearing the blindfold, I won't put it on. If she isn't, I will … at least until I'm close enough to stop her from running when she realizes who I am.

Time is moving slowly, and I don't even have Kellan here to distract me from watching my cell while I wait for the alarm to go off. I pace the room, end to end.

Maybe I should get there before her. But what if she sees me leaving the dorm? It might make her change her mind if she thinks I'm outside where she could run into me.

I've never felt so fucking conflicted in my life.

Gnawing on a thumbnail, I spin and stalk toward the door, then stop.

No, I should let her get there first. That way, I can check to make sure she hasn't been followed.

Maybe I should text her and make sure she's still meeting me?

Fuck.

I don't want her to think I'm putting her under pressure. It might make her start to question if I'm behind the other texts and trying to get her somewhere alone.

I stalk across the room again. I hate this out of control feeling.

Another glance at my cell tells me that my anxiety is too high for me to make sense of the numbers on the screen.

But my alarm isn't going off, so I know it's not time to leave yet.

Will she be there?

I sit on the edge of my bed, one leg bouncing up and down, my anxiety levels higher than they've ever been in my life.

Maybe I should *text her to confirm.*

I've purposely stayed out of her way today, to try and reduce the chance of her being told to do something to me. Kellan kept a watchful eye on her and reported earlier that she didn't keep checking her cell, so maybe they've left her in peace.

Or maybe they know you've arranged to meet her tonight, and this is all a fucking setup.

I shake my head, denying the whisper that tries to convince me not to go.

What if she already knows you're Sin, and this is just a way to get you outside without any witnesses?

She almost killed you once, with the GHB. Who's to say this isn't all part of the next step of their plan?

No, I don't believe she's part of this. No one could fake the fear I saw in her eyes.

What if the texts aren't from her? What if someone else has the cell?

What if ...

What if ...

What if ...

"No!" I snarl the word aloud.

Another time-check—nope, still can't make head nor tail of the numbers.

How do I tell her it's me without her thinking I'm fucking with her? Or worse, taking off through the woods. How do I explain that when all this started, my intention was to release the videos myself. She's never going to believe it wasn't me if I do that.

I rake a hand through my hair.

Fuck. I'm screwed, no matter what I do.

I jump to my feet.

I need some air, otherwise, I'm going to lose my mind. As I reach for the handle, there's a pounding on the door, and someone shouts my name.

89

Arabella

The second the clock hits an hour after curfew, I slip from my room. Every single tiny noise has me jumping out of my skin. I scurry along the hallway, my heart in my mouth, and make my way to the exit.

Please don't see me. Please don't see me.

The words chant over and over inside my head. It will only take one mistake for this all to go wrong. Stepping into the cold air outside, I suck in a breath. I have to be careful with the extra security the school now has. I duck back into the shadows by the wall of the building and scan the area slowly. Nothing moves. Nothing stirs. I stand frozen, willing my legs to move.

How many times have I done this before to go and meet Sin?

It feels like a lifetime ago.

I need to take this chance.

I urge myself to move. I barely have the energy to jog across the open grass in the darkness. By the time I hit the tree line, I'm dizzy and panting. Clutching at the nearest tree trunk, I steady myself and close my eyes. Maybe I should have tried to force myself to eat more than a chocolate muffin. Not that much of it had gone in my mouth when I'd picked at it.

I take a quick glance over my shoulder to check I'm not being followed. I see no one. Minutes tick by, and I remain staring nervously back at the school.

Got to keep going. Don't make Sin wait.

I set off along the path, the full moon lighting my way. It doesn't feel real being out here again. The wind is icy against my cheeks, its bite penetrating my clothes and making me shiver. Wrapping my arms around my waist, I keep a steady pace, not stopping until the bench comes into sight. It's then I remember the blindfold. I forgot all about it.

Will he still come if I don't have it? I'll just keep my eyes closed for him. I can promise him I won't peek. I did it before. At the movies.

I drop heavily down onto the bench and pull my phone anxiously from my pocket. I'm a little early, and he's not messaged me yet.

What do I say to him? Where do I start?

Everything is an ugly mess.

A chime comes from my other pocket.

No, no, no.

I close my hand around it inside my hoodie. I want to ignore it, but I don't.

I'll just see what they want.

Licking my lips, I check the message.

`Unknown number: We want you to attend the Valentine's Ball tomorrow night.`

Shock holds me immobile for a beat.

`Me: Lacy told me I'm not welcome.`

`Unknown number: You will attend.`

`Unknown number: We'll provide you with the perfect dress and makeup. We want you to flirt with Travers.`

I reread the words.

Me: Flirt?

Unknown number: You'll be messaged with further instructions in the evening. We will get the reaction we want out of him.

Lacy doesn't want me there. I can only imagine her reaction when I turn up. My thoughts shift to the jocks and their threats of what they plan to do to me on Valentine's Day. Panic claws its way through me, and I tremble, already dreading what's going to come.

Unknown number: You will make sure the Valentine's Day Ball is unforgettable. We want to see the monster unleashed.

They want to bring Eli down, and they are using me to do it. Anger surges, fracturing through the heavy fog of numbness.

Isn't this what Eli's wanted since he first met me? To see me groveling? Degraded? Beaten down? I'm nothing but trash to him. A gold-digger just like my mother.

I unblock his number on my phone, and all the old hate pours out of me like a festering wound that has never healed. My fingers fly over the screen, everything I've been holding in explodes out in my texts at my chosen target.

Me: Fuck you.

Me: Fuck this situation.

Me: You got what you wanted.

Me: You humiliated me.

Me: Hurt me.

Me: Took my virginity.

Me: Twisted everything with your hate.

Me: All I did was exist, and you hated me.

Me: You judged me without even getting to know me.

Me: All I wanted was to belong.

Me: It shouldn't have felt good to fuck you.

Me: You became a bad habit I didn't want to give up.

Me: Then you took it all away.

Me: I hate you for that.

Me: Well, you win.

Me: I'm done.

Me: You got what you wanted.

85

Eli

"They grabbed Kellan!" Miles blurts the words the second I pull open the door.

"*They?* They who?"

"Fucking Jace and Bret and the others. We were behind the pool, and they came around the corner. I was …" His white face turns red. "We were kissing. His pants were down, and I was—"

"I get the picture." I step out and slam the door behind me.

"They shouted at him to get away from me. Jace pulled him off me and then said they were sick of him trying to mess with me and were going to teach him what happens to anyone who fucks with their friends. I didn't get a chance to say anything before they dragged him away. He fought, but there were five of them. Eli, what if they hurt him?"

"Show me where they went."

We set off at a run through the dorm building and burst out of the door. A quick glance left and right shows security is nowhere near, and we take off along the path toward the indoor pool. As we draw closer to the building, a soft groan reaches us. We trade glances.

"What direction did that come from?"

Miles shakes his head. "I'm not sure."

We stop and stand, listening. A second or two later, there's another groan.

"Over there." I turn the corner, which takes us behind the building and into the small compound where the school's dumpsters are kept.

"Kellan?" I say his name quietly.

A soft moan echoes around the area.

"You go that way." I jerk my head to the row of dumpsters to the left, while I turn in the opposite direction.

My cell is in my hand, flashlight on high beam as I scan the gaps between the dumpsters.

"Over here." Miles' soft call has me sprinting over to him.

Kellan's been shoved between two dumpsters. His face is a bloodied mess, but his eyes are open. I crouch down.

"Fuck. Kell, can you look at me?"

I shine my light over him, checking for blood elsewhere. It all seems to be centered on his face.

"I think they broke my nose." His teeth flash in a weak smile.

"Can you stand?"

"Maybe?" He leans forward and I wrap a hand around his arm to steady him as he staggers upright.

"Let me look at your face." I grasp his chin and turn his head from side to side. "Definitely broke your nose. And you're going to need stitches. Does anywhere else hurt?"

"Ribs. Hurts to breathe."

I manhandle him until his arm is over my shoulders and mine is wrapped around his waist.

"Let's get you to medical."

Security appears just as we step out of the compound.

"What's going on here? You're supposed to be in your dorm."

"Kellan got jumped." Miles steps forward. "We're on our way to medical."

A flashlight shines in my eyes, then swings to Kellan, and the security guard swears softly.

"Do you know who did it?"

"No." I answer before Miles does. "I got a text from Kellan telling me he needed help." The lie flows easily off my tongue. "I asked Miles to help me find him."

Miles glances at me but doesn't say anything.

"I think they might have broken his nose and ribs. Can you alert medical?"

The security guard nods and pulls out his radio. "We have a situation around the back of section 1C. I'm bringing three students to medical."

86

Arabella

Me: Where are you?

Me: Please, Sin. I need you.

Me: Why are you ignoring me?

Me: It's been thirty minutes, and you're not here.

Me: I'm not leaving the cemetery until you come.

Me: They're texting me orders. They want me to go to the Ball tomorrow night.

Me: I'm nothing but their puppet.

Me: They want me to confront Eli. They want to see him react.

Me: I hate this school.

Me: You're the only thing I'm clinging to.

Me: Please don't take that away from me.

Me: Please come.

Me: I'm still waiting. It's been an hour.

Me: I'll do anything you want.

Me: I'll get down on my knees and suck your cock like a good girl.

Me: I'll suck your friend's cock too.

Me: I'd do anything for you.

Me: Please don't abandon me.

Me: It's two hours now, and I'm still here.

Me: I don't know who I am anymore.

Me: It hurts so much.

Me: I can't stop crying.

Me: I love you.

Me: Please don't do this to me.

Me: Sin, I love you.

Me: I feel so lost and alone.

Me: They've made me do things I'm not proud of.

Me: They have the videos.

Me: Please talk to me.

Me: Eli hates me so much.

Me: Maybe I deserve his hatred.

Me: Am I such a bad person?

Me: Is that why this is all happening to me?

Me: I can't do this anymore.

Me: I can't keep fighting.

Me: I'm so tired.

Me: I'm sorry.

Me: I'm weak.

Me: I'm not the strong girl you wanted me to be.

Me: I'm sorry if I did something wrong.

Me: I'm sorry if I'm a disappointment.

Me: I messed everything up. I'm not a bully. I didn't want to hurt anyone.

Me: I always make everything worse.

Me: Did they hurt you too, like they did Miles? Is that why you haven't come?

Me: Please tell me you're ok.

Me: I'm sorry. I'm so so sorry.

Me: I'm going to keep Zoey company.

Me: I like it out here, surrounded by trees.

Me: I'm so numb.

Me: I want to see the colors playing on the stone floor.

Me: It has to stop. I need to make this stop.

Me: Maybe it will just hurt for a moment, and then I won't feel anything anymore.

Find out what happens next in ***Dare To Fall***

Thank you for reading Dare To Take. If you'd like to keep up to date with L. Ann & Claire Marta, you can find both of them on Facebook.

L. Ann - https://facebook.com/lannauthor
Claire Marta - https://facebook.com/clairemartabooks

You can also join their active reader groups:-

L. Ann's Literati - https://facebook.com/groups/lannsliterati
Claire's Liquor & Lust - https://facebook.com/groups/clairesliquorandlust

You can find more books by L. Ann and Claire Marta on Amazon in paperback, ebook and audio.

Printed in Great Britain
by Amazon